R0082777574

10/2014

The Black Stars

ALSO BY DAN KROKOS

False Memory
The Planet Thieves

The Black Stars

DAN KROKOS

A TOM DOHERTY ASSOCIATES BOOK
New York

THE BLACK STARS

Copyright © 2014 by Dan Krokos

A Starscape Book
Published by Tom Doherty Associates, LLC
175 Fifth Avenue
New York, NY 10010

www.tor-forge.com

The Library of Congress Cataloging-in-Publication Data is available upon request.

ISBN 978-0-7653-3429-9 (hardcover)
ISBN 978-1-4668-0999-4 (e-book)

Starscape books may be purchased for educational, business, or promotional use. For information on bulk purchases, please contact Macmillan Corporate and Premium Sales Department at 1-800-221-7945, extension 5442, or write specialmarkets@macmillan.com.

First Edition: October 2014

Printed in the United States of America

0 9 8 7 6 5 4 3 2 1

To Suzie, Joanna, and Janet, for not giving up on me

Acknowledgments

Thank you to the teams at New Leaf and Starscape. It is an absolute honor and privilege to work with you guys.

Thank you to Antonio Caparo, for creating illustrations much cooler than anything I'd imagined.

And thank you for reading. I write because I want to show people a good time. Thanks for giving me that chance.

I've visited many solar systems throughout our galaxy. Most stars are kind, and happy to burn away for a few billion years. Some of these stars support planets. And some of those planets support life. But there are some stars in the galaxy that are not kind. These stars have planets that support life, but a kind of life that isn't content to live and let live. These solar systems contain life focused on extinguishing life. They destroy, even as they create. They are not necessarily evil: it may just be their nature. We are all familiar with these kinds of stars. I've taken to calling them Black Stars.

—Captain Joshua Reynolds of the Earth Space Command,
from his autobiography *I've Seen the Stars*

The Black Stars

Chapter One

Mason Stark had a problem with minding his own business. This problem had resulted in seven disciplinary actions since he arrived at Academy II just three months ago. As his friend Tom Renner had kindly pointed out, according to the Earth Space Command rulebook, Mason would be kicked out of Academy II if he received an eighth disciplinary action.

Mason would instantly become a citizen and be forced to leave the Academy and his friends forever.

That didn't stop him this time, of course.

Six of the seven infractions resulted from confrontations with older cadets. Academy II took six years to complete, just like Academy I had. The "first years" were thirteen years old, like Mason, or about to turn thirteen. The "last years" were eighteen, or about to turn eighteen. And they were big. And smart.

And jealous.

Because Mason and his friends had saved the day. Or at least, they'd brought a kind of tenuous peace between the Tremist and the humans. They were the most famous group in all the worlds. Reporter shuttles were permanently parked in low orbit over Mars, where Academy I and II were nestled in the foothills of Aeolis Mons, a mountain near the equator. The reporters weren't allowed to land, but they were able to take pictures from orbit. For the first month, the newsfeed had a story every day with an overhead picture of Academy I and II, which were only a few kilometers apart, accompanied by headlines such as

YOUNG HEROES BEGIN FIRST YEAR AT ACADEMY II

or

DOES MASON STARK CAPTAIN HIS OWN SHIP?

The rumors were nonsense, of course. Mason Stark did not captain his own ship. He was a student, with much to learn about command—he was the first to admit that. But humanity desperately needed heroes. Mason and his friends just happened to be the most available. Which wasn't exactly fair, in his opinion. How was he supposed to live up to the legend he already was? He wasn't even fourteen yet, and there were already movies and books about the exploits of the "Egypt 18."

And so Mason was not entirely welcome at Academy II. Respected, but not welcome. It did not matter who started the six fights that had led to six of seven disciplinary actions, or who finished them—Headmaster Oleg did not permit fighting outside of combat classes, period. Mason had thought he'd escaped the old man, but the headmaster had been pro-moted to Academy II right along with Mason.

It was 13:00 on Friday when Mason knew he'd be getting his eighth disciplinary action. He was in the gym used by both Academy I and II. The gym was a fat cylinder twenty levels tall, right between both academies. Cadets took a three-minute track ride through a tunnel in the mountain to reach it. Each level had different features to accommodate different needs.

Mason had just entered level 8, the workout room. He was sweaty from his last class of the day—Advanced Combat Techniques III—so it made sense to get a quick jog in before showering and meeting Tom, Stellan, and Jeremy in the mess hall. The quarter-mile track ran around the entire cir-cumference of the cylinder.

He was stretching out his hamstrings when he heard a commotion from the other side of the gym. It sounded like someone cried out, but Mason couldn't see through the forest of gym equipment. He paused, listening hard, until a familiar *fwump* sounded across the gym: someone had turned on a resistance pad. Then came a mean laugh—a cackle, really, and a forced one at that.

Mason made his way through the equipment, his footsteps quiet. Half of the gym was regular workout equipment—dozens of identical machines that could morph into any configuration to work out every muscle group. The other half was open space, but the floor was tiled with square pads. The pads created force fields that would provide resistance, so you could exercise without machines. Nobody used them.

They made your hair stand up for the entire day, and too much use would create itchy rashes on your skin.

The fact that someone was using one now was a red flag all by itself.

Tom's words came back to him now: "One more slip up, Stark, and it's game over. You're out. Be smart for once?"

Mason had argued back: "They'd kick me out? After all the good we've done?"

To which Tom had replied, "Do they seem to care about that here?"

"We're too valuable to the ESC. What's better for recruitment than the Egypt 18?"

Tom considered that, rubbing his chin. "Do you really want to find out how serious they are?"

Mason did not. Maybe they wouldn't make his expulsion public, just stick him in a room for a year or two. Who could know for sure?

But Mason's feet were driven across the gym anyway, and soon he was standing in the very middle, where the equipment met the line of pads.

Exactly six older cadets were gathered around the closest pad. The stripes on their sleeves said half of them were fifth years, the other half, sixth years. Mason was a first year again. But he recognized these fools. Just two weeks earlier, Mason found his locker completely filled with anti-bio fluid. The cream-colored gel had spilled out on his feet, a gelatinous wave that ruined his pants and boots. The news spread quickly through school, and everyone knew who did it— Marcus Jones, a sixth year. He was on a fast track to command once he finished his last year and joined the Earth

Space Command as an officer. Marcus was mean in a way Mason didn't understand. Cruel for the sake of cruelty. But he was smart and obedient and respectful . . . to his superiors.

No one would tell on Marcus, not ever. Mason couldn't either, as it would be seen as a betrayal to his fellow cadets. But once Marcus broke the wrist of Kevan Desoto, a small-ish cadet who talked too much, Mason knew he had to do something. So he hacked into the central computer, found the surveillance footage of Marcus throwing Kevan to the ground, and uploaded it to the wall screens in the refectory during lunch. It wasn't telling on Marcus—the footage was there. Mason just showed everyone.

For hacking into a restricted system, Headmaster Oleg awarded Mason with his seventh disciplinary action. Marcus's punishment was not made public.

Near the pad, the older cadets were gathered around a boy pinned on his side by the force field, knees pushed up tight to chest. The cadet was tall, but a first year like Mason, with white-blond hair and lanky limbs. It was Stellan, one of his best friends, one of the cadets who helped him bring the new peace. A member of the Egypt 18.

Anger struck Mason like lightning, and just as hot. He could only stand there as his pulse jacked, and a mechanism in his sleeve began to buzz, warning him to keep his vitals low. It was supposed to train cadets to maintain control in any situation—*A clear head is a living head,* they told him.

So Mason wanted to give the cadets a shot at doing the right thing. He wanted to try having a clear head. Stellan would appreciate that. Stellan had always told him to use his words, not his fists.

The cadets were chuckling to themselves while Stellan fought the force field. He couldn't move an inch. But his eyes could still see. They rolled toward Mason, and the cadets followed his gaze, turning around.

"Steak!" Marcus said with joy. "Steak" was the stupid nickname they'd given him. Mason didn't know what it was supposed to mean, but his current theory was that it played off his last name, Stark. "So glad you could join us. No surveillance cams in here. Did you know that?"

Mason stepped forward, closing half the distance. Two of the fifth years visibly backed away but then seemed to catch themselves and stand tall, shoulders back, chests puffed up a bit.

"Please remove the force field," Mason said. That was their one chance. He asked them nicely. He even said please.

Marcus stared at him with bright, intelligent eyes.

In unison, the cadets began to laugh. It sounded forced, like before.

"Mason, just go . . ." Stellan said, struggling to speak. It was clear the force field was too tight, and he was having trouble breathing.

"Another of the Fabulous Five," Marcus said. "We are honored by your presence." He made a low, mocking bow, and the others did the same. Marcus had curly black hair that was a little too long by ESC standards—just a centimeter— which Mason assumed he got away with because he was a rising star.

The Fabulous Five was a name the media invented for Mason, Tom, Merrin, Jeremy, and Stellan. Merrin Solace was Mason's best friend since before Academy I, though he hadn't seen or talked to her since that day on the Tremist space station, when the treaty was signed. He thought about her all the time, though. She was on the Tremist homeworld, Skars, with her father, the Tremist King.

Mason said it one more time. "Please remove the force field."

"Or what?" Marcus said.

Mason didn't say anything.

Marcus waited, then rubbed his hands together. "Tell you what. You just walk on out of here, and we won't make you get down next to him. How does that sound, hero?"

"Please, Mason," Stellan said. "You'll get kicked out. What's more important, huh? I can take this."

A lightbulb seemed to go off above Marcus's head. His eyes widened, then narrowed, and a slick smile spread across his face. "Ah, wait. You have seven demerits, don't you?" He didn't wait for a response. "Yep, seven. I've been keeping track. Why do you think you're at seven, Steak? You think it might be because of me?" Marcus hated Mason because he was direct competition that happened to be much younger, and that was *before* Mason had humiliated him by showing his cowardly act to the whole school.

He's even more dangerous now, Mason thought, but he didn't say anything out loud. Sometimes that was better. The mechanism was still vibrating against his arm, but not as intensely. He was allowing himself to stay cool, but his anger was bubbling just under the surface.

"I think it *might* be because of me. And I think you *might* want to walk away right now, unless you want to become a civilian before dinner."

Marcus was correct. No doubt about it. But Mason didn't care about that. He cared about what was right. And leaving Stellan behind was not right.

Mason let his Rhadgast gloves flow down from his forearms to cover his hands. A Rhadgast had given him the pair of lightning gloves on the Tremist space station, along with an invitation to join their school, if Mason wanted to learn the truth about his parents, which, other than Merrin, was all he thought about.

His gloves had been confiscated almost immediately. ESC scientists wanted to study their properties. The gloves appeared broken; when worn, they didn't conform to the user's hands and arms, and they didn't carry a charge. A story in the media appeared:

MASON STARK SEEN WITHOUT HIS
RHADGAST GAUNTLETS

with the subheadline:

WHAT DOES THIS MEAN FOR PEACE?

The gloves were immediately returned to him, and photographers were allowed into Academy II to take pictures of him wearing them. Then Mason was commanded to keep the gloves in his locker at all times, which of course he didn't do.

Each night he practiced with them for an hour, like he would with any weapon he wanted to master. He would lie in bed and feel the connection. That was all: he never brought electricity to the surface. The gloves came back to life once he put them on, but he was careful not to tell anyone, except for his crew. After weeks of practice, he was able to control the shape of the gloves. He could make them peel back from his hands and turn into bracers that went from wrist to elbow. Under his long-sleeved black shirt (standard ESC uniform, along with black pants and tall black boots) the gloves were undetectable. But always there. They made Mason feel safer, in a way, and were a constant reminder of his goal to find the Rhadgast once again.

Marcus's mouth dropped open once Mason's hands were covered in the purplish material, a kind of grippy rubber. They appeared violet-blue under the harsh gym lights.

"They work . . ." one of the fifth years breathed.

Marcus swallowed, recovering quickly. "You wouldn't dare."

No, Mason wouldn't. To attack a cadet with his Rhadgast gloves would ensure he was kicked out of the Earth Space Command for good. Beyond that, Mason didn't want to imagine how the story could be spun, or what it would do to a peace that had been shaky from its inception.

So instead, Mason pointed his index finger at Stellan's pad and let a single tine of violet electricity snap out from his fingertip. It shot between the grouped cadets and struck Stellan's pad. The pad hissed and sputtered and then flickered off . . . and so did all the other pads in the room. The new silence was deafening in a way; before there had been the hushed whisper of power coursing through circuits, and now there was nothing but a few cadets breathing a little too loudly.

Marcus was still smart, cruel or not. He swallowed. "I have

witnesses, Steak. This is it for you. I have three demerits. You have seven. It's over."

Stellan stood up on the pad and brushed himself off. His hair was sticking straight up, and he wasn't smiling. He looked sad.

Marcus started to say something else, but Mason just pointed at his chest and said, "Leave," with as much authority as he could muster.

Marcus held his gaze for another defiant moment, then said, "Let's roll." They walked away slowly, swaggering. Marcus threw a final glance over his shoulder, and Mason saw a fire burning in his one visible eye. *There's an enemy I've made for life.* Then they were gone.

Mason exhaled. Marcus wouldn't tell on him, not without receiving another demerit himself.

Stellan walked over, and Mason let his gloves slide back over his hands until they became bracers again. Mason held out his hand to shake, but Stellan just pulled him into a hug. "You risked a lot," he said.

"We're crew," Mason said, as if that explained everything. And, really, it did.

Stellan smiled. "How's my hair?"

Mason allowed himself to grin for the first time. "It's seen better days."

"Darn. You'll have to help me fix it. I'm going to talk to Juniper Mass at dinner. She kept looking at me in Cross Gates IV today."

They started toward the exit, and that's when Mason saw Marcus and his cohorts being cuffed by a security team, who must've been watching from a hidden cam. Marcus was already trying to talk his way out of it. He was pointing at Mason and Stellan. The five security guards didn't look amused.

Mason was contemplating the other two gym exits—they hadn't been seen yet, so escape was still a possibility, but escape to where?—when he heard a voice behind him.

"Mason Stark. You are in serious trouble."

Chapter Two

Mason turned around slowly. Commander Lockwood loomed over him, his face a rigid scowl.

"I've got it, Patrick, thank you," Lockwood said to the security guard walking toward them.

Mason would have rather gone with the guard.

Lockwood wasn't a bad guy—in fact, when they were on the SS Egypt together, he was the only officer who really gave the cadets any notice. But he was also fierce, with a hawkish face that was now more intense with his scars. Lockwood had almost died on the Egypt, a victim of several burns from the Tremist energy weapons, but some quick thinking by the cadets kept him alive. Afterward, Lockwood had asked to transfer to Academy II to continue working with the cadets. He taught Mason and his crew in Advanced Space Combat II, which focused on the smaller fighters in the ESC fleet.

"Sir," Mason said, snapping to attention.

Lockwood continued to stare down at him, which was hard because Mason was now almost the same height. "Son, do you realize how much it will cost to fix these pads?"

"No, sir."

"Sir," Stellan began. "I can explain, they—"

"Cadet Runeberg, you are dismissed," Lockwood said.

Stellan opened his mouth again.

"The word I used was *dismissed,* Stellan. I did not say *Please, I invite you to discuss this further with me.*"

"Apologies, sir," Stellan said, then stole a glance at Mason, who gave him a tiny nod. Then Stellan walked away.

Lockwood turned his gaze back to Mason. "You fired a Tremist energy weapon on school grounds. Can you even *fathom* the punishment that accompanies a charge like that?"

Mason was sweating now; it dripped down his spine. He wanted to say *Please don't make me leave,* but said, "No, sir," instead.

"They don't have a charge for it, because they can't imagine it ever happening, ever. Because the very idea of a Tremist energy weapon being discharged on school grounds is rather insane, don't you think?"

"Insane, sir. Definitely insane."

Lockwood drew in a long whistling breath through his nose, then exhaled just as slowly. Mason couldn't keep his eyes off the pinkish skin on his neck. Only six months ago, it was black, and Lockwood was on his deathbed, giving command of the Egypt over to Mason.

"Come with me," Lockwood said.

Mason did as he was told, for once. Lockwood led him out of the gym through a side exit.

"Eyes forward!" Lockwood barked when he caught Mason peeking back at Marcus and his cronies, who were being led toward a different exit.

They left the gym, and Mason bumped into a cadet right outside the doorway. "Sorry—Tom!"

Tom Renner stood with his arms folded, frowning deeply. Only Tom Renner could frown like that. "Who was right, Stark? I said you couldn't mess up again. Seven demerits. Yet you had to get that eighth one before the first year was over, didn't you?"

Mason couldn't argue. "What are you doing here?"

Tom shrugged. "I was summoned by our old pal Lockwood here."

"Excuse me?" Lockwood said.

"Sir. I mean I was summoned by Commander Lockwood, sir." Tom's attitude toward the rules had softened a bit since the Egypt.

Lockwood grumbled something unintelligible as they walked around the circular hallway that would lead them to the tunnels and to the headmaster's office, where Mason would quickly be ejected from Academy II and the Earth Space Command.

But why would Lockwood summon them both?

"What's this about, sir?" Mason asked Lockwood.

"It's not for me to say."

If Tom was here, there was a good chance Mason wasn't going directly to the headmaster.

"Are they going to kick me out?" Mason said.

"I guess you should have thought about that before damaging school equipment." Lockwood let that sit for a moment, while Mason sweated. Then he added, "But I don't think the ESC is dumb enough to give up their biggest propaganda tool since the start of the war."

Mason didn't like the sound of that. He'd been approached by several recruiting chiefs who wanted to use him in new ads. There was no shortage of applications to the ESC, but they were hoping to attract the best and brightest. Mason's accomplishments at such a young age, they said, were a real advertisement for Academy I. Mason had politely explained that he couldn't have done it without his team, but they didn't care. They wanted a face to go with their ads, a voice. Mason looked up to find Lockwood watching him.

"I didn't mean that," Lockwood said quietly. "You're more than that, Stark." And then, as if he remembered Mason was in trouble, he said, "Keep walking."

They followed the track back to Academy II, which was partially built into the mountain. Mason's heart started to pound when they took a lift to the top level, where the administration offices were located. *Yep, we're going to see the headmaster.*

"Have you done something wrong?" Mason asked Tom.

Tom made a face. "Please. Do you even know me?"

"There was that time you—"

Tom elbowed him in the ribs, and Mason fell silent. Lockwood raised a scarred eyebrow but said nothing.

The commander led them to the office at the far end. Mason had been inside before. It was Headmaster Oleg's new office, which had a wide, panoramic view of the red planet.

Lockwood shook their hands. He seemed upset about something, not quite wanting to make eye contact. "Boys," he said. "No matter what, it's been an honor."

Uh-oh.

Lockwood started away.

"You definitely did something," Mason said to Tom. Tom punched him in the shoulder. Mason thought about punching back, but then they'd be rolling around in the hallway on the administration level.

"I did not," Tom said. "But let's hurry this up. I have class in twenty minutes." His attitude toward the rules may have relaxed, but not his attitude toward classes.

Mason knocked on the door.

"Come in," said a voice from within. Not Headmaster Oleg's voice . . .

Mason opened the door. Sitting behind Oleg's desk was Grand Admiral Shahbazian.

Chapter Three

Mason hadn't seen Grand Admiral Shahbazian— or "GAS," to use the nickname given to him by students at A2—since they were both aboard the Will to sign the treaty. Talking to him had been awful then, and it didn't seem like this conversation was going to be any better, judging by the expression on his face. By all appearances, the grand admiral would rather be out on the surface of Mars right now, without a space suit.

"Sir," Mason and Tom said together, saluting. This man was in charge of the *entire* Earth Space Command.

"Sit down," the grand admiral replied sharply.

They did, taking the seats across from Shahbazian. Mason couldn't help but think of him as GAS. He felt a tickle in the back of his throat, the start of a laugh.

"Do you know why I've called you here today?" GAS said.

Mason had exactly zero ways of knowing why he was there. It was probably the dumbest question he'd ever heard.

"Let me get to the point," GAS said. "What I am about to share with you is classified beyond Top Secret. Do you understand what that means? It means sharing this information would result in imprisonment. For life."

Mason swallowed. Then he reminded himself that he was part of the crew that saved the Olympus space station from getting literally eaten by a Fangborn ship. So GAS couldn't be all that scary anymore.

Right?

"I asked you both a direct question."

"Yes, sir," Mason said.

"I understand, sir," Tom added.

GAS waited a dramatic beat, then nodded. "Very good." A storm was picking up outside, the barren reddish landscape blurry with fine dust. "One of our spies has discovered a piece of intelligence which indicates the Tremist are working on some kind of secret project. The nature of this project is unclear, but I believe it may revolve around some kind of weapons program. Normally there would be no way for us to verify this, but the intelligence sector is certain this project is taking place *inside* the Rhadgast school on Skars. We need to be aware if they plan to violate the treaty."

"The Tremist have been nothing but cooperative so far," Mason said. And then, as an afterthought, he added, "Sir." Tom kicked his leg.

It was true. The Tremist and humans were getting along famously, when you considered the circumstances. Earth had been stolen by the Tremist and transported to their solar system, to orbit the Tremist sun they simply called Renshas, which translated to "sun" in the Tremist language. Earth had adjusted, for the most part, since the calculations had been perfect. Tidal and seismic activity had not returned to normal, but that was because both planets were now affected by each other's gravity. The presence of Skars had overcompensated for the lack of the moon. But if the rumors were true, Skars hadn't completely adjusted to Earth, either.

Standing on the surface of either Earth or Skars, the other planet appeared like a tiny glowing marble in the night sky, smaller in appearance than Earth's moon, which was still back in the Sol system. In between both planets, Tremist and humans were working together to assemble a new planet-sized cross gate, which would allow Earth to return to its rightful solar system. Unfortunately, they were still *years* away from completing the gate.

Tremist were not allowed on Earth, and humans were not allowed on Skars, but the races mingled and conversed and traded and learned about each other on humanity's largest space station, the Olympus, and on the Tremist's largest space station, the Will. Both stations were parked midway between the planets, near the shipyard that was currently building the new gate. It was the unofficial line in space, and, so far, both sides were respecting it. There was even talk of visits to each other's planets in the coming weeks.

But still there was tension. Both sides had been at war for too long. It didn't matter that they had a joint ancestry and had originated from the same planet. Too many lives had been lost, on both sides.

GAS looked like he was about to have a stroke. "And how would you know they're cooperating, Stark? What information are you basing that on?"

"Nothing specific, sir, just a general observation. Forgive me. But may I ask what intelligence you have? How reliable is this?" He was careful to keep his tone neutral.

"Reliable," GAS said. "But I can't tell you where it came from. Don't ask again." He put his palms on the desk, clearly out of patience now. Mason wondered how he'd ever made it to the top of the ESC with that attitude. "Stark, you have an open invitation to the Rhadgast school. You are ordered to go there and enter the school as a student. Once there, you will report on everything you see with *this*." He held up a small disk-shaped piece of black plastic. "This communicator is quantum-synced to the one I carry on my person at all times. It is completely untraceable. While there, you will investigate anything odd you come across. If you discover proof of a project or weapon that violates the treaty, you will report it at once."

Mason couldn't believe his luck. *Come and find us, if you want to learn the truth about your parents,* the Rhadgast had told him, pressing the purple gloves into Mason's hand. *I've found you,* Mason thought now.

He didn't ask what would happen if they were caught, or if the treaty crumbled while he was on Skars. He didn't care. Or rather, he was too excited by the possibilities to really consider the risks. He was going no matter what, so the risks didn't matter.

"Uh, sir?" Tom said.

GAS turned his dark gaze upon Tom.

"Why am I here?"

"Because you're going with him," Grand Admiral Shahbazian replied.

Chapter Four

Tom began to splutter something incoherent, but Shahbazian cut him off. "I've been in contact with the Tremist King himself. I expressed my concern about Mason going alone into a strange new world, and he conferred with the Rhadgast. A committee decided Mason is allowed to bring along one of the crew who helped save the Will. And I have picked you, Tom."

Tom was suddenly a shade paler. "Why me? Why not Jeremy Cane? He's a better fighter."

Mason glanced at his friend. Tom wasn't the type to back down from a challenge, but not much time had passed since the death of Tom's mother, Captain Renner, at the hands of the Tremist. Tom would maintain peace with the Tremist, as was his duty, but to work side by side with them?

Shahbazian didn't look thrilled that Tom had forgotten to use *sir*. "Because I don't need a fighter, Cadet Renner. I need someone with guile and brains, someone who will stay cool behind enemy lines."

Mason couldn't tell if that was an insult to their friend

Jeremy, who was one of the smartest and bravest cadets he knew. It better not have been.

"What about our studies?" Tom loved school almost as much as Stellan, and he planned to get perfect scores for the next six years. It would guarantee he graduated as an officer. Tom looked at Mason in a near panic. "What if we're there for months? Or years! We won't be able to graduate."

Shahbazian actually grinned, or almost did: the corners of his mouth twitched in unison. "Son," he said, in a different, gentler voice. "I am in charge of the whole show here, and I don't intend to let this harm your future with the ESC. This is an incredible risk. You will be the first boots-on-the-ground soldiers since this whole thing started. I don't want to send cadets to Skars. Of course I don't. But this is our only option. And as the best the ESC has to offer, we're going to take the risk."

"They killed my mother, sir," Tom said. Mason suspected this was the real sticking point, not some silly classes.

Shahbazian was quiet for a moment. Then he nodded. "I know, Thomas. But the two of you are going to do your duty, all personal feelings aside. Isn't that right?"

"Yes, sir," Mason and Tom replied together.

"Great," Shahbazian said, leaning back in Headmaster Oleg's chair. "I'm glad I have your approv—" The chair was ancient and creaky and almost slid out from under him. He slammed his hands down on the desk to steady himself, glaring at the boys, as if they were the cause. Mason snorted but somehow kept his face placid.

"Your ship leaves in thirty minutes," Shahbazian said quickly. "Dismissed. I expect your first report this evening."

Mason and Tom stood up together and walked for the door.

"Boys," Shahbazian said.

They turned. Shahbazian tossed them each one of the black quantum communicators. Mason caught his, then immediately slid the disk into the secret compartment in the heel of his boot. Tom did the same.

"Good luck," Shahbazian said. "And be careful. . . ."

➤ "Tell me you're not a little excited," Mason said, once they were in the hallway. "Not even a *tiny* bit excited. I dare you."

"Oh I'm excited, all right," Tom said. "It's been a dream my entire life to visit the Tremist homeworld with no backup and be expected to go to *Rhadgast school*. Mason, have you forgotten that one time lots and *lots* of Rhadgast tried to kill us? Wait, it was much more than one time."

Mason hadn't forgotten. He dreamed of their blank, featureless faces, which pulsed with violet light. The Rhadgast were once thought to be wizards of some kind. To this day, they were legendary among the ESC. Mason would never forget the first time he saw one inside the gravity-free bay aboard the Egypt. The Rhadgast had flown through the air like a shark swims through water, firing off electrical blasts from his gloves, his black robe lashing around him as if the fabric were alive.

The memory sent a chill down Mason's spine, and for a moment Mason wondered if anyone would notify his sister, Lieutenant Commander Susan Stark, of his mission. He shook it off as their escort arrived.

The guard of six walked them to the shuttle bay, where they would take a shuttle to one of the bigger ships in orbit. They were not permitted to visit their lockers or to speak to any students they passed in the hallway. Their absence would be noted, of course, but that wasn't Mason's problem. Oleg could always say the two boys had been expelled, or suspended temporarily, for as long as the mission required. Mason had the disciplinary actions to back it up. Or maybe they'd go a different route entirely and publicize the mission as another step toward lasting peace. Either way, it wasn't Mason's concern.

Five minutes later, they were strapped into a shuttle. Fifteen minutes later, they were in high orbit above Mars, docking at a country-class vessel (identical to the one Mason was briefly captain of) named the Bolivia. Thirty minutes later they were in the new Earthspace, a quarter of the way across the galaxy. An hour after leaving Headmaster Oleg's office, they were aboard one of the Bolivia's shuttles, heading for the Will. Like Olympus, the Will was a ring-shaped tube. But unlike the Olympus, it had many rings inside one another. At the very center, inside the smallest ring, was a pod containing an artificial forest that Mason assumed was like the surface of Skars. *I guess I'll find out soon enough*, he thought.

The crew of Mason's shuttle was two members of the ESC intelligence sector. But they weren't normal intelligence analysts or number crunchers. These were true spies, known as Reynolds, named for the famous captain Joshua Reynolds. Like the Tremist, Reynolds always wore masks to conceal their identities. Their masks were featureless except for the two circular lenses over their eyes, which glowed softly with pinkish light.

They didn't speak to either cadet for the entire trip from the Bolivia to the Will. The shuttle coasted toward the Will slowly, giving the Tremist time to scan the ship and make sure it wasn't packed with explosives. The Will was still undergoing repairs from its encounter with the Fangborn ship, though the job was nearly finished. Only a few sections were open to space, the levels exposed, tiny worker pods crawling all over them like ants repairing a hive.

Finally, the shuttle connected to the Will with a bang and a hiss as the air pressure on both sides equalized. The door at the rear of the shuttle slid open, revealing a group of four Rhadgast.

Mason's heart rate skyrocketed. Tom threw him a panicked look. The two Reynolds were tense in their seats, looking back over their shoulders. The Rhadgast remained motionless, waiting. Two of them wore purplish gloves and masks along with their black robes, but the other two had gloves and masks that were a dark red, the color of old blood. It reminded Mason of the Tremist King's powerful armor. Mason had never seen a Rhadgast in red before—he'd never even known they existed.

You're going to be seeing a lot of these guys, Mason told himself. He hadn't laid eyes on a Rhadgast since the one aboard the Will had given him the gloves. His reaction now was involuntary, that was all. The two masks pulsing violet brought Mason back to the Egypt, and the gravity-free bay, where he had risked his life to save his fellow cadets.

What have you gotten yourself into, Stark?

"Go," the Reynold pilot rasped through his helmet speakers. The circular lenses over his eyes flickered briefly with white light.

Mason and Tom unbuckled their harnesses with thick fingers, keeping an eye on the Rhadgast the entire time. They crossed onto the Will, and the shuttle door slammed shut behind them. Yeah, the humans and the Tremist had a long way to go.

The nearest Rhadgast—one of the red ones—finally spoke. "Greetings, young rhadjen."

"Greetings," Mason said. Tom just stared with wide eyes. Mason wanted to remind him that they had faced several Rhadgast along the way and won every time. So Rhadgast school should be a piece of cake. Yet Mason knew it wouldn't be.

The red Rhadgast used both hands to remove his mask. The seal broke with a sigh, and then his face was revealed. The face was human, although pale and nearly translucent. Mason could see the purple veins in his neck, which branched up and across his cheeks. His hair was long and deep red, and a smile came to his face easily.

The red Rhadgast stuck out his hand. "How is it the humans do it? A handshake, it is called?" Mason went to shake his hand, but the red Rhadgast pulled it back. "But wait. If you're going to come with us, it's best to learn how we greet each other." He made a fist and held it out. Mason lightly tapped it with his.

"We do that sometimes, too," Mason said, and he would've smiled if it hadn't been for the other three Rhadgast looming over them.

The red Rhadgast's eyebrows shot up. "Perhaps we have more than just appearances in common! How about that. My name is Reckful. I am of the Blood. Before we take you to see the king, we must remove your gloves."

The closest purple Rhadgast snorted in disdain and muttered something in the Tremist language. Reckful frowned at him but said nothing.

Mason's gloves were currently retracted. "How did you know I was wearing them?"

The red Rhadgast only smiled.

Tom blurted out, "Excuse me, the king is here?"

Mason and Tom had met with the king before, and it wasn't always a pleasant experience. In fact, it had never been pleasant. But Mason wanted to give peace a chance.

"Reck," said one of the purple Rhadgast.

"Yes, yes, we're late. The gloves, please."

Mason removed them reluctantly, wincing as he severed the connection between the gloves and his mind. His forearms felt naked, his hands itched, and his brain felt as if it were missing a chunk. Now that they were off, the gloves had expanded to the default size. He held them out to Reckful, but one of the purple Rhadgast snatched them out of his hand.

"Those belong to us," the purple Rhadgast said, his mask pulsing brighter. For what purpose, Mason had no idea, but the glow felt aggressive enough that he had a sudden urge to either punch the Rhadgast in the stomach or run.

"Manners," Reckful said, but the Rhadgast ignored him. "Come," he said to Mason and Tom.

The group started down a hallway, through a series of thick

blast doors meant to slow enemy progression through the docking port (in the impossible event a human ship actually managed to dock at the Will uninvited). Tom caught Mason's eye and gave him a look, like *Well, no turning back now!*

The inside of the Will reminded Mason of the king's Hawk. Instead of the cool metal and plastic of an ESC ship, the Will felt alive. The floor felt like rock, and the walls were glowing, so the light came from everywhere. They passed no one on their journey to the center pod, and Mason figured the route had been cleared, just to be sure no Tremist happened across the group and made a fuss over the humans. For now, Tremist and human meetings aboard either space station were carefully regulated and confined to specific areas.

Mason and Tom rode a series of shuttle cars with the Rhadgast, taking them deeper into the Will. Reckful had replaced his mask and hadn't spoken another word, but he nodded at Mason once, when he caught Mason staring at him. Mason had a million questions but didn't know where to start, or rather *if* he should start. Rhadgast didn't seem like the talkative types.

Seeing the Rhadgast had been a shock, but Mason reminded himself they were no different from the Reynolds, in a way. He was heading to Skars to *become* one of them, so it was time to stop fearing them.

But his new, carefully maintained calm was shattered a moment later, when the shuttle finally stopped and the door opened.

Merrin Solace was standing on the other side.

Chapter Five

His surroundings temporarily forgotten, Mason threw his arms around Merrin and lifted her up in a huge hug. They spun in a circle, both of them laughing. Mason set her down immediately after, his face and ears heating up. Merrin's cheeks had flushed a pale shade of purple; Mason hoped she wasn't embarrassed. Her violet eyes were bright, and her hair, which was the same color, was pulled back in a ponytail, and much shorter than it had been. She looked older, even though it had been just six months.

"Hi. . . ." Mason had no idea what to say to her, even though he'd been imagining this moment for a long time. They stood on the border of the central pod, with the lush blue-green forest stretching out before them. Through the clear dome above, Mason could see Earth and Skars, on opposite sides, each glowing in the light of Renshas.

"Hi yourself," Merrin replied. She didn't seem at all shocked when the four Rhadgast stepped off the shuttle, even though she'd been in combat with a few Rhadgast herself not so long ago. Tom and Merrin shook hands, but then Tom was quickly pulled into a bone-crushing hug.

The idea was too good to be true, but Mason had to ask: "Are you coming with us?"

Merrin's face fell, and she tapped the badge on her chest. Mason hadn't noticed her uniform, which consisted of a formal blue jacket and pants. The badge was a small bronze image of two shaking hands, which represented the Coalition for Life, a new organization dedicated to the continuing peaceful interaction of humans and Tremist. They put out advertisements across the Internet on both sides, showing humans and Tremist working together. In every ad, the Coalition reminded viewers of the true enemy: the Fangborn.

"I want to," Merrin said. "I have an open invite as well. But I'm doing some good work here, Mason. We're gaining hundreds of new members each day. I can't just walk away, not yet. I'm of both worlds, they say. . . ."

Mason tried to keep the disappointment off his face, but the desire to see his crew back together was strong, almost a physical itch. It was bad enough they had to leave Stellan and Jeremy at Academy II. "Then what are you doing here?"

"My father has business at the school. He decided to escort you and Tom himself, to give you guys some credibility. He thinks the school might be . . . a little rough. But only at first."

Mason hadn't expected to be welcomed with open arms, but he couldn't worry about that right now. The king was walking toward them. King Tolovim ruled over the entire planet of Skars (minus one continent that had left the Tremist Empire a thousand years earlier, in a bloody war that lasted one hundred years).

The king was no longer wearing his incredible armor,

which had seemed immune to energy weapons. He was sporting a simple long tunic of green and purple, along with a black cape. He wore a regal smile on his face, as he bowed low to Mason and Tom.

After a stunned moment, they returned the bow. The king stepped forward and put his arm around Merrin. She looked up at her dad with a genuine smile on her face. *What in Zeus's mountain have I missed?* Mason thought. He'd hoped Merrin would be able to reconcile with her father in some way, but he still found it impossible to forget the things Tolovim had done, the humans he'd killed. Mason remembered the numerous times the king had threatened Mason's sister. Mason had even watched as the king backhanded her to the ground.

The king's eyes narrowed, and Mason became aware of his own expression. It was something close to anger. He quickly relaxed his brow, untightened his mouth.

"Boys. We meet again." The king gave Mason a knowing look, a look that said *Yes, we still have much to overcome.* "It's an honor to have you aboard the Will. Shall I escort you to the school?"

Tom saved Mason the trouble of responding. "It would be an honor, sir," he said.

The king smiled, and Mason was again struck by how human he looked. Without his armor, he wasn't all that tall—a much less imposing figure than before, especially without the empty black mask that seemed to eat the light from a room.

Another awkward moment of silence passed, until Reckful cleared his throat. "Your Grace, we'll be late for the ceremony."

The king nodded. "Then we'd better hurry."

. . .

⮞ Minutes later, they were aboard the king's brand new Hawk. This one was much larger than the previous Hawk, with an unfamiliar layout. But it was still the same bird-shaped craft Mason recognized, with wide swooping wings that curved to a forward point.

As the Hawk left dock, the king asked Mason to join him for a walk. Mason just wanted to stay with Merrin, since they would soon be separated again, but who was he to refuse the Tremist King?

Once they were alone, the king spoke. "My actions during the times we've met in the past, they were unbecoming of a king. And of a decent sentient being. My desire to find my daughter affected me over the years. I allowed myself to approach madness. For the last few years there was only . . . rage." He closed his eyes for a moment, though they were still walking forward. When he opened his eyes, they were clear. "I acknowledge my part in the damage I have done to your people, and to mine. Merrin has helped me see that."

Mason nodded. "It was war." He didn't know what else to say.

The king nodded back. "But how you fight a war matters."

They reached the front of the Hawk, where a window above the bridge gave them a panoramic view of Skars. It was a sickly yellow thanks to a single cloud of pollution that covered the planet like the peel of an orange. The planet was growing by the second as they sped toward it.

"Our home was blue once, just like Earth," the king said.

Mason didn't know what to say to that.

The Hawk entered Skars's atmosphere and began to shake.

Mason braced himself against the wall. All he could see through the window was fire, until the Hawk burst through the cloud cover, and the surface of Skars became visible for the first time. A city stretched out before him, hundreds of miles across, the buildings growing taller and taller as they moved toward the center of the city, which resembled a mountain, with a tower in the center that had to be miles high. The buildings were of every color, some of them clear as crystal, many of them purple, none of them the dull gray of steel or stone. The city was surrounded by a long, winding mountain range with snowcapped peaks, jagged white fangs against the yellow sky.

And then they were moving past it quickly, over the range, which revealed another city on the other side, this one just as magnificent. Mason heard his breath catch, because in the distance, another city faded into view through the air, followed by another.

Above the cities were narrow lanes of air traffic, small ships zooming back and forth, but not as many as Mason had expected. Most of their traffic was probably still close to the ground, like on Earth. They passed city after city, including one that was bigger than any Mason had seen before. The building at the center of it was needlelike, stretching higher than they were flying. In the dingy light, it still shone brightly, somehow appearing purple one moment and then red the next.

"And that is where I live," the king said, pointing at the needle, which was still shifting between purple and red, like the two Rhadgast colors. "I hope you can visit someday."

"It would be an honor." For one brief moment, Mason

couldn't believe where he was standing or where he was going. "Do you rule over all of this?" That was the legend the ESC spread, but Mason couldn't imagine one man ruling everything.

"Yes and no," the king said. "There are many kingdoms and many kings. And there is a council of these kings, of which I am the head. That's why I was the one to sign the treaty." Mason wondered if that was intel GAS would be interested in. Mason had always thought the king ruled over almost everything. "Only Fen, the continent that split away, is not under the treaty," the king added, "but they're of no threat to you."

Mason wanted to ask why, but he decided to stop asking questions lest he seem too curious.

After the last city, there was nothing but forest. Trees with blue leaves stretched out for miles in every direction. Patches of the forest were green, and some appeared red. Mason tried to imagine what Skars would look like from space, without all the pollution. It had to be prismatic. Or maybe all the colors blended together into a fuzzy brown.

"Mason, the Rhadgast school will not be easy. Many inside have never met a human and have only heard about them in classrooms, where antihuman propaganda is still taught in certain independent communities. It will be difficult, and it will be dangerous."

"I know," Mason replied, but he was still chilled. If the king thought it necessary to warn him, it was probably pretty bad.

The Hawk continued over hundreds of miles of forest, until it began to slow. "Almost there," the king said, and together they rejoined Merrin and Tom. But not before the king gave Mason another pair of purple gloves. "Put these on. The journey to the school may be a perilous one."

Mason took the gloves gratefully. When they remade the connection to his brain, he almost breathed a sigh of relief. But these gloves felt different somehow, not the ones he had grown to love over the last few months. He transformed them into bracers to hide them from his Rhadgast escort.

The four Rhadgast waited patiently by the exit. The king gave Mason and Tom a parting nod. "Be strong," was all he said, before turning away with a swish of his black cape.

Merrin looked distraught, her eyes a little glassy. She pulled Mason and Tom into a hug at the same time. "I wish I could go with you."

"Me, too," Mason and Tom said together.

"We will see each other soon." Merrin didn't sound convinced but followed after her father without looking back.

Behind Mason, the airlock hissed and thumped and then opened. Strange air rushed into the exit compartment, ruffling Mason's hair. When he turned around, the four Rhadgast were staring at him, two on either side of the open doorway.

"You want the honor?" Mason said to Tom.

"That's all you, my friend."

Mason nodded, then walked down the ramp and became the first human to set foot on Skars.

Chapter Six

The Hawk sat in a clearing surrounded by forest on all sides. Above, the sky was yellow and churning in every direction. Despite the visible pollution, the air smelled sweet. It was chilly, and goose bumps broke across Mason's back and down his arms.

Tom came down the ramp and stood next to him.

"So . . . alien planet," Mason said. "What do you think?" This was not like Mars, a place Mason considered home as much as Earth. Mars just had rocks and dust.

Tom shrugged. "I think we need to be careful."

"That's a nice, boring answer."

Tom grinned, but Mason knew he wasn't going to say anything bad about Skars while the four Rhadgast were within earshot. Or lightning shot.

"We're late," Reckful said. "Consider this your first test." He broke into a jog for the forest, his robes flowing out around him, and the three other Rhadgast followed. Mason and Tom shared a look, then took off in pursuit. The blue-green grass under their feet was short and springy, and the gravity seemed to be weaker here—Mason and Tom were almost flying across the grass. But they weren't nearly as quick as the Rhadgast, who had already crossed the tree line into the woods. Behind them, the Hawk's engines began to spool up, and wind pressed Mason from behind.

Mason and Tom entered the forest together. The tree trunks were widely spaced, but the branches above created a dense canopy that blocked the yellow light. He only saw the leading Rhadgast because their gloves burned softly, red and purple light swaying up and down as they ran.

"Why do I have a feeling," Mason puffed, "that they would leave us behind if we lose them?"

"Because that's probably what would happen," Tom puffed back.

The forest floor was thick with gnarly, curling roots, each one a hazard. Mason kept his knees high as he ran. They skirted the edge of a pit filled with bubbling black liquid. The smell in the forest was suddenly rotten, almost a feeling on his skin. Then all at once the lights ahead disappeared.

Mason realized something odd: there were no animal sounds coming from the forest. No chittering insects. The woods felt dead. The only sounds came from their lungs and feet and the rustle of their clothes.

Tom began to slow but Mason grabbed his arm. "Keep going!" he said, putting on a burst of speed.

A low moan came from the branches above them—*ErrmmmmmmmmUHHH*—and then thick vines were unfurling from the darkness, dropping down and lashing at Mason and Tom. One coiled around Mason's wrist, tightened like a fist, and tried to yank him off the ground.

"The trees are alive!" Tom yelled.

"You don't say!"

Mason skidded to a stop, and a vine took the opportunity to curl around his neck. Little barbs on the vine dug into his skin, drawing beads of blood. Tom was suspended in the air, two vines holding him up by the arms. Mason growled in defiance, but it turned into a choking sound when the vine constricted and tugged, trying to lift him off the ground. He closed his eyes, let his gloves slide over his hands, then he clapped them together; a blade of pure electricity appeared. The lightning sword shone brightly in the darkness, crackling in his hands. Mason flicked his wrist, severing the vine around his neck. He dropped back to his feet as the severed length slipped from his shoulders. Then he leapt forward, swinging the sword in an overhand slash. The blade bit through Tom's vine with a sizzle, and the tree actually *screamed*. The scream wasn't just a reaction: it sounded angry. Spinning leaves began to drift down from above, but Mason ignored them, until one spun toward his neck and drew another bit of blood.

Mason grabbed Tom's ankle just as the second vine pulled them higher toward the canopy.

"Just let me go!" Tom said.

Mason didn't bother with a response. He opened his right hand, and the blade snapped out of existence. Then he shot a bolt of electricity from the same palm. It hit the vine a few inches above Tom's hand, and together they fell hard to the forest floor.

Tom groaned. "I think a root just impaled my kidney."

"You're fine," Mason said, pulling him up, batting away a few razor-sharp leaves. More vines were snaking down from the canopy. "Let's move!"

They started to run again, but the vines weren't giving up. Mason shocked the ones that came too close, but he couldn't get them all at once. A vine grabbed his ankle, and he fell to one knee. The other vines seemed to sense his vulnerability, and they turned away from Tom and shot toward him.

Mason felt something in his gloves, a kind of yearning, an urge to break free. The material was humming against his hands. He lifted them up, palms out, and released the pressure. A crackling dome of electricity snapped into place around him, severing all the vines within its radius. The veins of light curled and wove together, making the dome more and more opaque, until the dome solidified into pure violet light with a deep metallic sound, like plucking the galaxy's biggest guitar string. But just as soon as it formed, it disappeared, leaving the ground around him smoking and scorched. His head felt swimmy and his hands were buzzing with energy. He held them up to his face and stared. Around them, the vines were retreating slowly, almost respectfully.

Tom was staring at him, mouth agape. "Um . . ."

"Well, that's new," Mason said.

"How . . . ?"

"I have no idea." Mason swallowed, then stood up on shaky feet. He shook his head to clear it and almost fell over. "We're too far behind."

Tom was still staring at Mason, not with shock now but concern. "Are you okay?"

Mason shrugged. "Okay enough to get out of this place." He thought he saw something then, a large shadowy form through the tree trunks. It had the shape of a man but was much taller and wider than any man could be. He blinked and it was gone, more shadows in its place. *Just nerves, and creepy trees,* he thought.

They broke into an easier jog in the direction the Rhadgast had gone. No more vines came near them. They ran for fifteen more minutes, until light appeared through the trees ahead. It grew brighter and brighter, until they stepped out of the forest. The Rhadgast school was just ahead.

Chapter Seven

The school was one enormous dome in a perfectly circular area clear of forest. It rose so high, Mason had to crane his head back to see the top. The dome was halved by a black line right down the middle, from top to bottom. To the left of the line, the dome was painted a deep crimson. To the right, the brightest violet. The dome was on the edge of a cliff: beyond it, the ground dropped away completely, and didn't rise again for many miles. In the hazy distance, an enormous mountain range was visible.

Mason suspected the dome was one half of a sphere, the other half hidden underground.

"I can't believe we're actually here," Tom said, echoing Mason's thoughts. He reminded himself of their mission: *It's not to learn the ways of the Rhadgast. There is something happening in this school that has the ESC scared, and you're going to find out what it is.*

He would also find the truth about his parents. No order would dim that desire or keep him from pursuing it.

The king's Hawk was parked next to the sphere, by a row

of Sparrows, which were the needlelike fighters the Tremist deployed in space battles.

"They made us take the long way on purpose," Mason said.

"Of course. If we couldn't make it through the forest, I guess we have no business being a Rhadgast, right?"

Tom had a point. Mason still felt weak from creating the electric dome. The gloves had taken something out of him to do that, and he couldn't help but wonder what else the gloves were capable of.

At the base of the dome, Mason saw the four Rhadgast waiting for them, so he just rolled his shoulders to loosen them up, then marched forward with his head held high. He might be here to train, at least officially, but Mason Stark was ESC first and always, and he would make them proud. If he couldn't live up to his impossible legend, he would still try his hardest.

Reckful began to clap as Mason and Tom approached. The four had removed their masks again, and Reckful was smiling. "How does it go? You clap your hands together, yes? To show approval?"

"You got it," Mason said.

Reckful clapped a final time. "Wonderful! See, I'm learning."

A huge door in the dome slid into the ceiling. Mason started toward it, but Reckful held up a hand. "I'm afraid we'll need those back, for the moment at least." He was pointing at Mason's forearms, which hid his gloves.

Mason didn't want to give them up, but there wasn't much choice. He pulled them off and handed them to Reckful, who tossed them to one of the purple Rhadgast. "Perhaps you'll get them back soon," Reckful said. "Though I'm hoping you have blood."

Mason had no idea what that meant.

The closest purple Rhadgast made a rude sound that was halfway between a laugh and a sigh, but full of contempt; he kicked at the dirt.

"He cheated!" the other purple one said. "I have his gloves right here!"

"Not my fault you didn't take my extra pair," Mason said. Reckful winked at him.

The open door was waiting. Together they walked through.

➤ The next hour was a blur. Mason and Tom were ushered through a series of hallways, where they were scanned by lasers of every color. Their possessions, including their boots, which held their hidden communicators, were taken to another room. Mason didn't know what to do. He couldn't just say, *Um, actually, can I have my boots back? There's a device I need in there so I can spy on you guys.* They'd figure something out; they always did.

Mason and Tom put their uniforms in a bin reluctantly. Tom rubbed his thumb over the ESC insignia, staring down at it wistfully.

"We'll wear it again," Mason said, before they walked into the next chamber, this one with hoses hanging from the ceiling. Here they were sprayed down with a sticky liquid that smelled a lot like pine sap. Once Mason and Tom were covered head to toe, they were doused in a second liquid that washed away the first.

The Tremist who decontaminated them (Mason assumed that's what they were doing, since they were definitely carrying germs alien to Skars on their skin) wore masks and never spoke to them, even when Mason tried to greet them.

"They must think we're dirty humans," Tom quipped, and got a face full of spray for it.

The whole time, Mason wondered what would happen if they couldn't recover their com devices. Would the grand admiral send in a small team of Reynolds to retrieve them? Would he think Mason and Tom were dead, and declare all-out war? No, you didn't get to the head of the ESC by being an idiot, of that Mason was sure, or at least partially sure.

Toward the end, Mason and Tom were fitted with thin belts that had silvery discs embedded on the surface. A Tremist technician, speaking to them for the first time, explained, "These belts will allow you to control your movements in zero gravity, and they are never to be taken off. Do not try to remove them."

So that's how they fly around! Mason almost wanted to laugh, having guessed belts the first time, when he and his crew fought their first Rhadgast in the gravity-free bay. Mason winced as the weird plastic heated up and fused around his abdomen. He picked at the edge, but the belt was firmly in place, like it had melted to the skin. The silvery discs began to glow with a soft blue light.

Tom was picking at his, too.

"Try not to break it, Renner."

Tom gave him a look; he was clearly not amused by all the poking and prodding.

The implants came last. Another Tremist, this one a tad

friendlier than the one before, said, "This implant will allow you to understand the Tremist language as if it were your native tongue. Everyone in the school is not going to speak human just for your benefit, understand? This will be the last time anyone speaks your language here."

Mason never saw the implant, but he felt the Tremist probing the base of his skull. "There is a two percent chance you will reject the implant and die immediately."

Mason was about to protest, but something punched him in the back of his head, and then a cool liquid sensation spread throughout his brain. It was a different feeling than when he downloaded the history of the People on Nori-Blue. He'd unpacked that knowledge while he was unconscious aboard the Egypt, and now it was always waiting in his head, a part of him. He didn't have to study it. As part of his mission to spread the truth, he'd shared his knowledge with hundreds of ESC, and the king had done the same with his people. Scribes on both sides were re-creating the book from memory, and soon everyone would be able to read the history.

The sensation faded to nothing, and he could actually feel the knowledge, a new weight in his brain. He thought of the Tremist word for "sky" and realized there were many different languages on Skars. Not just different dialects, but different languages entirely.

"Implant successful." The technician spoke now in the Tremist tongue.

"Whoa whoa whoa," Tom said, holding up his hands. "What did he say? About dying? Could you understand him just now?"

The technician held a cylinder to the back of Tom's head, and then Tom flinched, blinking rapidly.

"Congratulations," the technician said. "You have survived."

"Thank you." Mason used the Tremist dialect preferred by the school (which he also inherently knew; the dialect was called Mhenlo dai Cross, which roughly meant "People of the Fields"). Mason had to stop and think about it to realize the words for "thank you" came out sounding like *pelly vos*. That's how natural the language now felt. What Mason really wanted to say was: *Don't ever operate on us again without our consent,* but he didn't.

"There are two chickens in the garden," Tom said in the correct dialect. He caught Mason's eye. "What? Just testing it out."

"If you're quite finished," the technician said, "you're late for the address." He held two folded sets of clothes in each hand. Mason took his and unfolded them. There were simple fitted pants, an undershirt, and a jacket that buttoned up the front, with a high collar and a long, rounded tail in the back. It was almost a robe but not quite. All of it was gray, he noted, not purple and not red. His gray boots were softer than his ESC boots and ended mid-shin.

"What address?" Mason said, putting on his new uniform. *I need to find my boots.*

The technician was blank-faced for a moment, and then his upper lip peeled back in the loose translation of a grin. "All students must choose on their first nights."

"Choose what?" Tom asked.

But Mason already knew. Four Rhadgast had brought them

here, two purple and two red. The dome itself showed them the divide between the Rhadgast. Mason had no idea what the divide meant, but clearly one existed.

"Between Blood and Stone," the technician said.

Chapter Eight

Mason and Tom were told to follow a line on the floor. The line was yellow, and it pulsed as they moved along, fading behind them and growing in front of them. It showed them the way to the Inner Chamber, which was located in the exact middle of the sphere. It was there the rhadjen met once a week to discuss the current state of the school.

Mason kept opening and closing his hands, missing the comfortable snugness of his gloves, the protection they provided. His skin felt fragile without them.

Tom was just as jittery as they walked. "I don't feel prepared for this. At all."

"We can speak all the Tremist languages, so that should help," Mason said, though he knew what Tom meant. Mason didn't feel prepared either. Only a few months ago they were trying to take back the Egypt from Tremist hands. . . . Now they were here to learn from them? All the while executing a secret mission that Mason didn't know how to begin.

They followed the line through turn after turn. The walls in each section were made from different materials: some walls were polished metal, some were stone, some were glass, many of them glowed softly, providing dim ambient light. It was comfortable, warm, and inviting. Mason took that as a good sign.

Soon the line on the floor began to pulse faster, which probably meant they were getting closer. Mason's heart rate began to rise along with the line; thankfully he no longer wore the mechanism that so helpfully warned him to keep his vitals in check. The tail of his jacket touched against the back of his thighs weirdly, distracting him. *Focus, Stark. You're behind enemy lines.*

The line ended at a large set of double doors carved from dark alien wood, with whorls and spirals in the grain. If he unfocused his eyes slightly, he could just make out the details of some ancient battlefield depicted in the whorls, but as soon as he thought he saw something, his eyes would refocus.

Mason and Tom stopped in unison.

"Uh . . . do we knock?" Tom asked.

"I don't know," Mason replied. He lifted his fist to knock, then lowered it.

"Well we can't just stand here."

"I'm *thinking*—"

The doors opened under their own power, cutting him off. Before them was an enormous hall, with rows of benches to the left and right of a central aisle, almost like in an ancient church. A very *wide* ancient church.

The rows were filled with rhadjen, Tremist around his age, some younger and some older. On the left side of the room, some wore their hair in high ponytails, like Reckful did.

Over half of them had dark red hair, and their black robes had crimson accents on the collars and wrists. To the right of the aisle, the rhadjen were like the familiar Rhadgast he already knew, like Merrin and the king—mostly purple or violet hair, with purple accents on their robes. As far as Mason could tell, the hair colors were natural, and having purple hair did not necessarily mean you were Stone, especially since Merrin had purple hair; she was not a Stone, or even a rhadjen. Maybe once you chose a side, some were more likely to dye their hair to fit their new identity.

At the other end of the hall, a Tremist stood on an elevated platform. He wore neither red nor purple, but gray, like Mason and Tom. Two more Tremist were with him on the platform: the red one sat near his right, the other on his left. They were clearly the heads of each group of Rhadgast and wore the colors of their side.

The rhadjen all turned in their seats at once, staring at Mason and Tom, who were frozen just past the doorway. Then the room exploded into chatter.

The rhadjen were talking to each other loudly, but Mason could only hear snippets: *That's them, the humans are here, why are humans here, they saved the Will, I don't care, they've met the king, they know the king, Mason Stark, he doesn't look tough.*

The chatter seemed to go on for hours, but it was really only seconds. The gray Tremist on the platform suddenly lifted one booted foot, then stomped it on the floor. Mason could see the shock wave spread out from the boot as it rippled the dust in the air. Mason's ears popped and wind buffeted his face. The doors slammed shut behind him.

"What a wonderful im*pression* you've made on our two new brothers tonight, students." The gray Rhadgast did not have gray hair: his hair was a mix of red and purple. If the colors were any indication, and unnatural like Mason assumed, then he was the leader of the school and could therefore not take a side.

"Such discipline," he added.

No one spoke. It was so quiet Mason could hear himself breathing. His eyes roamed over the students, who were now facing forward, completely still.

"Welcome!" the gray Rhadgast said to them. "I am Master Zin, leader of our humble school." He gestured grandly at the Tremist—no, *people*. They were all people here, and Mason had to start thinking that way. Tremist were not really aliens so much as cousins.

Master Zin swept his hand toward the Rhadgast on his right. "This is Master Shem, leader of the Bloods." He made the same gesture to the man on his left. "And this is Master Rayasu, leader of the Stones."

Master Rayasu, a man paler than any Tremist Mason had seen so far, was drilling holes in Mason with his eyes. He had a vertical blue scar on his forehead, which matched his bluish hair.

"Thank—" Mason's throat was so dry the syllable turned to dust. He swallowed hard. "Thanks."

"Thank you, sir," Tom added, elbowing Mason in the side.

Master Zin nodded, seeming pleased, though his smile was hard to see across the room. He spoke to everyone now: "These two humans have come to train at our school. They have been afforded all the rights . . . and responsi*bilities* . . . of a normal student. Is that understood?"

"Yes, Master Zin," everyone replied in unison. Even the teachers. Mason noticed older men and women sitting at the outer ends of the rows, clearly not students. "Now, with the addition of these two, plus two more who have come to train from halfway across Skars, we will have . . ." Master Zin trailed off as a Stone rhadjen stood up.

It was a girl around Mason's and Tom's age, thirteen, if Mason had to guess. Her violet hair was done in two braids down her back. She looked over her shoulder at Mason and Tom, her eyes narrowed in disgust and hate.

"Yes, Lore?" Master Zin said with extreme patience. "You have something to share?"

"I do," Lore said, facing Master Zin. "It is well known that these two humans are responsible for the deaths of several Stones."

The words had barely left her lips before the room exploded into chatter again. *They don't exactly run a tight ship here,* Mason thought. But he was proved wrong a second later, when Master Zin stomped his boot a second time, much harder, rocking the students in their seats. Tom actually took a step back from the wind. Mason's ears were ringing.

"I will *not* ask for silence a third time," Master Zin said.

The effect was immediate, as before. No one spoke or moved. Lore didn't seem to know whether to sit or stay standing, so she just clasped her hands behind her back, then checked over her shoulder again, as if to make sure Mason and Tom weren't sneaking up on her. They weren't.

"Continue, please, Lore, if you have some point to make," Master Zin said from the front.

"As I was saying, Master, these humans are killers. They cannot be Stone. Not ever."

Mason almost expected chatter to break out a third time, but it seemed Master Zin's threat was enough.

Reckful was suddenly standing at Mason's left. Mason glanced up at the only Tremist who had been kind to them so far, looking for some kind of direction.

"Master," Reckful called out, giving a slight bow. "I offer to take these two under my tutelage, as my personal squires. I will mentor them, and they will be Blood. I think that may be best for everyone."

Mason wanted that to happen very much. He felt a sudden rush of warmth for Reckful, who was still a stranger but willing to risk himself for the two humans. Mason shared a look with Tom, who appeared just as pleased.

Please say yes, Tom whispered to himself.

"Reckful, you know that every student must choose his or her own path," Master Zin said, and Mason's heart sank into his lower abdomen. "If they are of the Blood, it will be apparent this very night. If they belong to Stone . . ." Master Zin looked over the purple side of the room, as if daring them to object. There were a few mutterings but no obvious talking. "That will *also* become clear."

Reckful bowed again. "Of course, Master." Then, to Mason and Tom: "I tried."

"Thank you," Mason said. "I owe you."

Reckful only winked like he had before, but it didn't feel natural, almost like he'd learned that some humans wink and was trying to appear more human to Mason and Tom. As if reading his mind, Reckful whispered, "Do you wink with your left or right eye?"

"I don't think it matters," Mason said.

"Now then," Master Zin said, rubbing his hands together. "We have a few more menial matters to discuss. Is there anyone here who would be kind enough to escort our newest rhadjen to their living quarters while we finish and prepare the rooms below?"

Please someone volunteer, please someone volunteer, Mason thought. The rejection was already stinging his face.

But then a member of the Bloods stood up, a tall boy already possessing the animal grace of the Tremist Mason had met in battle. Many of the students gasped, and Mason couldn't tell if that was a good or bad thing.

"I will take them," the student said.

Chapter Nine

The student looked over his shoulder at Mason and Tom but didn't stare at them the way Lore did (who, by the way, was still sneaking glares at them). Instead, he seemed to be enjoying the spectacle.

"Thank you, Po," Master Zin said, nodding.

Po bowed, then shimmied out of his row and into the aisle. Every eye was on him, and Mason heard more than one person mutter *traitor* quietly. From *both* sides. It only seemed to make Po smile. And then smile wider as he reached Mason and Tom.

"Shall we?" Po said, gesturing toward the doors.

"We shall," Mason replied. "Thank you."

"Don't thank me yet," Po replied. "C'mon, let's get out of here."

Mason and Tom opened the doors wide enough to slip through, then shut them as Master Zin began to talk. The feel of glaring eyes on Mason's back was severed like an electrical current.

The trio walked down a hallway in silence for a full minute. Mason didn't know if he should try to strike up a conversation or wait and see if Po was feeling talkative. He shared a look with Tom, who shrugged.

"Do humans have a hard time speaking?" Po asked finally.

"No, I—" Mason began.

Po grinned. "I'm kidding. You're nervous. You should be."

"Why did you offer to take us?" Tom said, a hint of accusation behind his voice.

"Maybe I'm just curious about you two," Po replied.

The line in the floor was once again leading them somewhere, though Mason had no idea how it could know where they were going.

"No really, why would you volunteer in front of everyone?" Mason asked. "Did you not hear what they were saying?" There had to be some underlying motive; perhaps Po wanted something from them.

For the first time, Po's face became somber. "You want the truth? Once, my older brother's ship was boarded by some ESC special forces. They had him cold. A few of the humans executed his men, but one human put a stop to it. He had to draw his weapon against his own kind." Po's eyes were far away, remembering. "My brother told me there was more to humans than we thought. He died three years later, but I still like to believe it's true."

"I'm sorry," Mason said. "It's true, though. Just as there is more to Tremist than humans think."

Po nodded. "You should hear the stories they tell about you guys—humans, I mean. Scary stuff."

"Oh, we have some stories about you, too," Tom said.

"In truth," Po said, "I don't like doing what everyone else does. It's boring."

Mason liked Po already; he wondered if they'd just made a solid friend, an ally. They would definitely need one.

"Master Zin seems nice," Mason said, hoping to keep Po talking.

But all Po said was, "Yeah. He is. But make sure Master Zin visits *you*. You don't ever want to visit *him*."

"What do you mean?"

"Exactly what I said," Po replied. "And one more thing—I'm assuming you're both considered pretty skilled back where you come from, but this place is different. There are fourteen million applicants from schools across the country each year." He smiled slyly. "About a hundred new students get accepted. I hope you brought your brains *and* your muscles."

Mason smiled. "If we were missing our brains or muscles we would certainly be dead."

Tom elbowed Mason. "Thanks for the warning," he said sincerely.

They walked down another hallway, this one made of warm wood, like a hollowed out tree trunk. It ended at a wide spiral staircase that went straight up. It too was made of warm wood; Mason thought he could feel heat through the soles of his boots. "I thought we have to choose something first?" Mason said. "How can you know where we're going to sleep?"

When Po spoke, it was like he was reciting something from a rule book. "In an effort to better integrate the two factions of Rhadgast, students will share sleeping quarters with students of an opposing faction." He made a snorting sound, like that was the most ridiculous thing in the world. "*Better integrate,* yeah right. It'll never happen."

"Why did you split in the first place?" Mason said.

The wooden hallway now had doors set into the curving wall. "That's a story for another time. I'm sure you'll learn about it in Lore class. Not *that* Lore." They stopped at the third door. "Here we are."

Po pushed the door inward. Inside was a large room with bunk beds lining the walls.

"Wait," Mason said. "Master Zin mentioned preparing 'the rooms below.' For what?"

Po hesitated.

"We've handled bad news before," Tom said bluntly. Too true.

Po spoke very carefully. "When students come to this school, they must undergo a test to find out which side they belong to. You have to earn your gloves." Mason had noticed earlier none of the students were wearing Rhadgast gloves, including Po. Which made him feel a little better about his surroundings.

"We saved the Will," Tom said defiantly. "Mason already earned his gloves."

"Yeaaah," Po said. "I heard about that. Very impressive and everything. It's just . . . you have to earn them the way everyone earns them." He looked pointedly at Mason's hands. "I notice you don't have your gloves now."

"They took them," Mason said, a little surprised at how angry it made him. He'd used those gloves to save lives. Tom was right: they *had* earned them. "Then what can you tell us about the test, if we have to take it?" Mason said.

"I can't tell you anything. It's different for everyone. Also, I'd get expelled if they found out."

"Well how do we get on your side?" Mason asked. "The Blood side?"

"Oh, I can't tell you that either. You have to find it in your heart." Po widened his eyes, and Mason knew he'd just been given a clue. Maybe not the best clue, but a clue.

"Can you fail?" Tom said. Tom prided himself on *not* failing tests.

Po shrugged. "I don't know. You probably don't want to. *I don't know.* I shouldn't be talking about it. Just take a second to freshen up, drink some water, meditate . . . whatever you humans do. Then find your way back. Be there in ten, and don't be late." Po darted back into the hallway, then leaned back through the doorway. "The heart," he said, tapping his chest, then disappearing.

It was a good thing Mason had paid attention to the many turns they'd taken. Tom looked at him quizzically. "Uh, you know how to get back?"

"Yep. Pay attention next time, Renner." He clapped Tom on the shoulder, who playfully shoved him back.

"I was just testing *you*," Tom said. "I know exactly how to get back."

They took in the room around them. The bunks were identical, the beds neatly made as they would be back at Academy II.

"So," Mason said. "Is this another test? Figure out which one is ours?"

"No idea," Tom replied. "If all the tests are like this, though, it should be a pretty easy ride."

Yeah, that isn't going to happen, Mason thought. Neither of them could afford to think anything was going to be easy. Or safe.

They spent a few minutes exploring the room, careful not to touch anything that wasn't theirs. Each bunk was big enough that a student could sit up and pull a desk out from the wall. Or at least it appeared that way; Mason and Tom didn't want to monkey with anything. He was sure they were still being monitored in some way. All he could really think about was the communicator: if they didn't get the devices back, things would go south rather quickly.

They drank from the bathroom faucets, which created neat little waterfalls that dropped into basins. Then they stretched, wanting to be prepared for whatever the test threw at them.

Mason and Tom walked back through the different hallways, coming across exactly no students or teachers or anyone.

"I do not like this," Tom said quietly, as they approached the great room where the rhadjen had gathered.

It was completely empty, not a soul in sight.

But there was now a circular door at the far end, behind where Master Zin had been standing. Mason couldn't say if it had been there before.

"Join the club," Mason replied. "I guess we go through there."

"A brilliant deduction," Tom said.

Mason did not know what lay beyond the doorway, and

the uncertainty made his stomach feel as if it were full of writing beetles. The deadly, spiky, smelly kind found on Nori-Blue. But he had a mission, and he would not fail, not if he could help it. The thought of being placed with the Stones made him start sweating, but he'd made it through worse. They both had.

Mason and Tom shared another look, then walked across the room to the circular doorway. Once they passed the threshold, the door slid shut behind them with the heavy sound of grinding stone. They were plunged into total darkness and a silence so vast Mason could hear the blood running through his veins and the quickening of his breath. The floor began to drop.

"Just an elevator," Tom said in the darkness next to him.

"Just a dark, *weird* elevator," Mason replied.

Tom gave a nervous laugh. They descended for a few minutes in total silence. Mason missed the gentle *whoosh* of an ESC lift; the absence of sound gave the unpleasant sensation of falling forever.

Finally, after the longest minute of his life, the doors opened on a small cave cut from the rock under Skars. The cave had two doors, one on the left, one on the right.

"I guess they want us to split up," Tom said.

"A brilliant observation," Mason replied.

They walked to the middle of the cave. The left door had a label on it that read MASON The right door read THOMAS

Tom stuck out his hand. "Good luck, my friend."

Mason looked at Tom's hand, then pulled him into a hug. After a moment, Tom hugged back.

Then they went into their separate rooms.

Mason's was dark like the elevator had been, but then it was lit. Mason squinted against the sudden light, but his eyes soon adjusted. And standing before him was Merrin Solace.

Chapter Ten

"Merrin! It's you! What are you . . . How . . . ?"

Mason trailed off, taking in their surroundings. It was another cave room, with a domed, craggy ceiling. At the far end was a chest of some kind, a treasure chest, if he had to call it something.

Merrin was wearing a Tremist suit of armor. The surface was black but shifted colors depending on the light. Sometimes it would appear an oily purple, sometimes green. Mason was familiar with the armor, having stolen and worn a set himself. The pieces were able to mold to the individual user, just like the Rhadgast gloves.

Merrin had a neutral expression. She was clearly not as happy to see Mason again as he was to see her.

"Merrin . . ." he said.

"Hi, Mason." Her arms were held weirdly at her sides, extended away from her body.

The sick feeling returned to his stomach. *Something's not right.* Why would Merrin Solace be part of his test?

"Mason, I'm really sorry. I'm really, really sorry."

Mason approached her like he would a wounded animal.

"Merrin, talk to me. Talk to me. It's me. Tell me what's going on."

Merrin's eyes were wet now. "They said you have to choose."

"Choose what? What do I have to choose?"

Merrin *screamed.* She fell to one knee, her left hand clutching her right. Mason stepped forward to help her, but he faltered, his lungs seizing, and he almost passed out right there. Merrin's right glove had contracted slightly, crushing her hand within.

Mason was on his knees next to her, trying to pry the material off. He cut his hand right away on the strange metal but didn't care. Merrin shoved him away, and he fell onto his back.

"No! Get away!" she said, nearly sobbing. "You can't get it off!" Her violet eyes were bright with pain, her forehead sweaty. She was taking quick, short breaths. Mason had never felt so helpless in his entire life. Everything was forgotten aside from his friend in agony.

"Tell me what's going on! *How do I help you?*" Mason said. He took a step toward her again but was careful not to get too close. Even as he watched, the armor over her forearm began to contract, and she grimaced, fresh tears flowing down her face.

"They told me you have to—that we *both* have to choose. You can either let the armor crush me to death . . ."

"Or what? Or what?" Mason would do whatever the other option was. He would never stand there and watch the armor slowly kill his friend. "Tell me what it is!"

She looked over her shoulder. There was a door in the

wall. An ancient door made of wood and banded with iron. Her voice dropped to a whisper. "They told me—they said there are five members of the ESC behind that door. Prisoners of war. You can choose to let them die to save me."

Cold spread across Mason's chest, as if he'd just been stabbed by a sword made of ice. Merrin screamed again as her armor tightened around her elbow now, the sound fading to a sob.

"It's a trick," he breathed. "There has to be a way to save you both." He knew the answer in his heart, even as he said it.

"Don't play their game, Mason! You have to let me die. Those soldiers are innocent!"

Who are they? Are they young? Are they grizzled veterans? Does it matter?

"What happens if I don't choose!" Mason said. He dropped to his knees in front of her.

She shook her head, her lips clamped in pain.

"Tell me!"

"Then you die. But me and the soldiers will live."

His path was entirely clear.

Mason took her face in his hands. Her skin was flushed violet, hot to the touch. They stared into each other's eyes for a long, clear moment, her face momentarily free of pain.

"If you don't let me die," Merrin said, "I will never forgive you."

Mason wouldn't have to live with that.

"If you were ever my friend," Mason said. His cheeks were wet, too. "If you ever cared about me, you'd understand. I won't let anyone die for me. Not you and not those soldiers."

Merrin looked at every inch of his face, as if searching for some deception. Mason was leaning on her now, a little. Their faces were so close.

"Mason . . ."

"I've never been so sure in my life," he said. "I pick myself."

She became blurry as his eyes welled again: this was it. He had made it to this point in his life, and nothing would come after. And he was okay with that. There were worse deaths than sacrificing yourself for your best friend—and for your fellow soldiers. Mason blinked to clear his eyes.

And when he opened them, she was gone.

Mason fell forward onto his hands and knees. A tear dripped from his cheek, darkening the stone floor. He looked around the room, searching for her, but there was only the chest. It was glowing now, with a soft white light.

Mason wanted to laugh, but he couldn't. He could barely move. *Stupid,* he thought. *You're stupid.* Of course the Rhadgast would never kill the king's daughter. They would never crush her hand. If he'd taken three seconds to think about it, he would've known it was an illusion. Somehow the Rhadgast had made him think his friend was here, in extreme agony. The implant in his brain felt hotter than before—maybe that was the thing responsible. Mason couldn't think of anything crueler.

But he found the strength to stand up.

He looked around the room, expecting someone to be there, to tell him how he'd done, but there was no one. He walked to the chest slowly, as if approaching a live bomb. It seemed to glow brighter as he got closer, a gentle light that felt good to look at. It was the only thing that felt good.

He kneeled in front of it, searching for some kind of clasp; there was none. So he gripped the top and lifted. The lid swung open on oiled, silent hinges. Inside was a folded piece of black fabric. He stared at the fabric, knowing what it was but not so sure he wanted it any longer.

But after a few seconds, he decided he had to keep going. He pulled out the fabric, which was a simple black robe like those the other students wore. This one had crimson accents on the collar and wrists. And beneath the robe was a new set of Rhadgast gloves. These were red, too, a darker red, not purple like the ones he was used to.

I am of the Blood, Mason thought.

Still alone, he stripped out of his gray initiate shirt and pants, then put on his new gear with shaking hands. First pants and a shirt, both black, then the robe, which was closer to a long jacket, open in the front so his legs wouldn't get tangled if he tried to leap on something. *This is serious now. You made it. You're a student.*

Right before he put the gloves on, his sleeves automatically retracted to right above his elbows, then stiffened. He pulled the gloves on, and they sealed against the fabric on his arms. He held them up to his face, then willed the gloves to peel away from his hands. Soon he had deep red armbands from elbow to wrist.

"Not everyone can do that," a voice said behind him.

Mason turned around slowly, not wanting to show how startled he was. It was Reckful, smiling at him from across the room, wearing gear not unlike Mason's. His red hair was pulled into a high ponytail.

"Do what?" Mason asked.

"Manipulate their gloves like that. We don't teach that in the first year. You already impress us."

Mason didn't care, but he didn't want to say that, so he said nothing. Probably because a part of him really did care if the Rhadgast were impressed. Mason clearly wasn't welcomed by many at Academy II, and he desperately wanted to feel welcome, even if it was in some creepy temple on Skars.

"So, I guess I'm Blood now."

Reckful nodded. "Blood believes in the heart," he said. That was Po's clue right there, the heart. "When presented with the choice between sacrificing ourselves or saving a loved one, we will always put the other person first."

"And a Stone kills the strangers," Mason said. Sounded about right.

Reckful nodded again. "Or they let their loved one die, for the sake of whatever five strangers we tell them is on the other side of the door. Stones believe in strength. They believe in our might, our importance. We Bloods believe in that too, of course, but in a different way. We are servants. To be Stone, you have to believe your life is more important, more valuable, than the person or people you sentence to die."

"I'm glad I'm Blood, then," Mason said, and he really meant it.

"But that means they believe in the greater good, Mason. The Stones are not evil. They make hard choices better than us. They will sacrifice thousands for the sake of millions. And you can't say they're wrong. It's no small thing to ask someone to die for people they've never met."

"I'm still glad." Mason thought back to when he was ready to sacrifice his crew against the Fangborn ship, in order to save the Olympus and the Will. Was that something a Blood would do, or a Stone?

"I am as well." Reckful crossed the room and extended his gloveless fist, pale and corpselike in the dim light.

Mason touched his fist to Reckful's, as a terrible thought occurred. Mason knew the answer before he asked. "What about Tom? What did Tom do?"

"What do you think?" Reckful said, raising an eyebrow.

"He sacrificed," Mason said.

"Indeed. You are both strong in your desire to help others. Stone is no place for you, though I have no doubt your conviction would let you excel there. Stone was also . . . no place for me."

"You were Stone?" Mason said.

Reckful looked away for a moment. "I am Blood, as you can see."

Mason decided not to push the idea. "It was still wrong. To make me see that and feel that. I thought it was really Merrin. How did you do that?"

"How is not relevant. We find the person most important to you and make you see that person. And you're right, it is a terrible thing. But how else do we find out what's truly inside you?"

Mason didn't know.

The light had faded from the now-empty chest. It was just a regular old chest.

"Are you ready to begin?" Reckful said.

Chapter Eleven

Tom was waiting for him outside the room. Next to him was another teacher, also Blood, a younger man with a cherry goatee and sculpted eyebrows. Tom was pale, eyes on the rock floor. He didn't even notice Mason at first, until Mason said his name.

Tom looked up, as if being woken from a dream. "Stark. Hey."

"You okay?" Mason said.

"He's fine," the teacher next to him said. "He did well."

"This is Karn," Reckful said. "You'll learn from him soon."

"The entire school watched both of you complete your tests," Karn said flatly.

The cold hand of embarrassment gripped the back of Mason's neck. He'd been crying during the test. Or maybe not crying, but there were definitely a few tears. Just some minor precipitation. Nothing noticeable. Probably.

"*What?*" Tom said. "You have *got* to be kidding."

"I don't kid," Karn said. "And you will have to soon learn

the proper way to speak to your teachers. The first day you get a pass, because you're human."

"Our apologies," Mason said, when it didn't seem like Tom was going to reply.

"Give them a break, Karn," Reckful said. He guided Mason and Tom back toward the elevator. "Come. Tomorrow is your first day of class. You need your rest."

They got into the elevator together and rode in the darkness back to the main level. The Inner Chamber was once again packed with students. When Mason and Tom appeared, everyone on the Blood side of the room stood up. They didn't clap like humans, but standing seemed like some form of recognition. Next to Mason stood two more new initiates: one a young boy who was wearing Stone robes, and a girl wearing Blood, like Mason and Tom were. The girl—who had reddish pink hair, smiled widely at Mason and Tom; the boy looked at them like they were a piece of gum stuck to his shoe.

Mason elbowed Tom and whispered from the side of his mouth, "So, Stones are pretty friendly types, eh?"

The students on the Blood side of the room sat back down. Master Zin was walking up the aisle toward them. Up close, he appeared neither old nor young, but there was something ancient about him.

"I am no longer shocked the Stones kept trying to kill us last summer," Tom said.

Mason couldn't hate the Stones. One had given Mason his old gloves. The very same Stone had told him to seek the Rhadgast out if he wanted the truth about his parents. They couldn't all be bad. And maybe "bad" was the wrong word.

Different. The Stones had the same goals, same desires, just a different philosophy about doing what was necessary to win.

Master Zin took center stage. He cleared his throat, looking out over his students. "Today, we glimpsed the hearts of our four newest students. Some of you know what they will experience in the coming days, weeks, and months, and some of you have also just started your journey. Remember who they are. Remember who *you* are. And remember why we're all here. To learn . . . and better our*selves* . . . and become de*fenders* of the things we hold most precious in this world. Though we may wear different colors and believe different things, we are the same. . . . We are *Rhadgast.*"

Mason heard a girl snicker from the Stone side and say under her breath, "Does he think he's the Great Uniter?" Which got a few hushed giggles.

Master Zin raised his hands, choosing to ignore this. "Now get to sleep. Tomorrow the sun will rise again."

The rhadjen rose in unison and began to file out of the Inner Chamber. The girl who had made the joke stood up, too, but Master Zin pointed at her and she froze. "You and your friends will be in my office within five minutes." Mason made a note: *Master Zin does not ignore things.*

"Yes, Master," the girl said, before joining the queue.

Master Zin turned toward Mason and Tom. Mason looked around: it was just the three of them up there. "Well done. Truly, well done." And then he walked away, his gray robes billowing behind him.

Mason and Tom followed the line back to their dorm. The halls were mostly empty, save for a few random rhadjen who were taking their time getting back to the dorms. No one looked at them for more than a few seconds, but it was clear they wanted to. One bigger boy, a Blood, stared at them the entire time they walked down one section of hallway. Mason asked him, "Do you have a problem?" before Tom pulled Mason along. The boy still seemed to be searching for an appropriate response.

When they were alone, Mason said, "Tell me about your test." They followed the line up the spiral staircase.

"It's personal," Tom replied.

Mason didn't say anything for five seconds. Then he said, "I'll tell you about mine."

Tom wouldn't look at him directly. "It was . . . it's stupid."

"You can tell me," Mason said, putting his hand on Tom's shoulder. When Tom remained silent, Mason let his hand fall and they climbed in silence. "It's just me and you, buddy. We have to trust each other if we're going to survive—"

"My mom."

"What?" Mason said.

Tom balled his hands into fists. "They convinced me my mom was still alive, that they brought her back to life, they . . . I believed it. It was her. She was wearing this armor that—"

"—began to hurt her," Mason finished.

Tom nodded, eyes brightening. "The same thing happened to you? Who did you see?"

"Merrin."

Tom's eyebrows shot up.

Mason only shrugged.

"Not Susan?"

"No."

They were almost to the dorm now.

"But—"

"How did yours end?" Mason said, before Tom could ask another question.

"I . . . told my mom I couldn't watch her die again, and that I wouldn't let the POWs die either. And then she disappeared."

"At least we're not Stones," Mason said as they reached the door. It slid open on their approach.

Po stood in the doorway. "Welcome! Nice robes you got there. Or nice colors, I should say. Come inside."

Mason and Tom walked through the doorway; Mason fought the urge to examine the room again. Searching for traps or listening devices would not make the best first impression.

Most of the rhadjen were already in their bunks. Two were hunched over a workbench in the corner, tinkering with a pair of gloves. Every eye went to Mason and Tom.

One boy on a top bunk on the left, a Stone, said, "Oh good, the humans get to stay with us." Which confirmed that the Tremist had a firm grasp on sarcasm.

Mason met every gaze without faltering, without looking away. He would not show weakness, not an ounce.

"This is your bed," Po said, pointing at a bottom bunk on the left. He pointed to Tom's bed, which was right next to Mason's, but Mason didn't hear what Po said. He was staring at Lore, and she was staring back. She was right above his bed, up on one elbow with a paper book open on her chest. She had taken her two violet braids and twisted them together.

Up close, Mason noticed the sharpness of her eyebrows, which gave her a look more severe than the other Stone, like she was always staring intently. Maybe she hadn't been glaring at Mason at all, and that was just how her face looked. There was nothing soft about her.

Mason held her gaze, and soon he felt everyone in the room staring at them. But he didn't look away, and neither did she. She was a pro, but she didn't know what human children did at Academy I. They had staring contests. They arm wrestled. They competed all the time, in everything.

Po cleared his throat.

Finally, Lore's eyes flicked away, then back to him. But it was enough. Mason had won the stare-down. *I will not be intimidated.*

"So that was super awkward," Po said.

No one laughed.

Po did introductions right then. The room housed four rhadjen, not including Mason and Tom, but there were enough bunk beds for twelve, three on each side. Two Bloods and two Stones, before Mason and Tom had to mess the whole balance up. Mason suddenly missed his crew very much. He missed Jeremy and Stellan the most, but also Willa and the other cadets who had helped him save the Olympus and the Will. He wanted his Egypt 18.

He made a mental list so he wouldn't forget a name and offend someone. Or just look plain dumb and forgetful. First there was Po, of course, but Mason didn't think he'd be forgetting Po anytime soon. The only other Blood was a girl named Risperdel. Her hair was black, which made her appear human, if you ignored the supernaturally translucent skin. She was the only Blood besides Po who didn't look upon Mason and Tom with some level of suspicion.

"Risperdel is the fastest girl in the school," Po said. "That's about all she's good at. That, and getting into trouble, or getting us into trouble." He laughed and ducked as Risperdel threw a sock at him. But she must've been fast, because it still hit him in the face.

Po threw it back at her. "The first of our two stony friends here is Lore, who you've already met. Hmm, what can I tell you about Lore that you don't already know? Lore . . . wins. Anytime there's a competition, she wins. Be on her team."

Mason nodded at Lore; he would not be forgetting her either, the girl who had called him out in front of the entire school five seconds after his first appearance. When they made eye contact a second time, she gave a grudging kind of nod, as if she had decided to accept his presence, but barely.

"And Jiric is the smartest person I know," Po said. He scratched his chin thoughtfully. "In fact, we're all kind of the best of the school, now that I think about it. I wonder if that's why you guys were put here."

Risperdel grinned. "So we make the humans look bad."

"That won't be so difficult," Jiric said.

Jiric's face was pinched, like he was smelling something terrible. He wore a pair of simple eyeglasses, which enlarged his eyes and made him appear human. When Mason looked closer, he could see data scrolling down the lenses. What data Jiric would need to be monitoring, Mason had no idea. The human look was helped along by the fact that he was the first Tremist Mason had ever seen to have shoulder-length brown hair.

Mason learned that a Tremist only had one name, but if he or she was part of a family descended from royalty, the full name held a part of that royal name. Like Risperdel was directly related to the House of Del, a minor royal family from a faraway kingdom.

The door opened. Reckful stepped inside their dorm.

"Sir," Po said. Risperdel, Jiric, and Lore slipped from their beds to stand at attention. It was so like the ESC that Mason had to blink the idea away.

"Stand easy," Reckful replied, "It's after hours." The students relaxed, Jiric and Lore crawling back into bed. "I'd like to have a word with our newest brothers for a moment."

Mason's heart began to pound: there was something about the way he said it. His usual smile was gone.

Reckful gestured toward the door, and Mason and Tom stepped past him into the hallway. Reckful followed, and the door shut behind them.

"This way, please," Reckful said, starting down the corridor. Mason and Tom shared a brief look, but Reckful called over his shoulder, "Move like you have legs."

Something was wrong. Very wrong. Mason began to sweat, but he took a series of calming breaths, his mind already picturing their escape route. He knew which direction to run for the exit, but then what? The school was surrounded by a living forest of trees intent on sucking them up into the branches.

Mason and Tom caught up to Reckful, who led them into a new hallway—not wood, but a metal that reminded him of the Egypt's decks, silvery and polished. A door opened in the wall, and Mason and Tom stepped through. The room began to brighten from everywhere, that strange ambient lighting present throughout what they had seen of the school. The room was some kind of storage unit, full of equipment Mason didn't recognize or understand.

When it was bright enough to see well, Mason looked at Reckful, then down at Reckful's hands. On each palm rested a small black disk. Their communicators. He had found them. Or someone had found them and given them to Reckful.

Slowly, Reckful curled his fingers over the disks, then let his hands fall to his sides.

"Do you think Rhadgast are feebleminded?" he asked, his tone ice cold.

Mason and Tom were frozen. Out of the corner of his eye, he saw Tom shift his weight onto his back foot. *Don't do anything stupid. Don't do anything we can't undo.* He had to trust Tom to be smart, because Tom *was* smart.

"I desperately want to trust you both," Reckful said. "I desperately want peace between our species. *Desperately.* You see, you two may be seen as heroes for the events that transpired this last year, but I have been on the front lines. I have seen the destruction of war." His face was twisted in a grimace, so strange after seeing his near-constant smile and easygoing demeanor. "I know what enemy we need to face together. They're coming for us right now."

"So do we, sir," Mason said. It slipped. The words just bunched up in the back of his throat, then came out in a tumble.

But rather than set him off, Reckful's forehead unwrinkled, and he gave a long sigh out of his nose. "I suppose you do."

Mason knew he had two choices:

1. Lie.
2. Tell the truth.

There were no other options. Reckful had come to them first, taken them to this room. Mason and Tom should already have been arrested. Or dead. But they weren't.

"Tell me the truth," Reckful said. It was like he was reading their minds. Or, more likely, it was just the most obvious request.

Tom looked at Mason, as if waiting for his call. It was up to him. But Reckful already had their communicators, so Mason had to assume he knew the truth.

"I'm here for two reasons, sir," Mason began.

Reckful nodded. "Go on."

"When I was on the Will, a Stone—though I didn't know he was a Stone at the time—told me that I should seek out the Rhadgast if I wanted to find out the truth about my parents."

If Reckful knew any of this, his face didn't reveal it. He just listened.

"So . . ." Mason continued, ". . . once I got permission to take the invite to this school, there was nothing that was going to stop me."

"And the second reason?" Reckful said.

Mason licked his lips. Telling the truth would be a direct violation of mission parameters. An ESC spy wasn't supposed to reveal himself to the first person who asked. *He already knows,* Mason thought. *If you lie, you're gone, and this is all for nothing.*

"If you refuse to tell me, or if I think you're lying, you're gone."

Mason began to speak. He had to trust his instincts, whether they were borderline treasonous or not.

Reckful lifted his hand sharply. "Let me finish. There is no play here. You will not overpower me and escape. You will simply be locked away until the leaders figure out what to do with you. So I want you to think about that first. The truth, and nothing less, or your time here is finished."

Tom nodded at Mason. "Do it, Stark."

Mason sighed. "The ESC has intelligence indicating the Tremist might be working on some kind of weapon or project that is in violation of the new treaty. A project that may be based *inside* the Rhadgast school. Since I'm the only one allowed to be here, I, along with Tom, have been tasked with uncovering the plot—I mean, if there is one."

Reckful was silent for a very long time, but Mason could see the cogs turning behind his eyes. "I see," he said after a long moment.

Mason and Tom awaited their fate. All Mason knew was that he didn't want to die here. Not after he already thought he was dying less than an hour ago. He wanted to see Merrin again first, to make sure she was all right. And Jeremy and Stellan, too.

"What Rhadgast told you about your parents?" Reckful asked.

"He wore a mask," Mason said.

"Would you recognize his voice?"

"I don't know," Mason said, though the memory was seared into his brain. "Possibly. Yes."

"I don't know anything about your parents," Reckful said. "Or about any secret project happening at the school. I would know about a weapon, I think."

Mason dared to hope they would be allowed back to their dorm.

Reckful opened his hands; the communicators rested on his palms. "What happens if you don't use these? Will there be a problem?"

"I don't know," Mason said. "We're supposed to report that we got here safely."

"If we go off the grid," Tom said, speaking for the first time, "there may be some kind of retaliation."

Reckful snorted, as if the very idea of retaliation against the Rhadgast school was hilarious.

A moment passed. Reckful took a breath, but Mason and Tom couldn't.

"I don't know if there is anything going on here or not, and I hope in time you report that there isn't. I sincerely hope that."

He extended his hands, presenting the communicators to Mason and Tom. "Take these. Hide them well. If you're caught, I will say I had no idea you had them, and I will stand by as you're both tried for espionage, the penalty for which is death."

A chill ran up and down Mason's spine.

"I can't help you," Reckful added. "But if there is something to this intelligence, I want to know about it."

Mason and Tom took their communicators. Mason

dropped his into the back pocket of his pants. His hand was shaking with relief now.

"I am choosing to trust you boys."

"Why?" Tom blurted. Mason wanted to slap him.

Reckful's eyebrows shot up. "That's a good question. Perhaps I have my own reasons, Tom. Did you consider that?"

Tom visibly paled.

"Not everything is right at this school," Reckful said. "I can feel it. And I want the truth."

"Thank you, sir," Mason said quickly. "We won't forget it." Reckful's words left a chill in Mason's gut.

Reckful nodded. "See that you don't. Now get out of here. You can find your way back, I hope."

Reckful opened the door, and Mason and Tom squeezed past into the hallway. The air was cooler out here. Mason took a big gulp of it, looking over his shoulder as Reckful shut himself in the small room.

"That was a pretty close call for our first day," Tom said flatly.

"Tell me about it. We can't do anything easy, can we?"

Tom didn't quite smile: they were both too tense for that. "I hope we know what we're doing," Tom said.

"I don't think we do," Mason replied. *But it's too late now.*

They got back to the dorm and found the rhadjen had hung their robes from pegs on the wall. They were all in bed, working at their pull-out desks. Mason and Tom hung their robes in two open spaces, and now they wore a uniform not unlike the one worn by ESC cadets. Mason and Tom took off their boots in silence, sliding them into the row of boots, careful to make them as neat as the rest.

"Welcome back," Po said, and Mason was grateful he didn't start asking a bunch of questions Mason couldn't answer.

The Blood girl known as Risperdel didn't mind. "What was *that* all about? An after-hours visit from a teacher?" She looked around the room as if trying to gain support for how crazy of an idea that was. It didn't seem so crazy to Mason.

"He just wanted to make sure we were settling in," Mason said.

"Reckful's manner was less than casual," Jiric replied, studying them with his huge eyes.

"Save your questions for tomorrow, please," Po said. "Lights out in thirty seconds." He seemed to be the captain of the room, or something. The rhadjen listened. Over the next thirty seconds, the lights began to fade. Mason caught Lore's eye one more time before crawling into the bed below her. He couldn't make out her expression in the dim light, but assumed it wasn't that friendly.

Mason listened hard in the dark. The sounds were familiar, since he'd been sleeping in a room with a dozen or so people his entire life. First there was the rustle of blankets and pillows, the sniffles and sighs. Then the change in breathing, indicating someone was unconscious. He listened hard for Tom, who was still awake but completely still. He could not see him in the dark.

After another five minutes, Mason pulled his blanket up over his face, then slipped the communicator into his hand and squeezed. He felt a tingle build in his palm as the natural electric field produced by his body linked with the machine.

Mason closed his eyes, and when he opened them, he stood in Grand Admiral Shahbazian's office.

"There you are!" GAS said, slamming his hand on the table. He was smiling. "I was worried. Are you safe?"

GAS's own communicator rested on a pedestal in the middle of his office, displaying a silvery-white re-creation of Mason's face. Mason didn't have to speak aloud, just think, and the head spoke.

"We're safe," Mason said. "I'm sorry, this was the earliest we could make contact." One problem with the communicator was that it blocked out the things happening around your body. Someone could be looming over him right now, watching, and Mason would be completely unaware.

Suddenly, Tom snapped into focus next to him. He was using his own communicator.

"Good, you're both alive," GAS said. Mason could tell his eyes were bloodshot, even though he was seeing them through a series of cameras on GAS's communicator.

"Were you expecting otherwise?" Mason asked.

GAS made a beckoning motion with his hand. "No, no. Just give me your report. In detail."

So they did. Mason and Tom gave a play-by-play of their experiences since leaving the grand admiral.

"I'll expect to hear from you when you have something useful to report."

Mason thought the revelation that there were two kinds of Rhadgast was pretty important, but maybe GAS had already known that.

"When do you want us to check in?" Tom asked.

"When it's safe. Get some sleep you two. Watch your

backs . . . and well done." GAS killed the feed, and Mason returned to the darkness of the room, surrounded by sleeping rhadjen.

He had expected to stay up the entire night. He was on an alien planet, in an alien school, on an impossible mission he didn't know how to begin. Using the communicator had left his head feeling buzzy, his skin itchy.

But once he closed his eyes, Mason slipped into a dreamless sleep.

Chapter Twelve

A loud buzzer ripped Mason from sleep, followed by a voice: *Welcome to the morning, rhadjen. Be in the refectory within five minutes.*

Mason jolted upright and banged his head on Lore's bunk, not used to sleeping with something above him again (at A2, he was given the top bunk by fellow cadets as a sign of respect, which had only made Mason feel more alienated).

The others were already out of bed, filing in and out of the bathroom. Mason could hear running water. He followed them in, found a stall, and went inside to take a five-second shower. The water blasted his body so hard it hurt. He bumped into Tom on his way out.

"Let's stick together," Tom said.

"You don't have to tell me twice," Mason replied.

"Watch it," Jiric said, bumping into Mason from behind. It didn't seem on purpose.

In the main room, the rhadjen dressed in their robe jackets. Mason thought the robes were cool, always seeming to hover a millimeter off the floor, but he couldn't understand the tactical advantage of them. The robes the full Rhadgast wore seemed even more complex, with layers that moved and flowed like they were alive. Mason remembered seeing his first Rhadgast, how his robes had rolled out from him like a tapestry of lashing snakes.

"We're already late!" Po called out. As they finished dressing, Mason worked a finger under his collar and tugged to get some air.

Mason pulled Po aside as the others pulled on their boots. "Where do we go?"

Po winked and patted Mason on the back. "You're with us, humans."

"Thank goodness," Tom said.

"We join you guys for class?" Mason said. "All day?"

"Yep. Bunkmates take classes together to build trust as a unit. One day when we graduate, we'll be deployed as a unit, too. For right now, I'm the team captain, until someone proves they're better for the job."

"And I'm coming for you," Risperdel said, grinning.

Genius, Mason thought. Academy I and II had units, but you didn't train with the same group of people during your entire time at school.

Po started for the door, but Mason grabbed his arm lightly. "Wait."

Po huffed a sigh. "Do you want to be late?"

"No, just . . . there's a lot of extra beds. Who else used to be here?"

The rustle of fabric faded away, silence took its place, and Mason realized everyone had stopped getting dressed and was now staring at him. Mason regretted asking, but if there were members of the team he and Tom had just replaced, he wanted to know. Mason and Tom didn't need another reason to be hated.

When Po looked at him, his eyes were solemn. "We don't know where they are. They're probably dead. Don't ask about it again." He looked at the others. "Finish up. Now." They listened.

Two minutes later Mason and his new team were in their first class of the day. There were no desks, no chairs. The classroom was a cylinder-shaped room on level 43, on the Stone side of the dome. Mason had assumed Bloods didn't travel to the Stone side of the sphere, and vice versa, but it appeared he was wrong. There were no "sides."

The seats were molded force fields that sprouted from holes in the floor. His teammates spread out and sat down in them, shifting around into comfortable positions. The force field chairs shifted along with them, molding to their bodies. It beat the crappy plastic chairs Mason had sat in his entire life, and they didn't even make your hair stand up.

The teacher's name was Broxnar, and he was by far the largest Tremist Mason had ever seen, with an immense pale bald head. He wore silky purple and blue robes, closed by an ornate sash that was ready to burst apart if he inhaled too deeply. But when he saw Mason and Tom, he gave a genuine smile, and there was excitement in his eyes. To Mason, it seemed similar to the excitement a child has when they visit a zoo for the first time and see some long extinct animal clone.

Broxnar rubbed his meaty hands together. "Welcome to our two newest students. How do you say your names— May-sun and Tome?"

The team laughed, almost all of them, including Po. It wasn't a mean laugh, which was a start.

"Mason and *Tom*," Tom corrected him.

"Yes, yes, May-son and *Tommm*," he said, tasting the words. "You'll excuse me, I don't have an implant for your language."

To Mason's extreme surprise, Lore giggled.

"Now, I have a special treat for you all, in honor of our new friends, our new brothers in attendance. Today we're going to experience the Divider and the Uniter."

A halfhearted cheer went up. Po actually started clapping. He leaned in. "Normally Broxnar teaches Rhadgast history, but with lectures and homework. Today we get to *live* something, thanks to you guys."

Mason had no idea what that meant, but he said, "Uh, happy to help."

Suddenly the room went dark and silent, and then a lone Tremist appeared in the middle of the room, like magic. Tom stiffened beside him, and Mason almost jumped out of his seat. But it was an illusion. It had to be. Just like Merrin had been.

When this Rhadgast, clad in robes of silver and sage, turned around and seemed to look directly into the eyes of every student in the room, they all cheered.

"Quiet!" Broxnar said. "You may have seen this before, but there will be a new test."

Over the next hour, Mason watched a series of events unfold right before his eyes, as if he were living it alongside the ancient heroes of the Rhadgast. The events told the story of the Uniter and the Divider.

Six hundred years earlier, the Tremist had not achieved space flight, but they had mastered electricity. Like humans once had, the Tremist warred on their own planet. The Rhadgast, elite warriors sworn to defend the people, were deployed to quell uprisings as they came, but soon there was a rift in the mighty order. Many Rhadgast were dying, and some wondered why they were sacrificing their lives for others when no real progress toward peace was being made. These Rhadgast wanted to get serious with their attacks and brutally strike at their enemies until the only option was surrender.

The other half of the order said these Rhadgast were hard as Stone and had forgotten *why* the Rhadgast had chosen them. Their power was given to them so they could protect people.

Today, Broxnar was quick to point out, the Stones no longer believe in such ferocious tactics, thanks to the leader of the Stones, Master Rayasu. They simply believe in the greater good. The value of one life does not compare to many, but they will still protect the innocent and die for them. Broxnar didn't elaborate on what involvement Master Rayasu played in changing the Stones to a less-extreme faction.

The first Tremist Mason saw in the room was the Divider, Jo-tep. He split the Rhadgast order one morning at the start of a long winter. There was no Rhadgast sphere in those days, just a series of wooden buildings linked together with tunnels underground.

Mason watched as the Divider walked up to the house of the Blood leader, put his hands on the wall . . .

. . . and let his gloves heat until the wood caught fire. The

Blood leader escaped with his life, but the war was on. It lasted forty-seven years, closer to thirty Earth years, since Skars orbited its star faster than Earth. Skars suffered as much as the Rhadgast, for they revered their elite warriors, and to see them fighting among themselves demoralized the entire planet.

It was a dark time. The king was assassinated, and for twelve years there was no leadership.

Until the Uniter, Aramore.

The Bloods in the classroom cheered when he appeared. He was riding what appeared to be a large jungle cat with red and black stripes, to match the red and black stripes in his hair. The cat reminded Mason of a saber-toothed tiger, but with the two big fangs jutting up from the bottom, not the top. The Uniter wore leather armor and a cape of crimson silk. He wore gloves more powerful than anyone else's, Broxnar said. The gloves were neither red nor purple, but black. Completely black. Where he got the gloves from was a mystery. Where he *came* from was a mystery. One day he just showed up, wielding the gloves of power.

The Uniter stood in front of a legion of Bloods. "I am here to put us back together. I am here to restore dignity to our order."

And that's exactly what he did. He warred with the Stones who would not cooperate. He warred by himself. Though there is no record, it was said the Uniter created an impenetrable dome of black lightning around himself, then walked directly into the Stones' camp, repelling any who came too close.

By then the Divider was an old man. He was wearing a different kind of armor than before, Mason noted. It looked exactly like the armor worn by the Tremist King, or at least the armor he used to wear.

"Yield," the Uniter said.

"Never," the Divider replied.

The Uniter killed him on the spot. Eyewitnesses said the Uniter had been corrupted by the gloves and began killing Stones left and right, even those who submitted to his power.

Soon after, the Stones agreed to peace with the Bloods, and the Uniter disappeared into the woods, never to be heard from again. It was said he joined up with a group of Tremist who chose to live a simpler life among the trees. It was said his gloves were still out there, waiting to be found by the next person who needed them.

Construction on what would become the Rhadgast sphere began. (Mason was right: half the school was below ground.) The Stones would retain their identities but war no longer. And so it has remained to this day.

But Mason's focus had drifted during the last parts of the lesson.

He couldn't stop thinking about the gloves.

Chapter Thirteen

"It isn't okay to show that," Jiric said when the lesson ended and the lights returned. "That is anti-Stone propaganda."

Broxnar chuckled, rubbing his hands together. "My dear rhadjen. I believe it's called history. You can't know where you're going until you see where you've been."

"It demonizes the Stones," Jiric said. "Just because we didn't choose to die."

Risperdel snorted. "You mean, just because you chose other people to die instead of you." But she didn't say it with malice, somehow; it was a friendly jibe. Jiric only fluttered his eyes and pretended to ignore her.

Broxnar cleared his throat. "That's enough, Risperdel. As I said, history. I myself made the hard choice. There is no shame in it. Some might argue letting yourself die is the easy way out. The way of not choosing at all."

Mason hadn't thought of it like that. He didn't really agree, but he could see where Broxnar was coming from. Perhaps the Stone decision isn't any easier than what Mason had done.

A bell chimed.

"That's all," Broxnar said, tugging on the sash around his waist. "Remember what you saw here today."

The students left with three minutes to reach their next class. The hallways were full of rhadjen running to and from classrooms. Many of them found the time to stop and gawk or point at Mason and Tom. It was day two, technically their first full day, but the attention was already getting old. They were humans, so what. They were almost the same species. But at the same time, it wasn't as bad as the attention they got at Academy II. Here Mason was an oddity, not a hero.

"So what did you think of our history?" Po said, sidling up to Mason and Tom as they climbed one of the many spiral staircases.

"It was definitely interesting," Tom said.

"And explains a lot," Mason said, a little too loudly, though he didn't mean anything by it one way or another. Lore, who was walking just a few paces ahead, turned around to give her seven hundredth glare of the day. Or maybe it was just her sharp eyebrows.

"Yes it does. Hey, listen. Tonight, if you want to have a little fun, meet me outside the Inner Chamber. You, too, Thomas."

"See?" Tom said. "Even he can call me by my full name. It's not that hard."

"I'm working on it, Tom," Mason said.

"So you'll be there?" Po asked. "Great!" he said, before Mason could answer. By then they were already at the next classroom.

Their second teacher, Grubare, wore robes of jade green,

no ornamentation, nothing to say whether he was for the Bloods or Stones. His eyes were black as coal, but his hair was silvery-pearl. He watched Mason and Tom as they found empty seats within the room.

On the desk sat a small, monkeylike creature covered in bristly blue fur. It was eating a small chunk of neon-yellow fruit that it turned over and over in its tiny paws. It's head had four eyes instead of two, one in front, in back, and on each side, so it could see 360 degrees. The eyes were sleepy, half-lidded, as it nibbled on the fruit.

"This is going to be amazing," Jiric said, before Lore hushed him.

"You're right, this is amazing," Grubare said from the middle of the room. "We're making history, isn't that right? Humans, not only on Skars, but inside our facilities, learning our secrets. It is so *amazing*."

"I'm sorry, sir," Jiric said.

"Silence. You're to write an essay about the meaning of the word *amazing* and its relation to the human race. By tomorrow." Grubare turned his dark gaze upon Mason and Tom. "I have been asked to tolerate you in my classroom. No, I have been ordered to tolerate you. Do not disturb the lesson."

"We aren't plan—" Mason began.

"You are disturbing it right now." As if to send the point home, the creature chirped and climbed up Grubare's sleeve to settle on his shoulder. And as soon as it was settled, it popped up and disappeared into a fold inside Grubare's robe. "And you are disturbing my gromsh."

Gromsh? "I'm—"

Tom nudged Mason with his elbow, a gesture Mason had learned meant, *Shut it, Stark, if you know what's good for you.* So Mason shut it.

Grubare went on with some lesson about the current socioeconomic climate emerging from the western continent and the impact it would have in trade over the coming decade.

Mason assumed this was some boring economics class (Academy I and II had their fair share of those), but then he heard Po whisper to Risperdel, "Why are we learning economics? We're supposed to go over defensive tactics for zero-gravity battles. We have a test this week." Mason, having missed the first four weeks of the semester, hoped he and Tom wouldn't have to take it.

Risperdel shrugged, then lifted her chin in Mason and Tom's direction. "Maybe he doesn't want to teach *them*."

Mason and Tom found the lesson interesting, though without context Mason didn't really know what Grubare was talking about. The rest of the lesson finished without incident, mainly because Mason was able to keep his mouth shut the entire time. Still, Grubare's eyes found him often, as if searching for some reason to scold. It was only at the end of the class that Grubare said, "Make sure your belts are operational. Tomorrow we will be in the gravity room, and we will see if you can continue your training here at this school."

Jiric and Risperdel exchanged worried looks.

Mason expected more classes throughout the day, but at lunch Po told him everything after this would be "physical" in nature. Meaning combat. Mason felt his blood quicken at the word. He was ready to show the Rhadgast what he could do.

"They're going to test us," Tom said beside him. "See what the humans are made of."

"Whatever gave you that idea?" Mason said.

Tom ignored him. "Oh look, they're testing us now."

A group of four Stones were walking toward them from across the refectory, which was at the very top of the dome, on the side overlooking the valley. One entire wall was curved glass that ended at the top of the dome. From this high up, Mason could see deep into the valley and the mountains beyond.

The lead Stone reached the table and said nothing.

"Hello," Mason said. Perhaps they just wanted to greet the school's newest rhadjen. Perhaps they wanted to be Mason's new best friend.

"Go sit down, Juneful," Lore said calmly. *Juneful.* Was he from the same royal family as Reckful?

She wasn't exactly defending them, but Mason appreciated the gesture.

"You're going to get *all* of us in trouble," Jiric added.

Mason caught Risperdel's eye, and she rolled hers. "Just be cool," she whispered. Mason nodded.

"You're on the Blood side now?" Juneful said to Lore, after taking five seconds to process her statement. He was clearly the leader of the four. His hair was long and black and flowed free. Mason was already imagining a series of defensive moves if Juneful attacked. Having long hair was a stupid choice, tactically. Mason could grab a handful of it, and from there the fight would be in his control. But maybe long hair had some kind of ceremonial significance. Or the Rhadgast were cocky enough to just not care.

Juneful seemed to notice Mason scanning all of his weak points, his pressure points. His eyes narrowed.

"Is there something you wanted?" Mason said. He'd been dealing with bullies his entire life and was a little sad to find out they were no different here. Tremist bullies were just as clever as the slow-witted muscle-bound morons he had dealt with at Academy I and II. He began to wonder what the true differences were between Tremist and humans.

Juneful didn't seem to know what to say. Po was staring at Mason intently from across the table—the whole team was—but Mason kept his eyes on Juneful. His three boys were behind him, safely. They were followers. They were no threat.

"I suggest you go back to your table," Mason said. "I know you're curious about what humans can do, but I don't think you want to find out right now, in front of all your friends."

Juneful's mouth opened in shock, just a tiny bit. "What about you, human?" he said to Tom, no doubt ignoring Mason until his dull, aggressive brain could figure out the correct response. "Do you need your boyfriend here to protect you?"

"No," Tom replied. "But I like to let him because it makes him feel better, and because he doesn't mind dealing with scum."

Mason laughed. He couldn't help it; it was the perfect thing to say. Had he not laughed, Juneful would've probably sat right back down. But he did laugh, and it felt good to laugh again. It felt good that Tom felt good enough to crack a joke. So Mason laughed, but he never lost his readiness.

As he watched, the gloves hidden inside Juneful's robe slipped down over his hands. During school hours, no student was allowed to have his or her gloves over their hands unless they were in a combat-oriented class. Mason didn't know the punishment for violating that rule, and he didn't want to find out.

There was a tray of food in front of Mason. Juneful's hand darted down toward the edge of it, and Mason anticipated he would try to flip it into Mason's face. Mason did not want this to happen for a number of reasons, including that the food here was somehow worse than the sludge they served on ESC spacecraft. The refectory had better food available— he'd seen strange and colorful fruits and vegetables being served to the older students—but he and his team got various protein-based gelatins. It would make quite a mess and ruin the robes he'd gone through hell to earn. So Mason grabbed Juneful's luscious locks and yanked down just as Juneful was starting to lift the tray with his fingers. Juneful's face smacked into the tray with a wet splat. Some of the gelatins flecked Mason's robe anyway, but it wasn't nearly as bad. As Juneful was bouncing up, Mason shoved him one-handed into his three friends, who all toppled onto their butts.

Everything stopped.

Juneful blinked goop from his eyes.

As every Stone in the refectory stood up from their tables.

"Now you've done it," Po said, stretching his arms and yawning. He seemed resigned to their fates.

"You with me?" Mason asked Tom quietly.

Tom sighed. "That was ill-advised, but I guess we've done stupider things. Of course I'm with you."

"Okay, then," Mason said, and stood up, letting his own gloves slip down over his hands. "Who's first?" he called to the room.

"Sit down," a voice said behind him.

Mason looked over his shoulder to find Reckful frowning down at him. "I don't think tactically that would—"

"Sit *down*," Reckful said. He put his hand on Mason's shoulder and pushed him into his seat. Mason instantly transformed his gloves into bracers.

"What is the meaning of this?" roared a voice from the other end of the refectory. It was the head of the Stones, Master Rayasu. He stormed into the empty space between the tables, his robes flaring out around him, violet eyes blazing in a way that had to be artificial. Mason saw Grubare, who still wore nothing to signify if he was Blood or Stone, standing in the corner, watching. His gromsh perched on his shoulder, staring at Mason with at least one of its eyes.

"A little altercation, that's all," Reckful said.

"Altercation?" Master Rayasu said it like he'd never heard of the word before.

Reckful seemed prepared with a response. "Well, I'm sure these four didn't come over to our newest students and say hello, only to have Mason and Tom dump food on them and push them on the floor from a seated position. I can't imagine one human, unprovoked, doing that to four Stones . . . can you?"

"How dare you . . ." Master Rayasu said to Reckful.

"Master Rayasu," Reckful said, not cowering before the leader of the Stones, "would you kindly ask your students to sit down?"

All the Stones in the refectory were still standing. Mason could suddenly feel his pulse in his ears and neck. If this had been an ESC cafeteria, the instructors would've ended the fight and sent all offending parties to the brig, where the details may or may not be uncovered. Here it seemed like the two instructors were about to tear each other apart.

Po stood up. "Sir, Juneful was about to smash the tray into Mason's face. Mason was just faster."

"He's right," Lore said. "I warned them. I told you to sit down, Juneful." Mason had a feeling she wasn't defending him so much as she was embarrassed by the Stones.

Once Lore spoke, Master Rayasu frowned, some of the anger draining from his face. It seemed that a Stone speaking against another Stone settled the matter, at least with everyone watching. "I see," he said.

Master Rayasu looked down at Juneful, who appeared to be waiting for permission to move. Bluish-green food dripped off the end of his chin into his lap. "Stand up. You embarrass every Stone." With that, Master Rayasu stalked away.

Juneful stood up along with his friends, but there was a new look in his eye. It wasn't the simple boredom that drives most bullies to bully. This was something new, something dangerous and calculated. Mason had just made fools out of them in front of the entire refectory, nearly a hundred rhadjen, who would no doubt spread the news throughout the school by end of day.

Reckful audibly breathed a sigh of relief.

Mason twisted around to look up at him. "I'm really sorry. They were going to ruin my robes."

Reckful sighed again. "Robes can be cleaned, you know. You realize this is still your first day of classes?"

"Yes, sir."

Reckful didn't say goodbye, he just left, following after Master Rayasu. Mason imagined them having some knock-down, drag-out Rhadgast fight in the hallways, away from the students. Wall-to wall-lightning, and all that. He wondered who would win in that situation.

When Mason turned back to the table, everyone was staring at him and Tom again.

"Do you know what you've done?" Lore said. "Juneful isn't dumb. He won't forget."

"Neither will I," Mason said.

Lore snorted through her nose, as if to say *You have no idea what you're talking about.*

Chapter Fourteen

After lunch, Mason was disappointed to find out that first-time rhadjen had to undergo stringent health and stamina evaluations. Mason and Tom spent three hours running and jumping while wearing biofeedback harnesses. They were of course in excellent physical condition, thanks to the ESC. Over the last few months Mason had noticed an increase in his muscle mass and strength. They finished the final test, dripping with sweat, and were told that they were cleared for combat exercises.

That night was the weekly free-for-all, held in a room above the Inner Chamber. The room was a perfect replica of a forest, much like the one Mason and Tom had traveled through, minus the strangling vines. These trees had bright red and purple leaves, and branches that appeared flat and sharp, like they were made from swords rather than wood. The perimeter of the room was thick with trees planted in what felt like real soil under Mason's feet. The trees became sparser toward the middle of the room, where there were only a few trunks that could be used defensively.

The rules were simple:

1. Any rhadjen of any age can enter the free-for-all.
2. You have to turn down the power of your gloves as low as possible, so you can only stun, not maim or kill.
3. Falling down equals disqualification.
4. Last rhadjen standing wins.

There was no actual prize for winning besides bragging rights, but that was enough to get plenty of teams involved.

Po pulled Mason and Tom aside as the participating rhadjen filtered through the trees. The room was immensely tall, and some chose to scale the jagged branches. Mason watched as they disappeared into the leaves.

"Hey," Po said, grabbing his attention again. "I think you should sit this week out. Juneful is already gunning for you, and I'm sure everyone else is, too. Because, you know, humans." He shrugged.

This was not surprising.

Mason looked at Tom. Tom looked at Mason.

"We've decided not fighting would show weakness, which would invite further harassment," Tom said.

"What he said," Mason added.

A slow grin spread across Po's face. "Fine with me. I've been wanting to see you guys in action, anyway." Po licked his lips, eyes narrowing. "What say we call a truce until only the three of us remain?"

"Sounds good to us," Mason said.

A stiff, artificial breeze blew through the trees. It ruffled Mason's hair.

Po smiled. "The game has begun." He slinked backward, disappearing around the trunk of a tree.

Without speaking, Mason and Tom did the same, moving to the perimeter of the room. They didn't even have to discuss tactics: six-plus years in the ESC had prepared them, and they already knew how to work as a team.

"You know how to use those things?" Mason said, jerking his chin at Tom's gloves.

". . . In theory. They're not big on instruction here."

"Stay close," Mason said.

From the center of the room, Mason heard the initial sounds of combat: sizzling blasts of low-voltage electricity, a yell, a thump, the cracking of a tree branch, the scrape of fabric against fabric or skin. Mason and Tom hunkered down in the shadows, waiting it out. Every few seconds, a buzzer would sound, which Mason assumed meant someone was knocked out.

This was confirmed a second later, when a Blood charged them from the right. He should've had Mason and Tom cold—his gloves were already sparking with red light—but Mason and Tom dived out of the way, circling around the trunks and coming at the Blood from behind. The Blood got a single lance of electricity off, but Mason swiped his hand in front of his own face, as if catching a ball. Mason's glove fired a tendril that met with the Blood's, and both streams of electricity veered sideways, cracking into a nearby tree trunk.

Before the Blood could fire another shot, Tom stepped forward, dropping into a low stance with one foot forward and firing twin blasts from both palms. The Blood yelped and fell back on his butt, furrowing the soil.

Mason expected the Blood to be angry, but he actually smiled. "Not bad—*look out!*"

Mason spun, dropping instinctively, getting his hands up in time to meet several fingers of electricity with his outstretched palms.

The fingers wound together, thickening, replicating, until a semisolid wall of light formed between the combatants. Mason didn't know how many were on the other side. His hands were instantly too hot for comfort, and he felt pressure against his palms, nearly driving him back. He'd been in this situation before with Merrin, atop the cube as it was transforming into the planet-sized gate. That time they'd been fighting full Rhadgast who were trying to kill them, so this should've been easy.

Tom was next to him, adding to the wall, their combined electricity braiding together, becoming stronger.

"Throw it up high, on three!" Mason shouted over the crackling. A rogue bolt hit a nearby tree branch, setting it afire. "One, two, three!"

Mason and Tom threw their hands upward, and the wall of electricity lifted along with their hands, dissipating in the branches above, which began to smoke. There was one brief second where Mason could see his attackers clearly, the wall no longer between them, the shadows of violet and crimson electricity fading from his retinas. Two Stones and two Bloods, side by side. Currently, three of them were looking at where the wall of electricity went, confused expressions on their faces: *How did* that *happen?*

Mason didn't waste the opportunity. He clapped his hands together, thinking hard about what he wanted. What he *really* wanted was to win the free-for-all on his first day, to show his fellow rhadjen that humans were not to be toyed with or taken lightly.

When he clapped his hands, it wasn't a sword he desired, but a whip. A thick vein of bright red electricity sprouted from his hands, and he swung it from right to left like swinging a baseball bat. The whip lashed all four targets across the chest, driving them back and knocking them out of the fight.

Mason was about to celebrate this fact when someone from behind clamped their hands on the shoulders of Mason and Tom. Neither had a chance to even turn before the sneaky rhadjen squeezed their shoulders, delivering twin blasts that made their legs turn to water. Mason hit the ground hard, right next to Tom, who was struggling to breathe, his lips against the dirt.

Mason blinked blearily until the person above him came into focus.

Lore.

She gave them both a smile before backing up into the shadows. Mason stayed on his side, looking up at the cinders that drifted down around them, forcing himself to take deep, slow breaths as the adrenaline turned sour in his veins.

Tom lay next to him, panting. "Not a bad first attempt."

Mason laughed breathlessly. "We need to work on our

situational awareness." He was content to lie on his back for a while (the soil was quite cool and comfortable), but he jerked upright at the sound of a scream, high and long and garbled with pain.

He'd heard a scream like that before. He would never forget the sound as long as he lived.

It was the scream of someone dying.

Chapter Fifteen

Mason and Tom were on their feet in the next second. Stillness had settled over the trees, as if the remaining combatants had frozen. Then a buzzer sounded, and a shrill voice said, "Leave the arena immediately!"

Bloods and Stones began to drop from the trees and slink between the trunks. Mason was shocked: no one wanted to find out who screamed? Was it a prank? He started toward the sound, but Tom grabbed his wrist.

"Wait," he said. "We've already gotten in trouble once today."

Mason locked eyes with Tom.

"I can't believe I just said that," Tom said. "They sounded hurt."

They sounded worse, Mason thought. They crept through the trees into the semiclearing, as more rhadjen jogged for the exits. From the canopy above, Mason watched as full-fledged Rhadgast began to drop straight down, landing on one knee and a fist, then flitting away into the trees. He caught glimpses of them circling through the trees toward the source of the scream.

"This is bad," Mason said.

"What gave you that idea?" Tom said.

"No, I mean something is very wrong."

Mason followed the Rhadgast across the clearing and into the trees on the other side. He saw slivers of their black robes through the gaps in the trunks. The soil muffled Mason's and Tom's approach. It was suddenly very quiet.

Mason rounded a tree trunk slowly, seeing a scrap of black fabric on the ground. Then another, and another, this one smeared with blood. On the ground was a shredded robe with purple accents and red blood, but there was no rhadjen in sight, no body. Four of the Rhadgast stood around the robe, staring at it, clearly puzzled. Two of them wore masks, which glowed red. The other two glowed purple.

"This isn't possible," one of the Bloods said.

"Clearly it is," a Stone replied. "Spread out. Find the owner of these robes."

"What do we tell the students?" the Blood asked.

That's when they noticed Mason and Tom standing halfway behind a tree. The Stone made a very unhappy sound in his throat, and they didn't waste any time. The Stone's hand shot forward, lightning bursting from his fingers, and Mason barely ducked behind the tree before the lightning shot past his face, making his hair stand up.

They ran.

Mason's heart was in his throat, and his breath was in his ears, because he was running for no reason. They had been seen, and there was nowhere to go. They couldn't fight back without being killed.

"Wait!" Mason huffed, knowing there was no chance to escape. Tom was right next to him. "We should surrender."

"Thank Zeus," Tom muttered. The two of them spun around, dropping to their knees, and placed their hands atop their heads, fingers interlaced.

An artificial mist had filled the room, probably some automatic effect to make it harder for the students who would've survived this long to find each other. The four Rhadgast burst from the mist, the vapor swirling around their passing. Mason closed his eyes, expecting them to burn him alive, but they only grabbed him with rough hands and jerked him to his feet.

"We didn't do anything!" Tom said. "The king said we're guests. I'm going to have your badge. Do you have badges?"

➤ Two minutes later they were in Master Zin's office. It reminded him of Headmaster Oleg's office, but instead of the barren landscape of Mars through the floor-to-ceiling window, Mason could see deep into the enormous canyon. His office must be right below the refectory.

One Rhadgast remained behind: "Master Zin," he said, "I ask that these humans be placed under guard in the detention center. One of their teammates is missing, only his clothes were left." Mason couldn't see the Rhadgast's face, just the pulsing violet oval of his mask.

Master Zin raised his eyebrows, one of which was purple, the other red. "You think these two killed a fellow rhadjen and disposed of his body *inside* the free-for-all room? I find that unlikely."

Mason liked Master Zin.

"I have a witness," the Rhadgast said, ignoring the logic bomb Master Zin just dropped.

The door swished open behind them. It was Lore, eyes cast on the floor, refusing to look at Mason or Tom. The world was turning red. Mason clenched his hands together. If Lore lied to make them look guilty . . .

"Tell them what you told me," the Rhadgast said to Lore.

"I didn't—"

"What we *talked* about," the Rhadgast prompted.

"They . . . they were on the other side of the clearing," Lore said. Her voice was soft, a little shaky. "I knocked them out myself." She gave a little smile, her fingers working fast on one of her braids that had come loose.

Mason took a breath, feeling a little bad he'd expected her to lie, though it sounded like the Rhadgast had wanted her to do exactly that. Mason gave her a nod, but she ignored it, still not really looking at either of them.

The Rhadgast was taken aback, spluttering for a second, before regaining his composure. "I will see you in my office later."

"Okay," Lore said, then turned around and walked out.

Reckful walked in a moment later. "Master, excuse me, is this really necessary? These two are personal friends of Princess Merrin. I'm sure—"

"I am not so old that I forget things so easily, Reck."

Just hearing her name made Mason's throat tighten. *Princess Merrin.* He still couldn't get over the phrase. Princess? Warrior princess was more like it.

Reckful bowed. "Of course, Master."

"Nevertheless, there is a violent predator in this school. I want it found and contained, whether it be another student . . . or something else."

What else could it be? How would a wild animal have gotten into the school?

"Dismissed," Master Zin said, and Mason felt his stomach unclench.

Mason turned to find Reck scowling. "It is still your first full day," he said.

"I know, I swear, we had nothing to do with it."

"I know *that*," Reckful said. "But you didn't leave the room when you were told. You snuck around like . . . *sneaks!* Do you how bad that looks? Is this common practice in the Earth Space Command?"

"No," Tom assured him. "Mason gets in trouble a lot there, too. He was about to be expel—"

"I'm trying to be good," Mason said quickly. "Trouble just . . . well, you know."

"Finds you?" Reckful said. "I've noticed."

➤ An assembly was called. The Inner Chamber slowly filled with students, and the teachers counted them one by one. The missing student was not officially revealed, but Jiric was not a part of their group. His name was whispered once or twice. This time, when they were sent away from the Inner Chamber, Mason and Tom followed instructions.

Po canceled their planned meet back in the dorm. No rhadjen were allowed out of the school after dark, not until Jiric was found. Well, they weren't allowed out at any time unless it was for a class, but with the added security, sneaking out would be impossible. Teams of students (always escorted by a full Rhadgast) were combing the school, looking for any sign of the missing student.

"Why aren't they saying who it is?" Mason asked.

Po half shrugged. "That's the way it is. They probably don't want us to start rumors, even though everyone already knows. Maybe Jiric is just somewhere else."

"You know he's not," Lore said. Her violet eyes were bloodshot.

"We don't know anything yet," Risperdel said. "They'll tell us—"

"They'll tell us nothing," Lore said, in a way that left no room for discussion.

"It'll be better if you guys stay in the room," Po told Tom. "Everyone knows you didn't have anything to do with it, but that doesn't mean we're not on edge, and, you know—"

"Totally understandable," Tom said. "No hard feelings."

Mason was here to figure out if the Rhadgast were developing some kind of secret project that violated the treaty. And now Jiric had disappeared, only his robes and some blood left behind to say he existed in the first place. The two had to be linked in some way. Unless students disappeared all the time, this wasn't normal.

"I miss Mars," Tom said next to him, quietly enough so only Mason could hear.

"We'll be home soon," Mason said, but he didn't believe it.

Chapter Sixteen

Juneful came for his revenge two days later.

Classes had continued as normal. Instructors gave the same response when asked about Jiric—*I don't know*—until Mason's team decided to stop asking. Mason still did not get any actual combat training, which his team was clearly becoming grumpy about.

"It's not your fault," Po said unconvincingly.

"It kind of is," Risperdel added helpfully.

Mason knew he was in trouble when Grubare kept Mason after class. Today Grubare had taught physics, an extremely useful subclass since the Tremist had figured out things humans were still trying to, like how to move faster than the speed of light without violating the laws of time and space (Mason was still trying to wrap his head around it).

Staying after class meant he'd be alone on his walk back to the dorm. "Do you want Tom to stay?" Mason asked Grubare.

Grubare rubbed his thumbs over his eyebrows, smoothing them out even though they were at maximum smoothness. "No," was all he said.

Mason's team filed out of the room, Tom giving him one

lingering look. Tom would wait outside the door for him, Mason was sure of it.

Mason approached Grubare's desk, which was a large semitransparent object that was a collection of glowing, rolling shapes that shifted between different colors during class. It was incredibly distracting. He sat behind his desk, hands flat on the shimmering surface, the light coming through his pale skin. The gromsh was not in sight.

"I just wanted to see how you're adjusting to your new surroundings," Grubare said, looking up at him. "I appreciate your attention in class. You . . . surprise me."

Mason was stunned. "Thank you, sir."

Grubare scanned the room over Mason's shoulder: they were all alone. "But I would like to make sure it continues. I first thought you were a detriment to this school. A spy." Mason's heart gave a hard thump. "That may still be true. But I am open to being proved wrong."

Mason nodded. "I will do my best. Was there anything else, sir?"

Grubare exhaled in a half sigh. "No, I suppose not. Enjoy the rest of your evening, Mason Stark." He smiled thinly. Mason saw a flicker of light from inside the folds of Grubare's robe—the glow from one of the gromsh's eyes. It was staring at him.

Mason found his heart beating faster. Never before had someone wished him a good evening while making it sound like such a threat. *He kept me here for a reason.* Mason's suspicion was confirmed a moment later, when he left the classroom, walked down one hallway, and came face-to-face with Juneful and his three goons.

Chapter Seventeen

Mason did not freeze, even though he wanted to. He simply stopped walking and faced the four Tremist with his hands held loose at his sides. The urge to let his bracers slip down over his fingers was strong and insistent, almost unconscious, like the gloves were ready to do the work for him. But he kept them in place, knowing that if he used his gloves against his fellow rhadjen, he'd get a one-way ticket back to Academy II, or worse.

Mason didn't say a word, either. He knew it would drive the Stones insane. He just kept his eyes open and free of fear.

"What are you doing out in the halls alone, human?" Juneful said.

Mason kept his lips sealed. It was hard, but he was ESC, and they were not.

"He asked you a question," Goon One said to Mason's left. He appeared to be second in command. All of them had black hair, long and loose.

Mason did not open his mouth.

"He must be brain dead," Juneful said after a moment.

"Come on, let's leave the little human alone before he tells on us."

Mason remained still as they walked past him on either side, banging their shoulders into his, jostling him. He heard their footsteps pause briefly after passing him, and that's when he knew the attack was coming after all. Mason bent at the waist violently, feeling air swish over his neck as one of the Tremist failed to strike the back of his head. In the same movement, Mason mule-kicked straight back and caught something soft—a stomach, he thought—and was rewarded with the sound of breath exploding from lungs—*"oof!"*— followed by a thump as one of them hit the floor.

That left three. Which was still a lot. Mason felt the adrenaline dump, as his blood became hot and his ears burned and his eyes became hyperfocused, the pupils jacking wide to take in more light.

But the other three weren't your regular bullies; they were Rhadgast trainees. As Mason spun, they caught him by the arms and walked him back against the wall. An elbow smacked him in the nose and his vision blurred with tears. He tasted blood on his lips. *Tom, I need you!*

He tried to kick out again, and someone caught his foot. Two more fists crashed into his stomach. His gloves almost slipped down over his hands, but he caught himself at the last second, refusing to use them against the students. Mason had a job to do.

But he was scared now. If he were at home, at Academy II, the fight would end safely. Maybe a bone would get broken, but it would be healed that same day. The combatants would be forced to shake hands and make up. There would be punishment. Here, Mason didn't know what was going to happen. It was an unknown, and that terrified Mason more than anything. He could die, right here, right now.

He decided to make sure that didn't happen.

Mason recalled the feeling he'd had in the forest with Tom, when the vines had been trying to strangle them both. Now, the gloves shot down over his hands without thought, and suddenly there was a wall of light in front of him; the rhadjen were on their backs in the hallway, stunned, their robes smoking lightly.

Juneful blinked rapidly, looking around, eyes unfocused.

"You just made a serious mistake," Juneful said, his wits, what little there were, returning. "The energy discharge was recorded. You're done." The anger on his face dissolved into a smile. A victorious smile. If Marcus Jones were here, he would definitely be friends with Juneful.

Mason made his voice very low. If he was going home, he wanted to get in a parting shot. "You attack me, then report me when I defend myself. If that's what this school is about, then I can't get home soon enough."

The goons all traded looks, as if they were unable to process this information without seeing Juneful's reaction first. Juneful couldn't deny Mason's logic, so he didn't even try. He just made a disgusted sound in his throat and stalked away. His goons followed, giving Mason looks that ranged from anger to what might've been some form of respect.

Mason watched them go, as his breathing returned to normal. The places they'd struck him still throbbed and probably would for some time. His skin would be bruised, but that was okay. If what Juneful said was true (and Mason had no reason to expect it was, other than Juneful seeming so confident), then Mason was going home, and nothing else really mattered. Hopefully he could see Merrin on the way back.

But his mission would be incomplete.

Mason stood alone in the empty hallway. It was quiet. And that's why he heard the footsteps coming from several corridors away. They were loud because they were heavy—the footsteps of men, not children, walking swiftly. They were traveling away from him, getting quieter. Mason set off down the hallway, moving with care, keeping his feet light. *Where are they going?* He had to know—they were marching with too much purpose. This wasn't a stroll to the next class.

Mason stopped at each intersection, where the hallway material changed and became something else: wood, glass, metal, and even what appeared to be ice. He was gaining on the footsteps. There were four of them, he thought, eight feet total. He caught his first and only glimpse of them turning a corner. Mason recognized the bluish hair of Master Rayasu. The other lead Rhadgast appeared to be Master Shem, head of the Bloods. *This is big,* Mason thought. He almost forgot about his throbbing nose and sore ribs.

They disappeared for a second, after reaching a set of stairs covered in springy, tough grass. Mason followed them down twenty seconds later.

The stairs led to more stairs and more doors. The doors were loud and clicked when they shut, but Mason made sure to give his targets enough of a lead. They had to be far underneath the sphere now.

Mason wished Tom was with him, not for the first or second or third time. He passed a sign:

NO RHADJEN BEYOND THIS POINT. STUDENTS WHO DISOBEY WILL BE STRIPPED OF THEIR GLOVES AND SENT HOME.

Oh well: Mason was going home anyway. Juneful hadn't been bluffing—he had seemed too confident, too pleased.

Mason's heart began to pound. Full Rhadgast, in the school, going to a secret, banned area? Maybe he was going to get a bit of intel after all. It was almost too much to hope for.

But his hopes were dashed a moment later, when he descended another flight of stairs—this one made of craggy rocks fused together—and came to a door that had what appeared to be a retinal scanner built right into the middle of it.

The door beeped, sensing his presence. *Oh crap!* Mason began to backpedal. His heels hit the staircase behind him, and he fell onto the steps. A readout above the scanner said:

COMPLETE SCAN OR ALARM WILL SOUND

A timer was counting down from five seconds. In five seconds, it would all be over. The Rhadgast would come back for him, and he would definitely not be leaving the basement alive.

There was really only one thing to do: try. Perhaps a false scan would buy him time and the system would reset. Mason pushed off the staircase and lunged for the scanner, watching as the number 2 flicked to 1. He pressed his face to the scanner and held his eyes open, and the scan initiated. But this wasn't an old-school retinal scan, Mason quickly discovered. That technology had been around for over eight hundred years, and the Tremist may have had it even longer. When the lasers passed over Mason's eyes, he felt them *probing;* they couldn't be lasers at all, not the way he knew them. It felt like tiny ants were walking up and down his optic nerves, plucking packets of information from his brain, intercepting the electrons traveling through synapses, pulling his very identity and reading it like computer code. There was no way to fake it. In an instant, the scanner knew Mason better than Mason knew himself.

The ants began to leave his brain, taking the itchy feeling with them. Mason stepped back, blinking rapidly as his irritated eyes began to water.

He waited for the alarm to sound.

But instead, a purple light in the scanner blinked, the lock clicked, and the door eased open.

Chapter Eighteen

Beyond the doorway there was darkness and a pinprick of white light.

Mason waited, listening for any sound that said he'd been discovered. But none came.

"Impossible . . ." he breathed. The machine had scanned him. And yet the door was open.

Like it had been expecting him.

I should get Tom.

But there was no time: the door was already beginning to close. Mason could go back for Tom, but who knew if they could both make it down here undetected again? Mason slipped across the threshold as the edge of the door brushed his chest. The door sealed shut behind him with a sucking sound, and he was left in the darkness with the single point of light ahead of him.

Only one way to go, he thought.

Mason started toward the light with slow, careful steps, not knowing what was around him in the dark. The walls could've been a few feet or a few hundred feet away. His footsteps did not echo, so there was no way to tell.

After a minute, the light was not a pinprick but a thumbnail. By the time it was the size of a closed fist, Mason could make out details: it was some kind of room with harsh, sterile lights in the ceiling. He could see reflections off a glass wall. Mason heard voices then, low and urgent.

A woman's voice, it sounded like.

She was arguing with the Rhadgast, just around the corner, out of Mason's line of sight. Mason stepped closer, crouching low. He looked down at himself to make sure no part of him was visible.

The woman spoke: "You're not hearing what I'm saying, so let me say it in whatever dialect you understand best—*I won't have another student harmed.*" She said the last part in the dialect of Mhenlo dai Kro, the People of the Mountains.

Mason inched closer, edging toward the line where darkness blurred to gray, until he could see most of the room. It was a laboratory, no different than a human one, with bare metal tables and various arrays of testing equipment, beakers, and containers of strange liquids. It smelled sweet. The back half of the room was separated by the floor-to-ceiling glass Mason had seen on his approach. Beyond the glass was darkness, with no way to tell how large the room really was.

In the corner a woman was talking to the four Rhadgast who had come down before him, once again two Bloods and two Stones. Their postures were tense, like they were in a standoff. The woman was facing away from Mason. She had black hair and wore a white lab coat tied with a crimson belt.

Mason saw Master Rayasu clearly. "Tell me again what you will and won't have, human," he said. "I'd love to hear it."

Human? Mason and Tom were supposed to be the first visitors to Skars. What was a human doing down *here*?

"She forgets her place," said another. "And her surroundings."

"And you forget your manners," Shem said to Rayasu—the other two Rhadgast Mason didn't recognize. He felt a bit of blood leak from his nose but dared not sniff it back.

"And everyone here forgets who I answer to," the woman said. "Now if you're done with idle threats, I will ask you to leave my laboratory."

The Rhadgast seemed like they were about to do just that, but, suddenly a dark shape stirred behind the glass, in the area where it was too dark to see. It was a man shape, hulking, and it crept toward the group.

The four Rhadgast and the woman turned to look, as out of the darkness emerged a Fangborn.

Mason clapped his hand over his mouth, but the sound didn't give him away. All eyes were on the creature. And a creature it was. Mason had only seen them in glimpses before, or through the thermal imaging system on the king's Hawk. He wished it had stayed that way. Now the beast was under crisp light, stepping out of the darkness completely. His arms and legs were impossibly thick and veiny, bulging with visibly striated muscle. His skin was bluish gray, like a stone, and it looked just as hard. His ears were pointed. The eyes were eerily human, but bigger. He had no nose, just two little holes beneath the eyes. Holes that flared with each breath.

But that wasn't what held Mason's gaze, what froze his blood and locked his muscles.

His eyes lingered on the Fangborn's enormous set of jaws, which easily took up more than half the entire head. The lips peeled back from rows of sharp yellowed fangs. He was drooling.

Mason knew nothing would ever be the same after that. The image would always haunt his sleep. This was what they were up against. An army of monsters in control of ships too powerful and huge to destroy.

Master Rayasu stalked toward the glass, then slammed his glove against it. "Are you going to stay put this time? Or must we kill you?" Electricity leaked from his glove, spreading over the glass.

Did this Fangborn kill Jiric? Mason wondered. *How?*

The Fangborn seemed to smile, though with teeth that big anything might look like a smile, and it made a low rhythmic chuffing sound. It was *laughing*. It was laughing at Master Rayasu.

Slowly, it melded back into the darkness, slipping out of sight.

The four Rhadgast shared a look, then stalked away as one—right toward Mason, who quickly retreated into deeper shadow. He kept walking, stumbling almost, but didn't hit a wall. With every step he expected to fall into an abyss that went all the way to Skars's core. Finally he stopped, and the Rhadgast walked past him, heading for the door, though it, too, was in darkness.

Mason waited, holding his breath. Master Rayasu paused and sniffed the air. He made a half turn in Mason's direction, paused again, then spun away with a swish of his robe. Mason didn't move until they reached the door and opened it, and he could see their silhouettes passing in front of the light. The door shut behind them.

Mason let out the breath he was holding. He was still shaking. A Fangborn *here,* under the school. How did it get here? *Why were they holding it?*

Mason knew where he could get his answers: the woman. There was just one of her and one of him, and he doubted she had the same gloves and training if she was working in a laboratory. Mason steeled himself, clasping his hands together hard until they stopped shaking. He wasn't over-reacting—it was a *Fangborn.* But his curiosity won out in the end. He walked toward the opening again and right into the laboratory.

The woman was working with a huge machine made of clear plastic. Inside were hundreds of tubes filled with liquids of various colors—rose, pink, green, lavender—all of them draining into a central chamber filled with a golden solution. Her back was still turned, as she entered different values on the front of the machine. The Fangborn lurked somewhere in the darkness on the other side of the glass.

Mason stood there, content to wait until the woman turned around. She was probably expecting him. How else would the scanner have approved him?

When she continued with her work for too long, Mason decided to clear his throat. The woman jumped and spun around, her hand jostling a beaker, which fell off the table and shattered on the floor.

Mason felt like a sledgehammer had struck him in the chest. The air went right out of him, and he almost fell to his knees. The woman had midnight hair and eyes. She looked like an older version of his sister, Susan Stark.

"Mason?" the woman said.

The woman was his mother.

Chapter Nineteen

"Mom...?"

It couldn't be real. It was another Tremist illusion. That was the only explanation. His parents were dead, and even if his mother had escaped the First Attack, she wouldn't be here in a laboratory under the Rhadgast school, in the company of a Fangborn.

Mason didn't run to her, and she didn't run to him. They just stared at each other. Mason tried to recall images in his mind, memories of her when she was still alive. He remembered her saying goodbye, giving him a kiss on the cheek, then leaving. Only to pop back in a moment later, say "I love you," and smile. That was the last time he saw her. April Stark had died that day. And yet here she was.

"Mom," Mason said.

His mother was crying. She kneeled next to the broken beaker and began to scoop the pieces into her hand. Mason's knees felt like they'd been replaced with water balloons, ready to burst at any moment and stop holding him up.

It could be a Tremist trick. How else did you get in this room?

"I know you're not real," Mason said.

The illusion of his mother stood up and put the broken pieces on the table. "I'm so sorry, Mason."

"You're not *real*." Mason didn't even care that a Fangborn lurked in the shadows near him; he was no longer afraid.

"Yes, I am." She held out her hands. "Come here."

Mason didn't want to, but he also wanted proof. He'd touched the illusion of Merrin, hadn't he? So how could he know for sure?

Mason crossed the room slowly, watching as his mother cried more tears. He stopped halfway. "If you're real, tell me how the scanner let me into the room. Then tell me how you're alive."

His mother seemed taken aback for a moment. But then she smiled. "Of course you asked that. You're just like your father."

Mason knew he looked like his father, that they had the same sandy hair and blue eyes. "Mom . . . if it's you, please. Tell me."

April Stark took a deep breath and paused, looking around the room, as if searching for the words in the air. "I . . . I've been allowed to follow your progress. You're famous here on Skars, too. When I heard you were visiting the school, I re-programmed the scanner to let in anyone who is a direct descendent of mine. I . . . was hoping you would find your way down here. They won't let me go to the higher levels. If a student saw me . . . I tried to come find you, but they caught me before I could leave."

"But how is this possible?" Mason said. "How are you here? You're a prisoner?"

She wiped at her eyes. "I guess the shortest answer is that the Fangborn threat has been known for a lot longer than you're aware. When the Fangborn were first discovered you were just a baby. We didn't know how dangerous they were at first. But when we realized, a small group of open-minded humans and Tremist decided to meet in secret, apart from both governments. Just those that understood what's truly at stake."

"What's truly at stake?"

"Your father and I were asked to be a part of this team, and we said no, of course. But they knew our specialties and they knew we were the best candidates to join the Tremist team—even though we were still at war then. They asked us again, and we agreed to six months. They agreed to six months, too. But then . . . the Tremist in control of the project didn't want us to leave. Our reappearance in the ESC would've brought too many questions. There was still so much work. We . . . we knew it was going to be important one day, that the future of both races were counting on us."

Mason let that sink in. She hadn't meant to leave him for that long. She had good intentions. He should be able to forgive that. But then she willingly stayed.

"Would they have let you leave?" Mason said. "If you tried hard?"

She turned her face away, briefly, and Mason wondered if whatever came out next would be a lie. "Things weren't easy in the beginning. The group didn't mesh. Someone tried to leave, quite violently, and I was too scared. . . . I didn't try, Mason. I thought I would've been able to finish and come home. But then more time went by, and I didn't know how to come back to you, how to explain, and there was so much work left. I . . . I'm sorry, Mason. There is no excuse. But I believe the Fangborn threat is paramount to everything, even my own feelings. I did what I did to protect you and your sister. To protect all of us."

Mason said nothing and felt nothing besides cold.

"I didn't know they faked our deaths at first," she said. "The First Attack was not staged, of course, they just . . . said we were there. When we were really on a shuttle to Nori-Blue. I was promised I could tell you I was leaving for six months aboard the ship—you and Susan were used to us taking long trips—but they *lied*. They said it was too big of a secret, too important."

"What's truly at stake, Mom?" He instantly regretted calling her that, wished he could pull the word back into his mouth, swallow it down. *But what am I supposed to call her?*

Her scrunched eyebrows relaxed slightly. "The Fangborn don't just want to eat us, they want to *change* us. Their fangs contain venom that, when applied to a human or Tremist, strips the evolved DNA away, reverting the victim back to its most primitive form. We hold the Fangborn code inside of us, and their venom reveals it."

A sick, cold feeling trickled down the inside of Mason's sternum. He was suddenly back in the free-for-all room, looking down at a bloody robe. It was the same feeling of helplessness.

"What happened to Jiric?"

"Jiric is no more. . . ."

Mason caught movement to his right; the Fangborn loomed out of the darkness again—no, a *second* Fangborn.

There were two of them, side by side. The one on the left was slightly smaller, his skin a little bluer. *They can speak,* Mason thought, as fresh goosebumps spread down his arms.

The smaller one had strange hands: the outer layer of flesh was translucent, showing a violet layer within . . . which ended at the elbows. Almost like it was wearing Rhadgast gloves inside its skin, as if the skin had formed around it . . .

"Jiric," Mason breathed.

The Fangborn cocked his head at the name, lips peeling back from fangs that were not yellow, but white.

"Subject One escaped the other day," April Stark said. "He was recaptured, but not before infecting another student. We're still investigating the breakout. There is no physical way past the safety glass without assistance." Mason filed that idea away for later.

His mother turned to him. She had to look up at Mason now. When he'd seen her last, she'd been able to pick him up. "I am *so close,* Mason. That's why I'm here. Because the fate of both our worlds is in jeopardy. The Fangborn are coming back, at this very moment. They are traveling to us *at this very moment,* and if I don't have a cure before then, I don't know what's going to happen!"

Mason took an involuntary step back, his heart dropping into his stomach. *They know where we are.* "Is the ESC aware? The fleet needs to be made ready! I have to—"

"Red light," his mother said. Any doubts he had that this wasn't really his mother were wiped away. Anytime Mason had been getting too far ahead as a kid, his mother would shout *"Red light,"* and Mason would have to stop in his tracks. Even now it shut him up, though it made him bristle. He was about to tell her she had no right to boss him any longer, but she spoke first. "It's not going to matter," she said. "You disabled their ship once. They won't let it happen again. They're coming, and there is nothing we can do to stop them, no technology we have that can compete with their ship and its weapons. They've been planning and building for millions of years."

Mason clenched his fists. "But we have to try."

"Yes, we will try. Warn the ESC if you can. I've been told they're aware, but . . . I don't trust *anyone*. Be careful, though. If the news leaks, there will be panic on both sides. The treaty may not survive it."

"I'm going to Master Zin right now to tell him you're leaving."

"No you most definitely are not! You're going to go back to your room and say nothing to anyone." She almost reached out for him. "You are here for the ESC, aren't you?"

"Maybe . . ."

"Then you're going to do your duty."

"Like you did? By faking your death?"

His mother reared back as if Mason had slapped her. "I . . . I sacrificed—"

"*Me.* And *Susan.* That's what you sacrificed." As he said the words, he tried to understand his mother. She was working on what was possibly the most important task in the galaxy. An ESC soldier knew what it meant to sacrifice, and his mother was an ESC soldier. So was Mason. But she left him behind. She left Susan behind.

"Why did you have to come *here*?" Mason said. "The ESC has resources, they could've—"

"I'm sorry, honey, it had to be this way. The Tremist tech is light years ahead of ours, but we had our own skills to bring, me and your father did. A human perspective for the research. If I was still on an ESC base, I wouldn't be where I am right now. *Days away.* Almost there. You have to forgive me."

Mason didn't have to do anything.

"Where is your team?" he asked.

"On their way. You can't be here when they arrive. I don't know what will happen."

"Is Dad with them?"

She blinked rapidly, like she was fighting sudden tears, and looked away briefly; Mason saw her trying to form some kind of lie.

"Is he dead? Don't lie to me. I want to know."

She swallowed three times before speaking. "You father . . . we were on Nori-Blue. That's when we made the discovery of what the Fangborn can do. How they can make us like them. He . . . he was infected. I last saw him on Nori-Blue eleven years ago."

"Was he . . . ?" Mason felt his throat tighten; any hope at seeing his father again faded like smoke.

"When I last saw him, he was not your father."

Chapter Twenty

Mason had to sit down. He did it right where he was standing. He simply folded his legs under himself and put his back against one of the metal tables. He did it a little too hard, and some weird instrument he didn't recognize clattered to the floor, a piece of it skittering away and pinging off the glass wall.

The two Fangborn had retreated to the shadows again.

"They don't like the light," Mason said, his words feeling hollow and automatic.

"They spend so much time underground, it's uncomfortable. The light isn't damaging to them, just annoying."

"What if Dad's alive?"

His mother was quiet for a moment. "Mason, that's the only thing that's kept me going all these years. Plus the hope that when I was reunited with you and your sister, I'd have created something . . . something that could protect our future together. But I *will* find your father and bring him back."

Mason heard a noise from the direction of the door he'd come through. It reminded him of where he was. He was still on Skars, in the Rhadgast school, deep below ground. As much a prisoner as the two Fangborn were.

"What happens now?" Mason asked. He had no idea what to do. How could he just go back upstairs and pretend like nothing had happened?

But that's exactly what his mother asked him to do. "You can't let anyone know you're aware of this secret. It could spread panic, and that won't help anything. You have to return to your team and continue your studies."

"How long do we have? Before the Fangborn arrive?"

"I don't know. We captured the one you've already met during the battle above Nori-Blue. In one interview, he began to taunt us, saying his brothers and sisters planted a tracking device on a Tremist ship during the battle. It's my theory they can communicate telepathically on some level. . . ." She paused. "Mason, I'm so proud of you. What you and your friends did."

"Thanks." He didn't know what else to say. "When can I see you again?"

"You can't. Not until this is over. If you're caught, I don't know what they'll do. You've probably been gone too long as it is. But I want a hug before you leave."

Mason went to her and his mom held him close. He squeezed her back, a crack appearing in the wall he built to hold back his emotions. He didn't want to know what would happen when it broke completely.

"Now go," she said.

Mason looked at the glass again, but the Fangborn remained in darkness.

"Please go. And stay safe." His mother's dark eyes were pleading.

Mason turned and walked toward the doorway, through the tunnel of blackness.

He did not look back.

➤ Mason didn't feel safe until he was back in the hallways of the school. He pictured his room in his mind, and the implant in his skull communicated with the floor: a new glowing line appeared, guiding him back to where he belonged.

Everyone was waiting for him when he returned.

"Juneful said he kicked your butt in the hallway, that you attacked him out of nowhere and he had to defend himself and you got *beat down.*" That was Risperdel.

"Of course he said that" Mason replied. He still felt stunned, slow to move, like he was walking through water.

The Fangborn are coming. That was all he could think now. It didn't matter what his mom said—the ESC *had* to be warned. Even if warning them only saved a handful of lives in the end, it was worth it. Grand Admiral Shahbazian would have to believe him.

"Where have you been?" Po came up to Mason but stopped short of clapping him on the shoulder.

"Yes. Where have you been?" Tom said just ahead of him, arms crossed. "I waited for you, but a teacher made me move on, said I was *loitering.* I tried to argue, but . . ."

"You saw," Mason said, his voice sounding hollow and fake. "I was kept after class."

"Yeah," Lore said. "Juneful told us in the hallway. So, is it true you attacked him?"

"Juneful didn't seem like the chatting type at lunch," Po said. "We can guess what happened."

"But he seemed sure Mason—"

"Yes!" Mason said. Everyone stared at him. "Yes. Juneful and his three friends jumped me in the hallway. I took care of it. They promised to report me. They said the school recorded the energy discharge of my gloves, and that I would be sent home." Mason had almost forgotten that last part: now there was no way he'd allow them to send him home, not with his mom inside the school and the Fangborn on their way. The stupid Tremist had brought Earth into the same solar system as Skars . . . which would make it so easy to wipe out both civilizations, or convert them into Fangborn, in just one battle. This was their fault. Yet the humans had created the gate in the first place. . . .

"They won't send you home . . ." Risperdel said, but she didn't sound so sure.

"But you beat them?" Po said. He was grinning. He had no idea what was happening. Mason had a mind to tell them all right then and there, to spread the word about their impending doom, but he didn't. His mother still had work to do. They both did.

➢ He spent the next two days in a fog. He told Tom everything he'd learned, and Tom just stared at him wordlessly. At the end, he put his hand on Mason's shoulder and squeezed. "You're angry," he said. "You have every right to be. But . . ." His eyes dropped. "She's still alive. That's what's important."

Tom had lost his mother six months earlier. And she was not going to magically reappear. The knot in Mason's stomach unclenched a bit.

Mason cocked his head to the side. "You know what? You might be the smartest person I know."

"No," Tom said. "I *am* the smartest person you know. Now, about that Fangborn invasion. What do you think we should do?"

"Tell someone, obviously," Mason said. "I just have to figure out who we can trust. My mom was right—if the news leaks, people will panic and start pointing fingers at each other. The treaty could crumble before they even get here. But we have to prepare." Mason thought again of the Uniter's gloves, how supernaturally powerful they had seemed. The Tremist and ESC could prepare all they wanted, but if the Fangborn ship was still impervious to energy weapons, it wouldn't matter much. They needed an edge.

Mason reported to Grand Admiral Shahbazian just once in those two days and decided the news of the coming attack was too great to keep secret. But Mason didn't want to tell GAS himself, not trusting the crazy old man to react in a normal, calm manner. For all Mason knew, he'd think the Tremist had been keeping the news a secret.

So Mason asked to speak with his sister, Susan, the following night. He was sore from zero-gravity exercises in the gravity-free room above the Inner Chamber. Lore kept gunning for him, barreling into his body then pistoning off before they both hit the wall. She'd done it twice in a row before Mason decided to focus solely on her. Not that it mattered much; she flew through the air like a bird.

Susan was in GAS's office, alone, when he activated the communicator. Seeing her for the first time since starting Academy II was almost too much. Mason wanted to break down when she smiled at him, even though she was smiling from billions of miles away.

"Hey little brother," she said. Her smile quickly disappeared. "What's the matter? Shahbazian was not too happy you asked to speak to me. How are you holding up?"

"I'm fine," Mason began. He was anything but fine, but how else are you supposed to answer that question? "I'm here to tell you something. It has to stay quiet."

She nodded slowly. "You've learned something? Why tell me?"

"Because you're in intelligence, and I don't trust GAS not to fly off the handle."

Her forehead wrinkled. "Gas . . . ? Grand—Grand Admiral Shahbazian?" She snorted.

"Yeah, sorry, him. Are you alone? No one is listening?"

"Yes, I'm alone. Talk to me."

Mason didn't know how to start, so he just said it: "The Fangborn are coming. I don't know when they'll be here, but they tracked the Tremist to this star system, and they're coming to finish us off."

Her mouth dropped open. "Are you—"

"Yes, I'm sure. You have to tell the Reynolds or something. Get people prepared in a quiet way."

"Great Mountain . . ." she breathed. "Where did you come across this intel? How can you be sure it's good?"

Our mother. Mason almost transmitted the thought but

held back. You had to will a thought, really focus, for it to go through the communicator.

Susan waited patiently. Mason had to tell her the truth. "Susan, I'm going to tell you something that's going to sound crazy. And insane. Insanely crazy."

"That wouldn't be a first," Susan said.

The words came out in a rush. "Mom is alive and she's working underneath the Rhadgast school on some kind of Fangborn antivenom because Fangborn have venom in their teeth that can turn humans and Tremist into other Fangborn."

A long moment passed in which Susan didn't do or say anything. Mason thought the feed had frozen. But then she blinked. "Are you sure?" she said quietly, in almost a whisper.

"Yes I'm sure! I snuck into an area I wasn't supposed to be in—"

"Shocking—"

"—and found her working in a lab. She says she's close to a cure! Wait. Why don't you look surprised . . . ?"

Susan put her hand over her mouth, then let it fall away. "There was a rumor I heard when I joined the intelligence sector. Something about humans and Tremist working together in secret, way before the treaty. I never thought . . ."

"It's real," Mason said. "Mom and Dad left us to help them. They thought it was that important . . . and I guess it is."

Mason couldn't help but remember the memorial for the victims of the First Attack, when he and his sister had stood side by side and mourned their parents. It had all been a lie. His feelings had been a lie.

"You only mentioned Mom before. . . ." Susan said. "What about Dad?"

The connection nearly broke, Mason's physical surroundings fuzzing into existence for a split second, replacing GAS's office. He'd rather be talking about anything else. He didn't want to see the look in Susan's eyes.

"They were researching on Nori-Blue eleven years ago," Mason said tonelessly. "Dad was . . . *changed*. Mom hasn't seen him since."

Susan's eyes were unfocused, distant. She began to nod absently. "Well . . ." She swallowed. "We have other things to worry about. Stay focused. And safe. You hear me? Eyes open, little brother." Her voice was steel. Mason knew it was the brittle kind, though. Ready to break.

His throat tightened. "I will."

"Tell me everything about the Fangborn one more time," Susan said.

Mason did.

"I'll get this information to the right people," Susan said when he finished. She paused.

"What is it?" Mason said.

She shook her head. "I don't know. I don't—we need something, Mason. We're not going to win like this. Without a miracle. Please stay out of trouble until I can see you."

"Only if you do, too," Mason said, though he knew neither of them would. Mason ended the link and was left with a hollow feeling in his chest. He missed the Academy. There he had a purpose. Here his mission was becoming lost in a haze of questions. Here he didn't know what he was doing, or what he was supposed to do.

Chapter Twenty-one

Mason woke forty minutes early—before the day had to start, but after curfew. He showered, brushed his teeth, donned his uniform, and was out the door while Tom and the others slept soundly in their bunks. The sleep of soldiers: completely unconscious, until they needed to be conscious. Though, as he was slipping out the door, he saw Risperdel watching him, one golden eye peeking around the covers.

The library was three levels down, in the middle of the sphere, where Blood met Stone. It was enormously tall, with pillars of what looked like creamy marble but probably weren't. A waste of space in Mason's opinion. The stacks rose fifty feet high around him. Hover platforms took you where you needed to go, but the highest books held a special risk, since the platforms had no railings.

The Tremist seemed to love paper books. This wasn't the reusable synth-paper the ESC used, which could display any book uploaded to its pages, but real paper that would tear if you weren't careful. The shelves were full of them, of all shapes and sizes. Tremist apparently didn't need or want all of their books to be rectangles of a similar size.

The library had a circular desk in the middle, usually staffed by several librarians, if the chairs were any indication. But today there was only one, a Tremist woman in her early twenties. She wore a long tunic of rich, velvety purple. Her hair was snow-white and piled around her shoulders. Her eyes were dazzling silver, catching and magnifying the dim light of the library. Mason was dumbstruck when he saw her.

She smiled, recognition in her bright eyes. "You're up early. Have a thirst for knowledge? You've come to the right place."

Mason cleared his throat. "Yes, hi, I am."

She folded her long, delicate fingers on the counter. "What can I assist you with?"

"I . . . was hoping I could find a book on Aramore the Uniter."

Her cheek twitched at the name, but her smile didn't break. "Aramore, huh? That is a broad subject, Mason—"

"How do you know my name?"

She lifted one eyebrow—*Really?*

"Right," he said. "One of two humans in the school. What's your name?"

"I'm Calora. Would you say we're well met?"

"Uh, yes—"

"Now, several texts cover this history of the Uniter and the Divider. Some written by Bloods, some Stones, so you can imagine there may be a slight disparity in accounts."

"What do you recommend?"

Her eyes lit up. "*The United,* by Sephaman. He remained

neutral through everything. But what *specifically* are you looking for?"

Mason licked his lips. "Information on his gloves. Where they came from, what they can do, that kind of thing."

"That kind of thing . . ." She quirked one side of her mouth. "You know what? I have just the *thing*." She came out from behind the counter, moving as if she were walking on air, then stepped onto the nearest hover platform. It dipped slightly under her weight. "Be right back." The platform rose up and away, cutting between stacks, disappearing from view. Mason stayed where he was, until Calora returned with a huge black book bound in leather. Gold and silver rivets adorned the front and back. She had to carry it with both hands. She placed it in Mason's arms, and he almost dropped it. She and Mason were of the same height.

"There you are," she said. "There is a table in the back you can read at, if you like." She went back behind the counter and bowed low over a sheaf of papers.

Mason went to the table and set the book down. He opened it and began to read. Two hours later, Mason knew what he needed to do.

Mason found Calora exactly how he'd left her. She tapped the counter without looking away from her papers.

"Can I ask you something?" he blurted.

She continued reading for another moment, then two, before looking up at him from behind her silvery eyelashes. "Hmm?"

"Are you a Stone, or . . . ?" Her purple tunic said yes, but she had been nice to him.

"Does it matter?" she asked softly.

He thought about it. "I guess not."

"Well, there you go. Take care, Mason Stark. Come see me again." Her eyes fell back to her papers.

➤ Mason got Po alone outside the refectory the next day. "Po, hold up," he said.

Po stopped and let a group of students slip past. The refectory was quieter than last time, a kind of thickness in the air that dampened the click of utensils and the clatter of plates. Everyone was still thinking about Jiric. *And only I know where he is,* Mason thought.

"I'm going after the gloves of Aramore," Mason said to Po. He waited for Po's reaction. Mason expected him to laugh, but instead Po smiled widely.

"My friend, join the club. That's *all* I've been doing for the last year, is looking for clues. I already invited you, if you remember."

The plans that were canceled upon Jiric's disappearance.

Po's grin fell away. "I have to warn you, it's more for fun than anything. The chances of finding them . . ."

"I have to try," Mason said. "As soon as we can get back out there."

"Why the sudden interest?" Po asked.

Mason had found something interesting in the book Calora had given him. A passage that described the gloves of Aramore. The Uniter had received his gloves from an outside source. No one knew from where. But they possessed a unique property. The electricity generated by the gloves was so powerful it could atomize anything. Any kind of matter at all. Scientists who studied the gloves, before they were lost, used their properties as a platform to develop the first shielding systems for spacecraft, even though the Tremist wouldn't sail the stars for another fifty years.

But it was the final line that made the path clear to Mason.

There is no matter in this universe, no electromagnetic field, no force at all, that can withstand the power of Aramore's gloves. Their origin is undoubtedly alien. Though I pray we never meet the species that created them.

Mason couldn't think of a lie fast enough. So he just shrugged. "You never know. We might need them."

Chapter Twenty-two

The next morning was the weekend, a time when rhadjen could continue their independent studies in whatever specialty they chose. Po planned a study for the team: they were heading into the woods to search for the fabled gloves of Aramore the Uniter. Not on paper, of course. Officially, they were going to explore some nearby ruins for a history credit, that was all.

Po usually went with Risperdel, but Lore didn't want to be left behind now that Jiric was gone and she'd be all alone with her studies. Lore and Jiric weren't particularly close, Po told Mason, but as the only two Stones on the team, they usually stuck together.

Lore had looked at Mason as if challenging him to have a problem with her tagging along, but Mason only smiled and said, "I'm glad, we'll be safer." Lore had turned away before he could see her expression.

They left the sphere through a secret underground tunnel that ended a safe distance away.

Tom eyed the trees as they got closer to the forest.

Po noticed. "Don't worry," he said. "The killer vines are on the *other* side."

"I'm so reassured," Tom said.

Mason wondered if they were just going to wander the woods aimlessly, looking for a pair of gloves on the ground that said PROPERTY OF ARAMORE, THE GREAT UNITER. He felt guilty participating in something that seemed so trivial: his mother was back at the school, toiling away at a cure, and he should've been spending his time learning a new skill, anything that could help when the Fangborn finally attacked. But something told him he needed the gloves, that they would help him in the coming fight. Something told him they would be found.

He looked to the yellow sky, where a space battle could already be underway. The fat clouds were rippled like vanilla custard, and they revealed nothing.

The group marched through the woods, over dead leaves and under low-hanging branches. The branches didn't seem to have vines, but Mason kept an eye on them anyway; once or twice he caught flitting movement among the dark branches.

The group didn't talk much, and when they did it was nothing of substance. Po told a story about the time his brother crashed the family sky car on the same day he got his license to fly. Risperdel talked about her first day at the school, when she had opened her chest after undergoing the test, but the chest had been completely empty. Grubare had come into the room with her robe in his hands, grumbling about some kind of lift malfunction under the chest.

The story was interrupted when a vine uncoiled from above and slipped around Risperdel's neck, jerking her off the ground. She gasped, both hands clawing at the vine, and it was Tom who attacked first, delivering twin blasts above Risperdel's head.

But more vines began to snake down from all sides, uncoiling and rearing back, looking for a limb to strike.

Above them, the trees began to scream. In the sound was glee, anticipation . . . and hunger.

"I thought you said they were on the other side!" Mason shouted to Po, eyeing the nearest vine, which dipped this way and that, thorns flexing.

"Uh," Po said, ducking under a vine that swung sideways at his face. "Maybe we're closer than I thought."

"I'll say," Lore said, but there was laughter in her voice. The team assembled with their backs to each other, palms out, fingertips bristling with hot light. Whatever intelligence lay within the trunks, the foliage of Skars knew when it was outmatched. There came a grumble from above, a low moan of frustration. And the vines slowly retracted into the canopy, more than a few scorched in places.

Po kicked aside the severed tip of a vine. They all shared a look, the kind a group of survivors shares after a battle— *We made it. No sweat.*—and then carried on.

After about an hour (the group bloodied, tired, and more than a little grumpy), Mason noticed a break in the trees ahead and what looked like some kind of stone structure.

Tom sidled up beside him, as the group spread out ahead. "Hey, what's your deal? You've barely talked. You usually can't shut up."

"I can stop thinking about . . . everything."

Tom nodded. "Roger that. But remember I've got a stake in this, too. I'm not your sidekick, I'm right here in it with you."

Mason felt his cheeks heat up. "Do I treat you that way?"

Tom shrugged. "I don't think you mean to . . . you're just a Stark. Born leader. You know what *those* are like."

Mason put his hand on Tom's shoulder. "You're a good friend, Tom."

"Are you kidding? I'm a *great* friend. Look at my shoe—I stepped in alien crap half a kilometer ago just so you wouldn't be alone."

Mason was about to respond that he'd also stepped in a suspicious substance, but right then they broke through the tree line. Mason lost his breath. A magnificent array of ruins spread out before them, rising and falling over hills, the stone structures glowing a soft yellow in the light. It was clearly once a large city. The wide streets were now overgrown with tough grasses. Trees now grew taller than the buildings, but it was hard to tell how large the buildings had been. Everything was worn by weather and time, and it reminded Mason of the skyscraper on Nori-Blue, Child's home, a building that made these feel new by comparison.

"I present to you the city of Darkai," Po said, flourishing his hand. Risperdel toed a crumble of ancient stone.

"How much area have you covered?" Tom said. "Do you think the gloves will just be under a rock or something?"

"Well, no," Po said. "I think they're going to be in the Tomb of Aramore, but that's sealed. Maybe with you guys here we can figure something out. We just have to document the stuff we find so it looks like we're doing homework."

"I thought Aramore disappeared?" Tom said. "Never to be seen again."

Po shrugged. "He did. But the lore books call it his tomb. Doesn't mean he has to be inside of it."

"What's the tomb sealed with?" Mason asked. Po was right. The gloves would be in the tomb, if they were anywhere.

"A very large stone," Risperdel said, pushing aside a few strands of the midnight hair sweat-stuck to her face.

"So we move it," Mason said.

Risperdel rolled her eyes. "Never thought of that one! It's sealed somehow, genius. And if we got caught tampering with it they'd probably put us to death or something." Her golden eyes brightened, as if this idea were somehow exciting and not terrifying. "*Look but don't touch* are the rules regarding the Darkai ruins."

Po seemed embarrassed, his cheeks a light shade of purple. "So, we just search in the other parts of the ruins in case we're wrong. We've already covered half the city. Hunt for clues that might lead to the tomb. There has to be some way to open it."

Mason and Tom shared a look. They were already here. So they joined the search. Mason went with Po deeper into the city, only to find many dusty rooms filled with collections of rocks and dirt. An hour went by, Po not saying much, consumed with the quest. Mason found that he was, too: every new room was another chance at a clue.

But every hour was an hour closer to the inevitable Fangborn attack. Mason made a decision then. He would get word to the king. He assumed the king didn't know what was coming, otherwise he wouldn't let Merrin stay on the Will, which would almost certainly be one of the Fangborn's first targets upon their arrival.

They had to be ready, and his mother would understand that. If both sides couldn't keep their cool as they prepared, then they didn't really deserve to win.

Already feeling lighter with the decision, Mason entered the next room of the castle they were combing. And that was when he heard the scream.

Chapter Twenty-three

Mason rushed out of the room and into the street, which was filled with knee-high grass. The others were right behind him.

"That sounded like Risperdel!" Po said.

They took off down the hill, listening for another scream, but instead Risperdel began shouting, "Help! I need help!"

The street wended through buildings and under arches that looked ready to collapse. Risperdel was still shouting when they reached the clearing at the front of the city. She stood side by side with Tom and Lore. They were facing off against something—a dark shape hunkered in the grass.

The monster was down on all fours, his head held low to the ground, drool dripping from jaws too big to close. The Fangborn jerked his head up as Mason and the others ran into the clearing. Slowly, the rhadjen began to spread out around the Fangborn.

"What is it doing here?" Lore shouted.

"Quiet!" Po said. "Stay calm!"

Mason's heart was pounding, but he forced himself to breathe and study his enemy. The Fangborn had bluish-gray skin like the last two he'd seen. And this one had the same strange purple layer of skin on his hands and forearms. *It's a Tremist!*

"Don't hurt him!" Mason shouted. "He's one of us!"

"*What?* How can you tell?" Po said. Each rhadjen had their gloves over their hands, palms alight with energy.

The team continued to box in the Fangborn. The creature spun with them, sizing up each possible threat/meal in turn, his eyes seeming to glow yellow from within.

"He's crazy," Lore said, glaring at Mason. "This thing isn't one of us!"

"Look at the gloves under his skin!" Mason said. The Fangborn also had a black mane of hair down his neck and onto his back. And those eyes . . .

Mason almost recognized him, but not quite.

The Fangborn, however, seemed to recognize Mason. It wasn't looking at anyone else.

"We need to capture it," Mason said, trying to muster as much authority in his words as possible. He hadn't used his captain voice since he was on the Egypt with his crew.

"Are you kidding? How do you suggest we do that?" Lore said.

"Imagine if we brought it in alive," Tom said. "We'd be heroes."

Risperdel and Po perked up at that. Tom looked at Mason as if to say *Hey, we have to convince them any way we can.*

The Fangborn was sinking lower to the ground, his muscles bunching up: he was coiling to strike.

"Well we can't hug it into submission," Po said.

"Stun it!" Mason roared, as the Fangborn launched himself off the ground. In the next instant, lances of electricity shot across the clearing, converging on a central point.

A point the Fangborn was no longer occupying.

The monster sailed over Mason's head, kicking out with his back legs and hitting Mason right between the shoulder blades. Mason's feet left the ground. He landed face-first ten feet away, attempting a roll but gouging the dirt with his shoulder instead. Mason staggered to his feet as the Fangborn jumped again. This time the rhadjen aimed true; purple and red electricity sparked over his skin. Smoke curled off his entire body. But the monster wouldn't go down. He planted his feet and arched his back, roaring at the yellow sky.

"More power!" Mason shouted once he could breathe. The Fangborn plowed into Po, who couldn't dive out of the way fast enough. He swiped his huge, veiny arm at Risperdel, who nimbly stepped back without breaking the coils of electricity flowing from her palms. The Fangborn lunged at Tom, who jumped straight up, using Skars's weaker gravity to his advantage, pushing off with one foot against the Fangborn's shoulder and executing a perfect backflip that momentarily put him at a safe distance. The Fangborn clawed air: the electricity was starting to have an effect.

But the beast wasn't ready to give up.

The Fangborn spun, tearing up clods of dirt and grass with his claws. He leapt directly over Po, who had to duck to keep his head. The Fangborn took off for the tree line; electricity crackled around his body, scorching the grass around him.

"Don't let it escape!" Po said, clutching his chest where his robes were shredded.

The rhadjen took off as one, giving chase. The Fangborn was much faster under normal circumstances, Mason assumed, and even though it was running on all fours, it was weaving, slowed by their initial assault. They followed the Fangborn into the gloomy woods, taking care not to trip over the bulbous roots that rolled in and out of the forest floor like waves. Vines unfurled as before, but the rhadjen were moving too fast to get caught. The Fangborn's claws tore through the roots, peppering his pursuers with sharp wooden splinters. Mason and the others knew what was at stake: if the Fangborn escaped and happened across a student or even a teacher that was all alone . . .

Mason and his team chased the monster all the way back to the school. They lost it three times and had to split up, and Mason thought his lungs were going to catch fire, but none of them slowed. The Fangborn crossed into the school's clearing, and Mason put on a final burst of speed, willing his glove to make a whip like before. He swung it sideways, flicking his wrist, and it shot forward and curled around the Fangborn's trailing leg. Mason tugged as hard as he could, digging his heels into the grass, and the Fangborn tripped and rolled. The rhadjen converged around it, delivering more power with their gloves, until the Fangborn was twitching and jerking on his back, clawing at the air.

"Enough!" Mason shouted after another moment. The rhadjen stopped their attack. The air smelled acrid, like burnt plastic. The Fangborn's eyes rolled back in his head and then closed, but his breathing became slow and steady.

"At least we don't have to carry it the whole way," Mason said.

Everyone looked at him.

Mason shrugged. "The Earth Space Command taught us to look on the bright side."

"This was just one," Risperdel said, her voice full of awe. "Does this mean they're already here? It has to." She looked at each rhadjen, but they had no answers. "What does this *mean*?"

"Look," Lore said. "The human was . . . Sorry. *Mason* was right, I mean. Look at the Fangborn's hands."

Now that it wasn't moving and trying to kill them, it was clear the Fangborn had Rhadgast gloves underneath the skin.

"How could it *be* somebody? And who is it?" Risperdel said.

Po nudged it with the toe of his boot. The Fangborn twitched, and everyone took a step back.

Mason looked at the school: there was no commotion, no sign anyone was coming for them.

"So returning as heroes is out of the question," Tom said. "If this is a rhadjen, we need to help him. But we need to do it quietly."

"Absolutely," Po said.

"No doubt," Risperdel added.

Mason faced the group again. "I think we can turn him back to normal, but you'll have to trust me. Here's the plan."

➤ Five minutes later they had a hover-cart to transport the Fangborn. It took all of them to lift the creature onto the cart. They pushed it toward the school, Po and Lore running ahead to make sure the way was clear. They got the Fangborn into the school (Po did some smooth talking and told the two guards he saw a student entering a banned area), and Mason realized that this plan was either really smart or really stupid. If the Fangborn woke up, he was betting it would be the latter.

They guided the Fangborn into a supply closet.

"Now what?" Tom said. "This thing is going to wake up, and then we're toast."

Mason found plastic sheeting rolled up in the back of the closet. "Help me with this," he said. Risperdel and Lore were quick to cover the Fangborn in plastic, which auto-sealed a moment later. The Fangborn was now shrink-wrapped under opaque plastic. But it still looked a little too much like a giant monster hidden beneath a tarp.

"We need to change the shape," Mason said. He looked around the closet for something to shove under the plastic, but everything was too large.

Tom looked at each of them. "How . . . how do you expect we do that?"

"You're not going to like it," Mason said.

Tom threw his hands up. "No! Nope. Not going to happen."

"Not it," Lore said, smirking.

"Not it!" Risperdel followed with quickly.

"Also not it," Mason said.

Tom swallowed. Then he lifted up the edge of the plastic and peered at the slumbering Fangborn within. "You have got to be kidding me."

"We're running out of time," Mason said. "It's going to wake up."

"Next time, you're cuddling with the monster, okay?"

"Deal," Mason said, though he was pretty sure this would be the only time.

Tom crawled under the tarp and nestled into the space between the Fangborn's legs and head. When they resealed the plastic, it looked like a bulky shape underneath, not something with arms and legs.

"It's going to get really hard to breathe pretty soon," Tom said, his voice muffled by the cover.

"You'll be under there for a few minutes, tops," Mason said. They pushed the cart out of the supply closet.

"This thing really smells . . ." Tom said after a moment. "Like its breathing smells. Or maybe it's just his face."

"Shhh," Mason said. "You're supposed to be an innocuous collection of inanimate objects. Or something like that."

They rounded the first corner toward the stairwells that would eventually lead to his mother and what he hoped would be a safe place to store the Fangborn until the cure was finished.

But right then an alarm went off. Mason froze, and Tom shifted under the plastic. The Fangborn stirred as the alarm—an extremely loud *WHOOP WHOOP WHOOP*—got even louder.

They were caught.

Chapter Twenty-four

Students began to fill the hallways, all of them heading for an exit. And Mason was right in the middle of everyone, with a stolen hover-cart that contained his best friend and a monster.

"Got any more bright ideas?" Lore said, flicking her double braid over her shoulder.

"Um . . ." Mason replied.

They stood there while the students flowed around them, a few giving the cart cursory looks. Mason hoped the hallway would clear again, and they'd be able to move forward and ignore the alarm.

"I'll check it out," Po said, sprinting ahead.

"What is that?" Mason whispered to Risperdel. "Is that a fire alarm?"

Risperdel's face was flushed violet. "Uh, no. I've never heard it before."

The hallway cleared out some, and Mason thought they were home free.

But then Grubare strolled around the corner.

Mason froze, then forced himself to keep pushing the cart forward. "Play it cool," Mason said.

"What does that mean?" Lore hissed, exasperated. "Is that like a human saying?"

"It means *act casual*. Pretend we're supposed to be here."

"We are supposed to be here," Risperdel said, sounding genuinely confused.

Grubare's eyes narrowed when he spotted Mason and his team. He started walking toward them. The gromsh galloped along at his heels.

"Stark," he said. "What's under the plastic?"

"I'm not sure," Mason said, not slowing down. "Broxnar asked for us to bring it to him."

"Hold it!" Grubare said. Mason stopped. The cart hovered in place. Risperdel and Lore were trying to figure out what to do with their hands. Down the hallway, Po rounded the corner and pulled up short.

"Show me what's under the tarp," Grubare said.

The gromsh plucked at the corner of the plastic with one paw, sniffing the air delicately, eyes closed. Then all four eyes snapped open, and it took a slow step backward, uttering a series of low chirps. *Stupid monkey thing!* Mason thought.

"Sir, we were asked not to unseal it," Mason replied. "You'll have to get permission from Broxnar."

Grubare's lip pulled back in a sneer. He looked down at the gromsh, which retreated behind the safety of Grubare's robes the way a frightened child would. "*Permission*. Interesting. A rhadjen saying I require permission. Do you know the punishment for disobeying a direct order from an instructor?"

"No," Mason said.

"A day in detention," Risperdel said.

"That's correct. You would know, Risperdel." Grubare turned his dark gaze onto Mason again. "You have one more second to change your mind, Stark. Or you'll be coming with me to visit Master Zin."

"Sir, what's the alarm for?" Risperdel said quickly. "Are we supposed to go somewhere?"

Grubare gave Mason more than one second to choose, but Mason didn't point that out. "It means two more students have gone missing. Their robes were found shredded." He said this in a tone one would use to describe the weather. Mason wondered how the warmth had been driven out of Grubare's heart, and if there had ever been any there to begin with. Mason couldn't be sure, but he still suspected that Grubare kept him after class so Juneful and his friends could get Mason alone.

Without warning, Grubare moved for the corner of the cart, his slender fingers reaching for the edge. Mason didn't know what to do. He couldn't attack Grubare. And he had no idea how the surly instructor would react upon seeing a human nestled in the arms of a Fangborn. Maybe he'd drop dead from shock.

"What's going on?" The voice came from the left. Mason turned, and his heart dropped further into his stomach. It was Broxnar.

Grubare straightened. "Ah, Brox. These students were just on their way to deliver this cart of . . . whatever it is they're delivering. I was curious about what they are transporting. It must be very important for them to ignore the alarm."

This was it; they were done for.

"Yes, that's right," Broxnar said.

Mason fought hard to keep the surprise off his face. He made eye contact with Grubare, whose nose was now scrunched up. Mason had to close his mouth.

"It is?" Grubare said.

"Yes, thank you for checking on them." Broxnar nodded to Mason. "You may proceed, young rhadjen."

"Thank you, sir," Mason said. They each grabbed a part of the cart and began to push it forward.

"Wait—" Grubare began, holding up a finger. A foot off the ground, the gromsh was doing the same thing, mimicking Grubare. Mason swallowed the urge to laugh.

"Now now, Grubare, they have to deliver that, and *then* make it back to the Inner Chamber in time for the assembly."

Mason risked a final look over his shoulder: Grubare's eyes were on him. He was still suspicious, so much so that Mason half expected him to give chase at any moment. But Broxnar put a large arm around Grubare's shoulders and began to walk him away toward the Inner Chamber. The gromsh followed, the eye in the back of its head never leaving the cart.

Mason didn't know why Broxnar would lie for them, but he was incredibly grateful.

"Why would he do that?" Risperdel said, echoing Mason's thoughts. They were hurrying down the hallway, side by side. "That gromsh is going to be the end of us."

"Maybe he has a soft spot for humans," Lore said.

"Or finds us a little too fascinating," Tom said. His voice was shaky. "How much longer?"

"Not much," Mason said. "Can you breathe?"

"No," Tom replied. "I mean, I can, but I don't want to."

Po caught up to them as they neared the stairs that would lead them down to the secret lab.

Mason stopped walking. "Here's where we have to part ways. I'll tell you everything later, but for now you have to trust me. There's no time, and I have to do the next part on my own."

"*Excuse* me?" Lore said. "We just risked our butts helping you sneak a *Fangborn*—"

"Shhh!" Po said.

"Sorry, a Fangborn," she said, much quieter, "into *our* school. You don't even belong here."

"Mason and Tom earned their robes," Po said. "They are Bloods, period."

"Even so," Lore said. "Not so long ago we were enemies, and now you just want us to trust you?"

Risperdel didn't seem to have a problem with it.

"Po?" Mason said.

Po looked at each of them in turn. "I say we trust them. On the condition he fills us in later. There's no time to argue anyway, like he said."

"Done," Mason said. He held his hand out to shake, but the others didn't seem to know what to do with it. After a second, Po made a fist for Mason to bump.

Lore snorted in disgust, then stalked away. *Just when I thought we were getting along.*

Risperdel leaned in. Her golden eyes were pale in this light, like crystal. "I hope you know what you're doing," she said, putting her hand on Mason's arm.

Mason tried to not look at her hand; he swore he could feel a dangerous charge from her gloves coursing up his arm. He swallowed. "I do."

Risperdel nodded, the charge fading as she removed her hand. She and Po followed after Lore.

"Seriously." Tom's voice came from under the tarp. "Can't breathe. Fangborn stinks. Want out."

"Hold on, buddy," Mason said, swinging the cart through the door and down the stairs. "This is going to be weird. Just go with it."

"Oh, I can't wait," Tom said.

Mason's mother was in the lab, using the same mixing machine as before. This time, the central reservoir held a magenta solution, not golden.

She spun around when Mason cleared his throat. "Mason! What are you doing here? We talked about this."

Mason still couldn't believe he was looking at his mother. She was right there in front of him, alive. She was whole, not trillions and trillions of separate atoms, like he'd been led to believe. Even now he felt anger brewing in his stomach at the deception. All these years, what he knew had been a lie.

"I didn't know where else to go," Mason said. He peeled back the plastic, and Tom tumbled out onto the floor.

"Hello," April said. "Who is this?"

Mason peeled back the plastic a little more.

"Great Mountain," his mother cursed. "Where—? How—?"

"It attacked us in the woods outside the school. Two more students have gone missing."

His mother was staring at the slumbering Fangborn, her

eyes wide. Tom picked himself up off the floor and dusted his robes. "Hi, Mrs. Stark," he said. "Tom Renner, pleased to meet you."

"Likewise," April said.

Mason waved his hand. "Mom! How could this be happening?"

"I . . . I don't know. Yet. Someone is obviously changing students. But how? Why?" She asked herself the last two questions. "There hasn't been another breakout—I know for a fact."

"Well how close are you to the cure? Where is your team? I don't want to hand this one over to the school if we can save him. Who knows what they'd do."

"No, you did the right thing." Mom pushed the cart over to the glass wall. The Fangborn within were hiding in the darkness. She ignored the question about her team, Mason noticed. Did she even have a team?

"Mom, I had to tell someone. I . . . may have already told Susan."

April Stark turned around. "Did she—? Was she—?"

"She was angry," Mason said. "But she hid it well, as always."

"Mason, I'm so sorry."

"I know you're sorry," Mason said. "You've said that more than once." He was sick of hearing it. It didn't change anything.

Tom shifted from foot to foot, clearly uncomfortable. "We should get back, Mason. Before Grubare decides to keep digging."

Mason nodded. "Mom?" Saying the word out loud still

felt weird. He wondered how long it would take to feel normal. If it ever would again.

"Go," she said. "I'll contain this one until the cure is ready."

April Stark wheeled the cart through a doorway, leaving them alone. She didn't look back, her mind already on the task at hand.

Mason's eyes immediately went to the glass wall. The Fangborn were there, just beyond the line of darkness. He could feel them watching. He made sure to stare into the darkness and not flinch, to not show an ounce of fear. Then he and Tom left the lab behind.

Chapter Twenty-five

Master Zin sat still as a statue at the head of the Inner Chamber. His eyes were not on the students; he appeared deep in thought. The whole room was filled, like it had been upon Mason's and Tom's arrival. The two humans sat in the back with their team—Po had saved them seats. The students were chatting idly, exchanging false rumors and coming up with new ones. Something was happening, that much was clear. The instructors had done their best to quash any rumors surrounding Jiric's absence, but now they couldn't hide the fact that students were disappearing.

Mason and Tom got more than a few suspicious looks; it was no secret things had been normal (or at least, relatively normal, since this was a school for alien space wizards) before the humans had arrived here to learn and train.

"We have failed at protecting you," Master Zin said, and every voice in the chamber dropped away to silence.

He stood up from his chair and opened his arms. "We have failed at pro*tecting* the students of this school, and for that I am sorry."

The assembly erupted in chatter, everyone looking at

everyone else for answers. Master Zin raised his hands. "*Please.* Please. I ask for your patience."

Slowly, the room quieted.

"Someone in this school is infecting students with *Fang-born* venom. This venom, once administered, scrubs away the genetic parts of you that make you Tremist." Somehow, Master Zin found Mason and Tom in the back. His eyes rested on them. "Or human. It turns you into one of them. Jiric was turned into one of them."

Mason could see the expressions on the instructors standing around the border of the room. Some of them seemed shocked that Master Zin admitted the truth, and some of them seemed shocked by the actual truth.

More chatter. A student stood up. "Where is Jiric now? Can he be saved?"

"We're working on a solution for that. Right now, Jiric is alive," Master Zin said, as rhadjen began to murmur. Master Zin did his boot-stomp thing, ruffling the hair of everyone and getting the silence he'd asked for. "Listen carefully. There will be no more roaming the school by your*self.* You will have a partner at all times. You will travel in groups as large as possible, with a minimum of two."

Lore stood up. Mason was not surprised. "But who is suspected of being behind this? A student? Or . . ." She looked around, not daring to accuse any of the teachers.

Mason felt a presence watching him, and when he turned his head, he saw Reckful standing next to Grubare. Mason couldn't read his expression.

Master Zin waited a long time before answering. "I don't know. Until we find out, things will continue as *normal,* or as close to normal as possible. You are dismissed. Tonight's free-for-all has been canceled, and all *future* matches are as well. For now."

"Sir." The first student who had spoken, a younger boy, stood up again. "You haven't told us who is missing in addition to Jiric."

Master Zin swallowed; Mason noticed all the way across the room. "Juneful and his friend, Dakor."

Mason's mouth dropped open. He'd been right: the Fangborn *had* looked familiar. It was Juneful. He'd helped sneak Juneful into his mom's lab. Would he have done the same thing knowing who the monster really was? *Talk about an improvement of character,* Mason thought, then immediately felt guilty. Juneful might be terrible, but no one deserved to be turned into a monster. Or at least not forever.

Five days passed. Mason spent every free moment in the library, fruitlessly searching for a clue that would allow him to open the door to Aramore's tomb (he only saw Calora twice, and when he did, she was helping other students). And then, on the evening of day five, another student went missing. It was a young girl named Keliandra, who nobody seemed to know very well. Her robes had been found, shredded. There was a rumor that two students had seen her roaming the hallways in Fangborn form, and they'd been so scared by the sighting that the medical staff sent them home.

Fangborn weren't escaping from the laboratory, Mason knew. There was an outside force at work.

➤ Mason wanted to visit his mother to see her progress, but classes went late. After class, rhadjen were forced to stay in their rooms. Groups of Rhadgast patrolled the halls at all hours. Mason focused on his studies, discovering the ways of the Rhadgast. He used his communicator and learned that Susan was on top of things: the Earth Space Command was quietly preparing for the coming battle.

Now all Mason had to do was make sure the Tremist were prepared, too. If they caught on that the humans were gearing up for war, they might take it the wrong way. The humans and Tremist made a treaty because they had a common enemy. Yet it seemed like there wasn't enough trust to fight that common enemy side by side. Mason wanted to laugh, even though it wasn't funny.

Six days later, Mason sent a message to the king through Reckful: *Sir, we need to talk.*

On the seventh day, Mason got the best and worst news of his career as a rhadjen: his friend Merrin Solace was coming to the school.

Chapter Twenty-six

News spread within a day.

The king's daughter. The princess. The princess is coming here to train!

Mason felt a little jealous. Several girls who called themselves the Stone Squad, for a reason Mason hadn't been able to figure out, officially declared Merrin a member of their group, even though Merrin hadn't taken the test yet. Mason wanted to tell them that Merrin already had friends, thank you very much, and would have no interest in joining their squad.

Mason got his first glimpse of Merrin in the Inner Chamber, when she was about to take the test.

Two new rhadjen were with her, boys who looked like twins, with bright green hair. Mason almost waved, but he didn't, and Merrin never noticed him. Seeing her again made his stomach flutter in a way he wasn't quite sure he liked. He felt a little sick. Her violet hair was pulled back in a ponytail, with two locks that escaped the tie and framed either side of her face.

Mason wanted to warn her about the horror she would

surely face inside the cave. The powerlessness ate at him. He tried to reach her, but there was simply no way to make contact. His only hope was that she'd be placed on his team, since Jiric was currently a monster and all.

The assembly of students left, and Merrin went down into the elevator with the two green-haired boys.

Mason caught up to Tom on the walk back to the dorm. "All we need is Stellan and Jeremy now, huh?"

Tom shook his head. "She shouldn't be here. Not with all this happening."

Mason felt the same, but he wasn't about to tell Merrin that.

In the dorm, Lore played some kind of card game with Po, and the others were reading textbooks in their bunks. Mason sat on his bed with his legs folded underneath him, feeling very much alone. He missed his crew.

Mason sat like that for thirty-four minutes. He counted.

And then the door opened and Merrin appeared, clad in new robes.

Chapter Twenty-seven

"Congratulations," Lore said, rising and walking toward her. "Welcome to the Stones."

Mason stopped breathing. Merrin's robe had violet accents on the wrists and neck. There was no mistake; he was not suddenly colorblind. *What happened in that room?*

Merrin looked shaken, her nearly translucent skin somehow paler than normal. The skin around her eyes was flushed purple, like she'd been crying. When she saw Mason, she walked toward him and pulled him into a fierce hug, pressing her cheek to his. He could feel her trembling.

"Missed you, too," he said softly.

"That was awful," she said, pulling back. She squeezed his shoulders, as if making sure he was really there.

"Yeah," Po said from his bunk. "It's never a good time."

Mason took Merrin's hand and pulled her back toward the door. "We'll do introductions later," he said.

He shut the door once they were outside, and Merrin sniffed, wiping at her eyes.

"You can't be here, it's dangerous!" Mason said.

Merrin raised an eyebrow. "Dange—Do you know who you're talking to? Did you forget what we *did* last summer?"

"Well, no, of course not—"

"Then why would you think I can't handle anything that comes our way?"

Someone was currently turning students into Fangborn, that was reason enough. Any one of them could be next.

"I don't think that. You're right. But this place *is* dangerous. More than you know. The test isn't even the start of it."

She pressed her fingers to her forehead. "The test . . . yes, the test . . ."

"Merrin?" He reached out to put a hand on her shoulder, but her eyes were closed, so he let it fall.

"It was my brother. He was there."

Mason's mouth fell open. "Your *brother*? You have a *brother*?"

"Yes. I've only met him a few times. He's older than me, and . . . cold. I had to choose between him and several people from the Coalition for Life, the organization I've been working with? I chose to let him die."

That didn't make sense. The test was supposed to show the person you cared about most—why would Merrin see a brother she barely knew? *They did it on purpose*, Mason thought. *They wanted to make sure the princess became a Stone.*

What had Reckful said? *We find the person most important to you.* What a scam. If it had been someone Merrin truly cared about, she would've picked Blood.

Right?

Mason heard the whispers of multiple robes and turned

to see a Rhadgast patrol of four moving down an adjacent corridor, passing out of sight.

"How did it end?" Mason said. "The test." He wanted to know why she was wearing robes of the wrong color.

She shook her head, biting her lip.

"You can tell me," Mason said.

"He began to cry, and I tried to explain. I—I told him I couldn't let five people die just because he was my brother. And he said . . ."

"What?"

"He said I could choose to die myself. But I told him I have important work to do with the coalition. And I just . . . I didn't *want* to. Every time I've talked to him, he's complained about humans." She dropped her voice to a whisper. "*My* people."

Something cold trickled down Mason's chest, behind his sternum. Mason hoped he never had to meet Merrin's brother.

"My father is coming to talk to you soon," Merrin said, clearly trying to change the subject.

"Oh good, I've missed the king," Mason said.

Merrin laughed shakily, still wiping at her eyes.

"Come on," Mason said. "Let me introduce you to the team."

➤ That night, Merrin joined the group in their hunt for the gloves. Po had taken a liking to Merrin, Mason could tell. Mason kept catching Po staring at her. Mason did not like this. When Po looked at Mason, Mason was sure to convey

how much he didn't like this with his face. Po only smiled
sheepishly and whispered, "The king's daughter . . ." as if
that somehow explained everything.

The walk back to the ruins had no idle chatter this time;
everyone was tense, eyes flitting to the shadows, postures low
and ready. Merrin, being a Tremist herself, had fit into the
group immediately. Lore was very kind to her, but Risperdel
was slightly aloof.

Once at the ruins, Po pointed out where the battle with
the Fangborn had taken place. Merrin nodded as Po told the
story.

"They seem to be getting along splendidly," Tom whispered
to Mason. They were trailing behind the group.

"So?" Mason said.

"So, nothing," Tom said, but he was grinning like an idiot.

They split up, Mason, Tom, and Merrin forming a group.
It was nice to be just the three of them again. Mason liked
his dorm mates, even Lore, but now he felt like he was part
of a team again. *You need them,* he thought. *You can't do
everything yourself.* As they stalked the ruins, Merrin told
them about the work she'd been doing in the coalition. "It's
like saving the world in a different way," she said. Mason
preferred saving it the way they were used to.

➤ The search was uneventful. Until Merrin stepped on a
rock in the room of a random house, and the stone pushed
through the dirt floor. She lifted her foot and looked at the
stone. After a moment, the stone sank deeper, disappearing
into the floor with a mechanical grinding sound that was not
natural. The mechanisms sounded a million years old. Ma-

son and Tom were with her, and they all shared a look: *Of course we're the ones to find it.*

Mason was about to call for the others when the ground began to vibrate under them. Small pebbles dropped down from the ceiling. Dust filled the air, rising off the floor in a sandy mist. A square in the floor the size of a table began to slide toward the wall, opening a hole right in the middle of the room.

The hole had a set of stairs leading down into pitch-black darkness.

"I'll get everyone else," Tom said, but suddenly the hole began to close.

"Did the stone pop back up?" Mason said urgently. He looked at where the stone had been, but there was only a small round hole.

This could be their only opportunity. Mason thought about the gloves, and what the Uniter had been able to do with them. Having them would change everything, he knew it in his heart. Calora's book had been clear. When it came time to face the Fangborn head on, Mason wanted to be ready.

He was prepared to sacrifice himself if it meant the survival of both races. But he couldn't ask that of Tom or Merrin. He didn't *want* to.

Without the gloves, they were truly lost.

The hole was half shut now.

"Mason . . ." Merrin said, but she knew him well enough. Tom made a grab for Mason's arm, but Mason dodged it, jerking away and sidestepping for the stairs. *Please let this be the right call.* It was possible the room was just some kind of secret storage area. There had been nothing special about the house, nothing to say it had belonged to the Uniter. But it was worth the risk to find out for sure.

Mason slipped down the stairs on his butt to avoid getting crushed by the door.

"Mason—!" Merrin screamed, but her voice was cut off when the door sealed shut.

Chapter Twenty-eight

The darkness was complete. He could hear thumps through the stone above him, probably Merrin and Tom running to get the others. Then there was silence, a silence so perfect Mason could hear his heartbeat. He could hear the air traveling in and out of his lungs. If he'd been wearing his ESC uniform, the built-in vitals monitor would've been vibrating like crazy: *calm yourself.*

Mason's eyes adjusted, but he still couldn't see anything. He held his hands out before him and fed power to his gloves, hearing a low buzz echo off the rock walls. His palms glowed with red light that painted the walls in blood. A corridor was in front of him. Mason took a calming breath and started forward.

The first hundred feet were featureless, but then out of the gloom he saw a door. It was ornate, like the doors to the Inner Chamber, with swirling patterns and pictures that were hard to see in the crackling red light.

"Why are you here?"

The words came from the door, a recording. The quality

was nearly perfect, but Mason could tell it didn't come from an organic being.

Mason figured he should try telling the truth. Why not? "I seek the gloves of the Uniter."

The door said no more, and several long seconds passed.

"Why do you want them?" the door said at last.

"Because we face a grave threat . . . and we need all the help we can get."

"Who are you?"

"Mason Stark, cadet of the Earth Space Command, and now a rhadjen."

The door was quiet for a moment.

"Many have found this door, but none have passed. What makes you different?"

Mason didn't know how to answer that. It reminded him of the application for officer-specific classes at the Academy. *What makes you uniquely qualified to be a leader in the ESC?*

Be honest, Mason thought.

"Probably nothing. My people think I'm a hero, but I was just in the right place at the right time, with the right crew. There is nothing special about me. But I know that if I don't find the gloves of Aramore, we're all going to die."

The door was quiet for a longer moment.

"Do you truly believe that?"

"Yes," he replied. "We're all going to die."

"Do you believe there is nothing special about you?"

Did he? Mason couldn't be sure. Maybe there was, and maybe there wasn't. *Be honest.* So he said, "I can't say for sure."

Something clicked in the door. Mason took a step back, his hands already up, ready to feed more power to his gloves for whatever lay behind the door. He waited a moment, then nudged it with his toe. The door swung inward, revealing a brightly lit chamber much like the one in which he'd taken his test. It was completely empty, save for a dusty glass cabinet at the far end. Inside under bright lights was a set of black leather armor and a cape of crimson silk, suspended upright as if an invisible person were wearing them. And there, hovering below the sleeves, was a pair of Rhadgast gloves, identical to the ones he was wearing but pure black.

Mason's heart pounded. Why would the door open for him, after all this time?

He approached the cabinet slowly, reverently, not wanting to make too much noise for some reason.

He took another step, and the glass surface turned into a screen, displaying a video image of a Tremist with red and black hair, as tall as in real life. Mason recognized him from Broxnar's class. It was Aramore the Uniter.

"Greetings," Aramore said. He spoke in a rare dialect, Mhenlo dai Fen, or People of the Forest.

"Hi," Mason replied.

"You're probably wondering why you're here, why you're the first one to be allowed through the door."

"Yes, I am," Mason said.

"Before my death, I built a program that would judge a person's worth simply from their answers. Twelve people have reached my door before, and when asked why they deserve the gloves, they all recount their feats of strength. Their achievements. Their glorified battle stories. Their pride makes them unworthy to wield my power. After nearly five hundred years, you are the first I've judged worthy of entrance."

Mason was floored. He didn't know what to say. He tried, "Thank you."

"Don't thank me yet. I'm afraid it won't be that easy. Because words are one thing. Now I need to see if you mean them."

Mason's heart immediately began to pound faster.

"Would you like to proceed?"

A fleeting thought: *Turn back now.* But Mason knew he couldn't. Not after coming this far. "I am."

A hundred tiny doors around the chamber snicked open. Mason spun around. In each hole was darkness.

"Then show me what you're made of," Aramore said, dimming along with the lights in the room. Mason heard chittering from within the holes, and the first creatures poked their heads out.

Gromsh.

Not dangerous. Grubare has one, after all.

They began to jump down from their holes, one after another. Fifty were in the room, then a hundred. When they opened their mouths Mason saw they had rows of needlelike teeth. He ignited his gloves, which now provided the only light in the room. *What am I supposed to do?* Mason thought. *Fight them all?* Hundreds of eyes reflected the light of his gloves back at him. It made the floor appear as if it were covered in a bed of moving sparks.

And then the creatures struck. Dozens launched themselves at Mason, grabbing on and tearing at his clothes. He fell to his knees as they swarmed over his head and face, sharp claws digging at his ears and eyes. He called forth power from his gloves . . . but there was nothing there. They felt inert on his hands, lifeless. Mason swung his arms, batting two away at a time, but four gromsh would take their place. He fell onto his side as they began to bite at his fingers and neck, chattering excitedly to each other. Strangely, there was no pain.

They were inside his robe now, crawling along his skin and biting at his flesh. So many standing atop him it felt like a hundred pounds. The room had to be four feet deep in gromsh. He inhaled sharply, and the head of one got stuck in Mason's mouth. He inhaled through his nose, but the fur of another blocked the air. *This isn't real! This can't be happening!* But if it was an illusion, it didn't feel like one. His chest grew tighter with trapped air, a burn that spread to his brain. His face tingled and then went numb.

As the gromsh began to drown him, he realized the truth: heroes, however much a society needed them, were just people. He was going to fail his test, and the sum of his past accomplishments would not be able to save him. His last thoughts were for his team: Tom, Merrin, Stellan, and Jeremy. And now Po, Lore, Risperdel. Without them, he was nothing.

The gromsh were weighing him down so heavily now he couldn't draw breath, even if his mouth and nose weren't full of fur. Spots exploded in front of his eyes. He shut them against the end.

And all at once, the gromsh disappeared.

Mason opened his eyes. He was alone in the room. The doors were gone, and he could breathe. He looked down at his clothes—they were intact. Maybe a little dusty from lying on the floor.

Anger bubbled up inside him; sweat popped on his fore-head. The implant was warm inside his brain. *They tricked me again,* he thought. *I let them trick me again!*

"Ah, well done! I was hoping you would pass the second part." Aramore was back. "I apologize for the deception. My computer was able to interface with your implant. Even though yours appears to be much, much newer."

"How did I pass?" He forced himself to stay cool. It was over now. And if there was a next time, he'd be ready.

"You simply can't win against the gromsh. Instead, your final moments are judged . . . including your thoughts. I sense arrogance in you, Mason Stark. But there is also humility. One of them will grow and be the driving force behind your actions. Make sure you choose the right one."

Mason stared at the image of Aramore, wishing the man were really here so he could talk to him in depth, ask his advice. Mason bowed his head, an instinct. "Thank you," he said, still shaken and sweating.

"You don't know the risks yet."

Risks?

"The armor is yours, do with it what you will, it holds no special powers. But the gloves are powerful indeed. They tap into a dark place. That place is inside your mind. You will require great mental fortitude if you choose to wear them. If you lack the strength, they will overpower you. They will turn you against yourself. . . . They will be your undoing."

Aramore's words sent a chill across Mason's shoulders.

Aramore stared at him, and it seemed for a moment like the image was actually seeing him. That they were making eye contact across hundreds of years. "Heed my words. For if you fail, it won't mean your doom. It will mean the doom of everyone around you."

Mason didn't know what to say.

The image disappeared and the glass case opened.

Chapter Twenty-nine

Mason stared at the armor and gloves for a moment. *I can't believe I found them.* What a huge responsibility to be the one finally admitted to the room after all these years. He was a little afraid to take the items; it wouldn't make the other students accept him: if anything, wearing them publicly would be an enormous risk.

Remember his words, he reminded himself.

Mason knew that the gloves would be taken from him as soon as they were seen in his possession. Maybe that would be for the best—a full Rhadgast might be able to wield them better. But he decided to wear the gloves at least for a time and keep the armor and cape hidden. He was still a rhadjen, and rhadjen wore initiate robes. Mason peeled off his regular gloves and folded them into an inner pocket on his robe. He grabbed the first of Aramore's gloves and tugged it onto his left hand. It felt exactly the same as his red gloves, just black. As soon as it was on his hand, it shrunk to fit him snugly, and then it linked to his brain.

It was different.

This was much more complete. The glove was his skin.

He could feel different parts of his mind unlocking and reaching out for the glove, and the glove reaching out for those same parts. Mason inhaled sharply and blinked rapidly. It felt great. Better than great. He had nothing to worry about.

Mason hurried to put on the right glove and fell to one knee when it joined the other in his brain. He held his hands up in front of his face, turning them back and forth. His hands were black and smooth. He'd never felt so good, so right, in all his life.

Instinctually he knew the gloves were his to command. They wouldn't work for anyone else, because *he* had taken the test. He could hand them over to Master Zin himself, and they would only function as an ordinary pair of gloves.

And yet, Mason wondered if he *could* take them off. They felt . . . permanent.

Afraid of the answer, *knowing* the answer on some level, Mason did not try to find out.

He pulled down the supple leather armor pieces and folded them up inside the crimson cape. He swung it over his back, then took one last look around the room. He might never come here again.

He didn't use the gloves to see, just guided himself by the echoes of his footsteps on the rock floor. He made it all the way back to the stairs, which he found by stubbing his toe on the bottom step. He stood in the darkness for a moment, and then the door in the floor retracted automatically. The purpose of his visit was finished, after all.

Mason squinted against the light, holding up one hand to shield his eyes.

"No. Way." That sounded like Po. Mason opened his eyes and saw his entire team standing around the hole, looking down at him.

"Those gloves aren't red," Risperdel breathed.

"What is that on his back?" Lore said. "That's a crimson cape. . . ."

Mason climbed the steps into the room. Once he was clear, the door slid shut.

"So . . . I found them," Mason said.

"You should've waited for us," Po said, looking none too happy. Mason felt a twinge of guilt: he knew how long Po had been searching for the gloves. But the door had been closing; there'd been no time to wait.

"Who gets to keep them?" Tom asked.

"Mason does, of course," Risperdel said. "*He* found them."

"Are you kidding?" Lore said, sticking her head out a window to check the sky. The air felt heavy with coming rain, and Mason wasn't eager to discover the chemical composition of whatever water fell from those yellow clouds. "As soon as we get back, the instructors are going to take them. What, you think they're going to go, 'Oh sure, little rhadjen, you get to *keep* and *wear* the gloves of Aramore the *Uniter*'? Get real."

"Hide them," Po said.

Mason immediately made the gloves into bracers. But he knew that wouldn't work for long. "I shouldn't hide them— I'll just get in more trouble. And I . . ."

"You what?" Po said.

Mason swallowed. "I don't think I can take them off."

"Well *try*," Lore said.

"I don't want to just yet," Mason said. Everyone looked at one another, puzzled. "I just put them on," Mason added quickly. "I don't feel like they should come off right away."

Mason looked to Merrin for advice, but she'd been silent thus far. She gnawed on her lower lip, a sign she was thinking through every possibility. "My father is coming to the school, to, um—well he's coming. He can have the final say."

"You dad's *say* doesn't overrule Master Zin," Risperdel said. "His rule here is absolute."

Merrin didn't bother to respond; she just arched a purple eyebrow. Mason didn't know who was right.

Outside, the first raindrops began to plunk down in the street. "Let's be quick," Po said. "We're already going to get in trouble with the laundry department for bringing them muddy clothes."

The rhadjen jogged out into the rain, through the forest, and back to the sphere. Thankfully, they came across no more loose Fangborn in the woods. But the rain lashed them sideways, stinging and hot. Back at the sphere, Mason let his gloves slip down over his hands. It felt better that way. He had nothing to hide. The crimson cape was soaked and dripping on his back. It was a five-hundred-year-old artifact worn by one of the greatest Rhadgast heroes to ever live, if not *the* greatest hero, and Mason had already dirtied it.

"Everyone, make sure you wash off the rain," Po said. "You'll get a rash."

"It's not my first storm on Skars," Lore replied.

Mason could already feel his exposed skin tingling.

The school day was over, but students were still roaming

the halls, on their way to whatever activities they had planned. A group of older Bloods noticed them coming in from the rain, and they were laughing a little, until one of them spotted the gloves on Mason's hands.

The older boy squinted. "Those gloves aren't standard issue. . . ." His eyes went to Mason's face, then narrowed once he realized Mason was one of the two humans in the school.

"The king's beard . . ." another boy cursed. As far as Mason knew, the king didn't have a beard. "Hey!" the boy said. "Why are his gloves black? Are those the gloves of Aramore?"

Risperdel sighed. "Yes. Yes they are."

"They found the gloves of Aramore!" the boy shouted to the entire school.

Groups of students up and down the hallways, a mix of Bloods and Stones, froze on the spot. Then they converged.

"Now you've done it," Lore said, rolling her eyes at Risperdel, who shrugged.

Students began to hurl questions at Mason—*How did you get them? Where did you get them? Can I try them on?*—but his team surrounded him, protecting him from the mob. Better to get this out of the way now, Mason figured. Surely a teacher would hear the ruckus and investigate.

The thought hadn't left Mason's mind when he saw Grubare marching down the hallway straight for them, pushing through a group of Stones. Mason immediately scanned around Grubare for the gromsh, but the little devil was nowhere in sight. Mason breathed a sigh of relief: if he never saw a gromsh again, it would be too soon.

Grubare didn't say anything at first. The students around him hushed, waiting to see what the instructor would do.

Mason just stared back at him, but Grubare's eyes were on the gloves. Mason watched as he swallowed. There was a glint of something in Grubare's eyes. Fear?

"Come with me," Grubare said. Then he turned around and walked away. The crowd made a surprised kind of sound in unison—*Did that really just happen?* Mason shrugged, then followed after Grubare.

Merrin and Tom were quick to follow.

Grubare seemed to sense their approach, because he stopped and spun around quickly, his robes flaring out around his legs (revealing the gromsh hugging Grubare's calf). "Not you, just him."

"I don't—" Tom began.

"This is *not* a discussion," Grubare hissed.

"Let him go, Tom," Merrin said.

Mason patted Tom on the shoulder. Tom flinched away as a spark of black energy burst between them. "Ow! Dude."

"Sorry, sorry!" The glove was alive on Mason's hand, begging to be used. He curled his fingers into a fist and lowered his hand.

Tom's mouth was hanging open. "Maybe you should take them off. For a bit."

I don't want to take them off. And I don't think I can.

"NOW!" Grubare roared from the other end of the hallway. Mason jogged after him, giving Merrin a parting glance. Her face held the same concern as Tom's, and she was chewing on her bottom lip.

Mason followed at a safe distance as Grubare led him up and down stairs and through hallways packed with students who stared at Mason's gloves with confusion.

When Grubare finally stopped, it was outside a giant wooden door banded in what appeared to be iron. The door was different than it was the last time Mason had visited Master Zin in his office. Po had told Mason you didn't want to visit Master Zin, you wanted Master Zin to visit you. His mouth suddenly became very dry.

Grubare lifted his hand to knock, but the door swung open before he could, slowly and creaking. Inside was a spacious, circular chamber. Every piece of furniture was made of wood.

Behind a massive desk carved in the likeness of some alien beast sat Master Zin. And across from him sat the Tremist King.

Chapter Thirty

"Ah, the human!" Master Zin said. He didn't say it the way some of the rhadjen did—*human*—like it was a dirty word or a curse. "Welcome, Mason. Please sit."

Grubare cleared his throat. "I'm afraid this isn't a social visit, Master. Look at the boy's hands."

Everyone did. The king's eyes grew wide and his lips parted in a small gasp. Master Zin kept a placid face, showing no reaction.

"Take those off," the king said.

Mason did not want to take them off. He'd had them for just over an hour, and two people had already suggested he take them off. What was the problem?

"He *can't*," Master Zin said.

"He must!" the king said. "You know what my armor did to me, Zin. You know how I struggled. Legend says the Divider and the Uniter were an even match because their gloves and armor were of the same technology. . . ."

Was that why the king had seemed so evil before? Had

his armor been influencing him the way Aramore said the gloves might influence Mason?

Grubare snorted. "Yes, legend also claims the technology is alien in nature, so advanced even *we* can't understand it. Go ahead. Take them off, Stark. It's just legend." His words were dismissive, doubtful, but his face held the same fear as before.

Mason figured he could take one off, just to show them it wasn't a big deal. He pressed his thumb against the glove where it ended at his elbow, and tried to peel the material up. But it was stuck fast to his skin. He tried harder, really digging in, until he felt both gloves warming to a dangerous level. They had melded to him the same way the belt had melded to his torso.

Aramore's words echoed in his mind: *The doom of everyone around you.*

"You remember how long it took to remove your armor?" Master Zin said softly to the king. "You were here for days. In agony."

Mason felt his blood turn to ice. When the king looked at him, it was with sadness and pity and a weariness around his eyes that chilled his blood further. *What have I done?* Mason thought.

"What insight do you have, Grubare?" Zin looked at Mason. "As a descendant of the Divider, Grubare can choose no side. He is both sides."

Grubare had fire in his eyes. "You reveal my secret so freely?"

"There are secrets and then there are *secrets*. This is the former. It is nothing to be ashamed of. Every day you atone for the evil acts of your ancestor."

Mason watched as the fire turned to ash. Grubare seemed tired. "In truth, I do not know. I thought the gloves were lost forever."

"Aramore warned me," Mason blurted. "Or his AI did. He told me the gloves were dangerous but that he thought I was worthy enough to wield them."

Master Zin folded his hands on his desk. "Then you will be watched. Carefully. The king is a grown man, and he struggled. You will have a much harder time."

Mason felt his defiance rising. "I can't say having the gloves is a bad thing. Since students keep getting turned into Fangborn against their will. Sir."

The king blinked. "I was under the impression that problem was under control."

"It is being handled," Grubare said.

"How?" Mason said. "How is it being handled?"

"*Silence,*" Grubare said.

"Silence indeed," Master Zin said. "From *every*one, if I may be so bold to request it."

Mason almost revealed that he knew about his mother and her lab but wasn't sure what would happen if he did. He didn't know who knew about the lab or who was allowed to know.

"There. Isn't that better?" Master Zin almost smiled. "Mason, will you visit me each day, willingly, to track your progress with the gloves?"

"What do you mean *progress*?" Mason asked, a little harsher than he'd intended.

"With their removal from your body," Zin said flatly.

Do I have a choice? Mason doubted he did. "All right," he said. *After the Fangborn come and I destroy them.*

"Good, then that's settled. Now if I may get back to my meeting with our king, I would be *extreme*ly grateful."

Mason had to tell the king about the impending Fangborn attack. The king probably already knew, but Mason wanted to know for sure. He wanted to know how *much* the king knew. "Actually," he said, "I would like to speak to the king. Alone, if that's all right."

Everyone looked to the king, who nodded. "May I borrow your office?" the king asked Master Zin.

Master Zin nodded. "You may." He rose and headed for the door. Grubare followed, after giving Mason what probably passed for a sympathetic look, if you were Grubare.

"Now, tell me what this is about," the king said. He looked paler than usual.

"Sir. The Fangborn are coming. They know our location and are coming to finish us off. I don't know when."

The king didn't seem surprised at all. His face betrayed no emotion.

"You knew. . . ." Mason said.

"Yes, I did."

"Did you get that information from my mother?"

"I—" The king's gaze dropped to Mason's hands, and his eyes widened with an emotion Mason had never before seen on the king's face. It was fear.

Mason looked down; his hands were glowing black.

"Calm yourself," the king said.

Mason made his hands into fists, then relaxed them. The black light faded.

"Your mother reports directly to me," the king said. "We are as ready as we can be for a Fangborn assault. I contacted your sister, Susan, to share this knowledge, so that the humans might prepare as well. Imagine my surprise when she already knew. . . ."

"I may have mentioned it," Mason said.

"Mmm. Susan knows how frail our peace is right now. We are trying to work together while keeping it intact. We *are* working together, Mason. Because of you and your friends."

The rubber band around Mason's heart loosened, but just slightly. It was a weight removed, a problem for other people now. More qualified people. And yet, when the Fangborn came, Mason would still have to fight.

"When this is over, I want my mother to be released," Mason said. "She can finish the cure back on Earth. Where she belongs."

The king seemed hesitant, unsure of what to say.

"It's not up for discussion," Mason said. He could barely believe the words coming out of his mouth. He used to fear the king, and now he was talking to him like this? *How much of this is the gloves? I just put them on.* He felt the gloves probing deeper into his mind, knocking on doors, poking around, making themselves quite at home. With a thought, Mason pushed them back. *I'm wearing you,* he thought to the gloves. *Not the other way around.*

"Mason, it is true that we need your mother. *Desperately,* I might add. But she is not a captive. At least, not anymore."

Then why didn't she come home? Mason didn't know what else to say. He tried: "Before, I thought you were the most evil creature I'd ever met. How much of it was your armor?"

The king was stone-faced. "I can't be sure. I wish I could blame all of it on the suit, but that would be a lie. That doesn't mean I'm not afraid for you, Mason. Aramore's avatar may have judged you true, but he was an exceptional man. I want to believe you're just as exceptional, but only time will tell how strong you are on the inside."

Once more, Mason was without words.

"The Fangborn aren't coming, Mason. They're already here. They've already begun their invasion, but in a slow way. A terrifying way. I'm tempted to send everyone in this school home . . . that's why I'm here. To decide."

"Why are you telling me this?" Mason said.

The king almost smiled. "You were once wise enough to show me one truth. Now I hope you can help me discover another. What would you do, if you were king?"

Sending the students home was the best idea Mason could imagine, but it wasn't the answer he gave. "I would find who was responsible, and stop them."

"So would I," the king said.

Chapter Thirty-one

Four days passed without a Fangborn sighting, without an incident, without a transformation. Space was empty, too. The Fangborn did not come.

In those four days, half of the students left the school to return home until the Fangborn threat was ended. There was a rumor Master Zin was sending students home so they wouldn't be asked to fight once the war started.

In those four days, Mason felt the yearning of his gloves. The old gloves, the red ones, were safely locked in the storage compartment in the wall next to his bed. Those gloves never wanted anything. They obeyed. They were tools. These new gloves were alive, Mason was sure of it. Somehow, some way. He hadn't seen his hands once in those four days, and yet his skin didn't sweat in the gloves; they didn't feel unclean. Because the gloves were his skin now.

Each afternoon, Mason sat with Master Zin and recounted his interaction with the gloves for that day. Master Zin never let his face slip, never showed how troubled he really was, but Mason knew.

Mason and his team went to class. He endured the whispers and the sideways glances, the rumors and the alienation. *Tom and Merrin are here, and we are alive, so that's all that matters.* Mason didn't have an opportunity to practice with the gloves, but he wasn't worried: he knew that when he needed the gloves, they would respond.

He visited his mother's lab on the third day, but the lab was empty. Which felt strange, with the threat so imminent. The Fangborn behind the glass stayed hidden in the dark, but Mason knew they were there, watching him.

On the fourth day, Broxnar visited Mason's dorm. He knocked on the door and opened it a second later, the way adults did, whether human or Tremist.

"Hello everyone, how are we this evening?" Everyone was not so good, almost the entire team having been eliminated in the free-for-all (which had just been reinstated) right away, when a group of older Bloods made them their first targets. The team was feeling the consequences of being associated with Mason and Tom now. They were becoming outsiders, and Mason didn't know how to fix it. He had not been allowed to participate in the free-for-all, since his gloves were still an unknown factor. In a combat situation, Mason worried he might actually kill someone, not stun them.

Lore, however, was doing great. She'd won the game, having escaped from the team and hidden herself in the trees for most of the match, a fact the rest of the team wasn't going to let her forget.

"That good, huh?" Broxnar said.

"We're okay, Broxnar," Po said, tossing a ball against the

wall and catching it. "Is there something we can help you with?"

Broxnar nodded, his jowls jiggling up and down. "Actually, yes, Po, thank you. I was hoping I could have a word with Mason Stark."

"Me?" Mason said, sitting up in bed. He pointed at his own chest, and when his finger touched his robe, a great warmth spread from his fingertip through his body.

Broxnar smiled. "I don't know any other Mason Starks."

Mason got out of bed and followed Broxnar, who was already waddling down the hallway.

"Is something wrong?" Mason asked, once he'd caught up to him.

"No, no, nothing is the matter." Broxnar smiled again, but it didn't quite reach his eyes. "Unless you count the madness this school has descended into. I must confess, I am quite embarrassed. The first time a human visits our school it has to be during a crisis like this. You must think so poorly of us."

So Broxnar didn't know April Stark had been here for years. Or more likely, he just picked his words carefully. Mason wondered if Broxnar was really embarrassed: horror at what was happening to the rhadjen seemed more appropriate.

"I don't think poorly of anyone. The school is trying to handle it, I guess." Mason said.

"The students should be sent home," Broxnar said. "All of them, including the older students."

Mason had to agree with that. The hallways were almost deserted, which made everyone feel less safe. The one they walked down now was like an enormous, hollowed-out tree trunk, but halfway through it became what appeared to be ice that was not cold or wet.

"Here we are," Broxnar said, stopping outside a door in the fake ice. He gestured for Mason to walk in first. A chill ran across his shoulders.

Mason entered an office that appeared like a meadow you might find on Earth. The floor was grass, the walls paneled in tree bark. Birds chirped all around them. The only furniture was a simple desk and two chairs across from it. Mason sat in the left chair, and Broxnar squeezed himself into the chair behind his desk.

They stared at each other for a moment. Mason did not like the light behind Broxnar's eyes.

He decided to be blunt. "How can I help you, sir?"

Broxnar shrugged. "I was hoping we could talk, you and me. One-on-one. You know my affinity for the story of the Uniter and the Divider. I believe it was your first lesson from me, was it not?"

Broxnar's eyes lingered on Mason's gloves.

"Yes," Mason said. "I enjoyed it very much."

"So what is it like, Mason Stark, to wear *history*? To wield *legend*?" For the first time since Mason had known him, Broxnar's face was harsh, tense with an emotion Mason couldn't quite place.

Mason looked over his shoulder at the door.

"Do not look at the door again," Broxnar said. "Now answer me."

Mason decided to be honest. "It's unlike anything I've experienced before. It's . . . power."

Broxnar was nodding, his lips twisted in something that might've been another version of a smile. "Go on."

"The gloves feel . . . alive."

"I would like to try them on. Just once." Broxnar leaned forward in his chair, which creaked. "You wouldn't deny me that simple pleasure, would you? Did you know I am a descendant of the Uniter? Not direct of course, but I have his blood. I know of the chamber you found those gloves in. I have been trying to access it my entire life, since I was a rhadjen myself. And then a human comes to the school and finds it within a few *weeks*. And now you have my birthright. You have what belongs to my family. So I'm sure you will understand my desire to just try them on, to just wear them for a moment. Surely you understand."

Broxnar's lips glistened with spit, and his forehead was beaded with sweat. A manufactured breeze pushed through the office, rustling Mason's hair. Broxnar had no hair to rustle.

"I understand," Mason said slowly. "But I can't take them off. They won't come off."

"That's interesting. Has anyone tried to remove them by force?"

Mason had felt uneasy at first—Broxnar had been his favorite teacher—but now he was beginning to feel the stirrings of anger deep inside his gut. "I don't think you'll be able to do that, either," he said.

"But there is fun in trying, isn't there? Know that if you strike me, every Rhadgast in the school will come to this location, and who will they believe? Me, a respected teacher, or you, a human wearing gloves that could be corrupting your mind with each passing second."

Broxnar was right. Mason felt a cold, sinking sensation in his chest.

"I don't know what you want me to do," Mason said. "They *won't* come off!" He stood up.

Broxnar rose with him. He reached for Mason's wrist; Mason let him. There was a small explosion of black energy between them when Broxnar's skin touched Aramore's glove. He yelped and pulled back his hand, but the yelp turned into a low growl, and Broxnar lunged across the desk, reaching with both hands for Mason's throat. It felt like an iron collar had been locked around Mason's neck. Instantly he felt pressure in his head, behind his eyes, in his ears. His breath was stuck in his lungs, unable to move in or out.

This is not the end, Mason thought, as he grabbed Broxnar's wrist. The glove, seeming to sense its master was in danger, automatically sent out a pulse of energy. Broxnar flew backward, knocking over his chair. Some things slipped out of his robe and rolled in the grass. Mason stepped around the desk, taking deep breaths, the pain in his head fading but his heart still thrumming. He was not afraid of getting in trouble anymore: Broxnar was clearly insane.

The gloves were hungry. They were hot on his hands, bursting at the seams with energy that was begging to be used. *Finish him off,* the gloves seemed to say, but Mason knew that was only a voice in his own head. *Finish him before he hurts you.* Mason stepped closer.

Broxnar struggled to one knee, his eyes on the items that had slipped from his robe. Three vials filled with a milky blue liquid. Mason knew what they were instantly, even though he'd never seen them before in his life.

They were vials of Fangborn venom. Broxnar was incredibly huge, but he was quick. His hand darted out for the vials and was already pulling them back when Mason unleashed the first bolt, this one intentional. The grass was set aflame. Broxnar rolled away behind his desk as Mason fired a second blast, scorching another patch on the floor. *Again! Again!* the gloves cried, but Mason forced himself to maintain control. Broxnar stood up slowly on the other side of the desk . . .

. . . And let the three empty vials fall to the grass.

"It was you all along," Mason said. "*Why?* Why hurt the students?"

"I wasn't hurting them," Broxnar said. "I was remaking them the way they're supposed to be." He held up his thick hands. "Look at these fragile tools of flesh and blood. We were *supposed* to be Fangborn. But the lesser race escaped and settled our planets and now . . . now we're *this*. Disgusting, weak creatures. When your mother slept at night, the Fangborn allowed me to spread their gift. And what a gift it is, Mason."

"You didn't even know any of this until we brought the truth to everyone," Mason spat back. His hands were almost rising on their own, itching to fire a volley of black lightning, but he kept them at his sides.

Broxnar sneered, his mouth already larger somehow, elongated. "You think you're the first one to discover the history of the People?" His words came out slurred, a bit garbled by his teeth, which were also much bigger than before.

Kill him now! Before he changes!

"The Fangborn have known about us for a long time,

Mason Stark. They've been watching. Preparing. Their ship took generations to construct, but they are patient beings. And now they're on their way to reclaim us. We will be saved from this miserable existence . . . and those that fight will *die*."

Broxnar was now a foot taller. Then two feet.

"This is the only way to survive, Mason. They will win. Join the winning side, like I did, and I will give you an incredible gift. But first . . . I need your gloves."

Mason knew he couldn't let Broxnar have them no matter what. With the gloves, Broxnar might be able to fight his way out of the sphere, killing dozens along the way. Even without them, he was an extreme danger to everyone in the school.

Broxnar's silk robes began to split in different places, accompanied by the sound of crunching bones and shifting tissues. His skin darkened, becoming gray and hard. Fingers became claws, and two curling horns sprouted from his bald head. Mason had to crane his head back as Broxnar grew taller still. *He took three vials.*

When Broxnar spoke, his voice came from deep within his throat. His cavernous mouth barely moved at all.

"Are you ready to change?" Broxnar said. He bared his huge teeth. Venom was already dripping off the fangs.

Mason was not ready to change.

He finally let his gloves do what they wanted to do. He raised his hands, palms out, and fired two blasts at Broxnar's chest. Broxnar stumbled backward, twisting aside and ducking under the twin lances. As he rose upright, he flung the desk at Mason with one hand. Mason threw himself to the still-smoldering grass as the desk exploded into a million splinters against the wall.

Broxnar let out a mighty roar that shook Mason's brain and tickled his skin. It was so loud it hurt. *Good, bring everyone.*

"GIVE ME THE GLOVES!" Broxnar lunged for Mason, who didn't think, just pushed out with both hands and closed his eyes. *TWANG!* A dome of black crackling energy formed around him, and Broxnar bounced off it harmlessly, careening back into the wall. He roared, shaking his head from side to side.

Mason stood, letting the dome dissolve around him in tiny black explosions of light. He didn't waste any time. Broxnar was still regaining his balance when Mason unleashed everything he had; every ounce of fear and anger funneled through his gloves and out his palms. Mason's brain was on fire, red hot with rage that felt bigger than himself. The gloves were practically singing on his hands. After a few seconds, Mason let off. Parts of the office were on fire, and black smoke crawled along the ceiling. Broxnar was heaving, gray smoke rolling off his broad shoulders.

"You will need more than that to kill me, human." He either smiled or just showed his gigantic teeth.

Mason decided it was time to run. He fired again at Broxnar—the gloves seemed just powerful enough to keep him at bay. And while he was running for the door, he had a terrible realization: *How will we ever beat them? If these gloves can't kill one Fangborn, what weapon can?*

He flew through the doorway into the hallway and heard

Broxnar crash through the door's frame right behind him. He was double the size of any Fangborn Mason had seen before, and the sight of Broxnar galloping after him almost took the strength from his legs, almost sent him stumbling into the wall. He preferred rage. Mason let the gloves ignite again, throwing volleys over his shoulder. Broxnar dodged all but one: a direct hit to his head. He snarled, jaws snapping at the residual electricity on his face.

Mason rounded the corner and came face-to-face with Reckful.

Along with Masters Zin, Rayasu, and Shem.

Yes! Mason had never been so happy to see a group of Rhadgast in his life.

"Lend us your power, Mason Stark," Zin said, stepping aside so Mason could join the line.

Broxnar pulled up short when he saw the four Rhadgast (and one rhadjen) standing shoulder-to-shoulder. **"You won't be able to save your student this time, Zin."** His voice was painful in Mason's ears, low and grating. **"Kneel before me, and I will reveal your true form."**

"This is my true form," Master Zin said. "And the only person I will not be able to save today is you."

Broxnar crouched, coiling his muscles to leap, and the five warriors unleashed their power. Purple and red and black electricity lanced across the space, winding together, spiraling into Broxnar's chest. Broxnar backpedaled from their combined might, until his back hit a wall. **"NO! I MUST HAVE THE GLOVES. THEY BELONG TO ME—"**

He collapsed, nearly covered by a blanket of prismatic electricity. The others let up, but Mason was still firing, wrapping his electricity around Broxnar's arms, pinning them to the floor. He didn't stop when he felt Reckful's hand on his shoulder. He only stopped when Master Zin lashed out, knocking Mason's tendrils aside with his own. Mason snapped out of it, heaving, the rage burning hot and black in his hands. He noticed Master Zin was wearing a Stone glove on his right hand and a Blood on his left.

"I *assure* you, he is quite incapacitated," Master Zin said to Mason.

"I'm sorry," Mason said, but he wasn't, not really. Broxnar had tried to kill him. Broxnar had tried to take his gloves.

His gloves.

The others were looking at Mason strangely. Shem had a hint of unease behind his cool gray eyes. Rayasu's hatred was mixed with a dash of grudging admiration.

"The boy has skill," Shem said. Mason couldn't help but feel a little thrill of pride. The head of the Bloods had never spoken to him before.

"But lacks control," Rayasu replied.

Shem raised an eyebrow at Rayasu. "I seem to remember a young rhadjen who was not so different."

"That was a long time ago," Rayasu said.

Master Zin cleared his throat. "Are you *finished*?"

They had more important problems. Namely an overlarge Fangborn slumbering in the hallway.

"We need to get him to the lab," Reckful said. "The cure is almost ready."

Chapter Thirty-two

Jiric was a Tremist again. So was Juneful and the other students who had been transformed. Their skin was paler than usual, their eyes bloodshot, but they would survive. They would continue their lives.

The glass cage in the lab held only one person now: Broxnar. He was lying in the corner of the room, still unconscious, his skin blackened in places, fangs glinting, a puddle of drool leaking from his gaping maw.

Mason was standing in the lab with Shem, Rayasu, Master Zin, and Reckful. They watched as April Stark administered the cure to the last student, who was strapped to a table, unconscious. His huge Fangborn chest rose and fell with each breath. Soon he would be Tremist again.

The other newly nonmonstrous students had already been taken to the medical room, where they would be under careful surveillance for some time, to make sure their cells did not alter. Only Juneful was still on a table, groggy from the transformation, his rhadjen robes neatly folded next to him. Mason watched as Juneful held up his robes and looked at them as if seeing them for the first time. Juneful probably thought he'd be a monster forever, but now he'd returned to his old life, hopefully leaving his bullying ways behind with the monster.

"Did you know about my visits here?" Mason asked Reckful. His visits to April Stark and her lab were not a secret, he had discovered. Master Zin had known the whole time, along with Rayasu. No one had stopped Mason because they wanted to see how he would handle it, what he would do with the information. *Everything is a test.* But they had no way of knowing Mason had the communicator, and had shared what he'd learned with Susan, unless Reckful or the king told on him.

Reckful folded his arms behind his back, staring at Broxnar where he slept. "You were on the Will once. After you and your friends saved it. Do you remember?"

"I don't think I'll ever forget," Mason replied.

"A Rhadgast told you to come to our school, if you wanted to know the truth about your parents. . . ."

Mason's mouth fell open. Only two people knew that—Mason and the Rhadgast on the Will. "But . . . no. You're—you're Blood!"

Reckful nodded slowly. "Yes. I am now. But I wasn't always. A part of me will always be Stone, but I don't think a Rhadgast should be any one thing. The day Blood and Stone are no longer divided is a day I will finally be happy." He faced Mason. "The test determines where you start, Mason. Not where you end."

Mason remembered something from the autobiography of Captain Joshua Reynolds: *There are no good men or women. Just people. And any person is capable of a great many things.*

"Thank you for telling me," Mason said quietly.

"I was supposed to keep it secret. But after everything you did, I wanted you to know the truth."

Juneful walked over to them slowly. He was clad in his robes once again, though his face was paler than it should've been, and his skin seemed loose in places, like it hadn't yet fully adjusted to his old form.

"Thank you," he said, looking Mason in the eye. "I was wrong." He nodded to Reckful. "Cousin."

Reckful nodded back. Juneful left without another word; Mason understood. *People are just people.*

Soon there was nothing more for his mother to do. She washed her hands at the sink and then put her hands on her hips, staring blankly at the cure, which was lined up in two dozen test tubes on the table. She didn't move, didn't seem to breathe.

"Mom," Mason said softly.

She jumped, eyes fluttering as if waking from a dream. "What? Sorry. I'm sorry. I just . . . I can't believe it. Years of work. Thousands of failures. And there it is. The cure. It's done."

It almost sounded like she was going to miss working on it. Even though its completion meant she had no reason to remain in this dungeon.

"What happens now?" Mason said.

"Well, I guess I report for duty. I'm still in the ESC after all." She pulled him into a hug. "I'm sorry. For everything."

Mason nodded against her shoulder. He'd thought about it long and hard, over many nights: the pain came from thinking his parents were dead, from not knowing they were still walking around with beating hearts, drawing breath. For years Mason had imagined their atoms somewhere on Earth. He had always believed they'd been vaporized. But even if Mason had known they were alive, they would still be strangers to him. The ESC allowed six weeks home every year, until graduation. Six weeks. He'd missed less than a year with his parents, total, assuming they wouldn't have been on some kind of mission during those six weeks.

Mason would find a way to make up the time. He would get to know his mom. And once his dad was human again, he would get to know him too.

Next stop, Nori-Blue, Mason thought.

"I have to go," Mason said. "Master Zin has called everyone to the Inner Chamber."

"Of course. Go. I need to make a report anyway." April pushed a bit of Mason's hair off his forehead, like she had when he was young and his hair would get too long and floppy and fall into his eyes. "I am so proud of you, Mason. Here. Take these. Just in case." She pressed three vials of the Fangborn cure into Mason's hand. "Press the button on the side, and a needle will pop out."

Mason slid the vials into his robe. "When will I see you again?"

"Soon," she said. "That's a promise."

Mason hugged her one last time, then left the lab behind, wondering if it was a promise his mom could keep.

➤ The Inner Chamber was half filled with restless students, most of them older. The younger rhadjen were on their way back to the school, if the rumors were true. Mason assumed they were: Broxnar was safely behind the glass, and the room was guarded by no less than five Rhadgast, even though Broxnar was next in line to become Tremist again.

Master Zin stood in front of the assembly, his eyes passing over them, back and forth, until Mason thought he was never going to speak. He guessed there would be some kind of announcement. Something that said the school was safe again.

But Master Zin didn't say any of that.

He took a deep breath and said, "The Fangborn have found us."

Chapter Thirty-three

Mason's heart stopped beating for a moment, or so it seemed. He was glad to be sitting down.

I thought we had more time.

A stretch of peace had seemed so close, but now there would only be war again . . . or the imminent destruction of both races.

The room was full of chatter. Master Zin stomped his boot, but no wind buffeted them this time. It was a soft stomp. The room quieted anyway. "Their ship is currently halfway between Earth and Skars. It isn't moving. It seems to be *waiting* for something. The Will and the human space station, Olympus, have left to regroup with *both* fleets. We are working to*gether*. Make no mistake, rhadjen. This is the most important battle we will ever fight."

Lore stood up. She was sitting in the row with Mason. His whole team was here. "Sir! How can we help?"

"That you *can* help, I have no doubt," Master Zin replied. "But patience. When the time comes, you will be called upon. For now, prepare yourselves. Mentally *and* physically."

Master Zin left the Inner Chamber, along with all the

instructors, who were no doubt preparing for battle. Mason felt a tingle in his palms, as if Aramore's gloves were nudging him: *You have the power now,* they seemed to say. *You are the Uniter. Unite your people. Together we can pierce the Fangborn ship. No other energy weapon can. You just have to let me in.*

Mason realized his eyes were closed. Someone was saying his name—*Mason, hellooo, Skars to Mason.* His eyes snapped open: Tom and Merrin were standing in front of him, both grim-faced.

"Are you ill?" Tom asked.

"Mason, what's wrong?" Merrin said.

"We have to get up there," Mason said. "We've beaten them once before."

Tom raised an eyebrow. "I'm not sure disabling their tractor beams and then getting blown up constitutes winning."

"If they need us, they'll call us," Merrin said, but Mason heard the doubt in her voice. If the Tremist called upon the rhadjen for help, it was already too late. Mason could help *now.* They all could.

It was good battlefield logic to not put all your forces in one location. The enemy could wipe you out in a single battle. There would be no second chances. But Mason had a feeling this was an all-or-nothing fight.

The walls on the way back to the dorm had changed: they were no longer ice or grass or wood or metal or any kind of throbbing colors. They were now floor-to-ceiling video screens that showed space. They showed the Fangborn ship from many angles, all one hundred miles of it. It was four times as long as it was tall, close to a rectangle laid on its side, but it was much too large to be considered any one shape. The bottom of it had several enormous engine platforms all in a row, facing "down." Mason couldn't imagine the amount of force required for the ship to break free of a planet's gravity.

On both sides of the ship were raised circular areas, pushed outward into domes, like the very dome they were inside of now. Judging by the size of the ship, they had to be twenty miles tall. Mason didn't remember seeing them last time, when they encountered the Fangborn ship above Nori-Blue. But he did recognize the red horizontal line at the front, which could swing down like a giant jaw, then swing up twice as fast to swallow entire ships whole. The front of the ship had control towers on top, like the horns of a demon.

The students were walking back to their dorms, but they stopped as the Fangborn ship began to glow white around the huge domes. The light grew brighter and brighter. Mason searched the screen for other spacecraft, knowing what that light meant. Soon it would unleash a blast from particle beams so enormous they could vaporize entire ships with one hit.

But Mason was wrong.

White light began to spill out from the left and right sides of the ship, from the two domes, almost as if it were growing wings before their eyes. The light grew and grew and stretched, and then suddenly it shot out from both sides in thick white columns.

The beams hit both Skars and Earth at the same time.

They're attacking us on the ground! They're blowing up the planets! Every muscle in Mason's body tensed; he expected to become space dust in the next second.

But Mason was wrong again. Everyone was still there, frozen by what was happening on the screen. Students were asking questions: *What is it doing? How are we still alive?* But no one had an answer.

It was Tom who figured it out first. "Great Mountain . . ." he whispered.

"What is it?" Merrin asked.

"Those aren't particle beams. They're tractor beams."

Which meant . . .

"They're pulling the planets toward each other. If we don't stop them, Skars and Earth are going to collide."

Chapter Thirty-four

The school had a shuttle bay on the side facing the valley. Mason had always thought that was a faulty design: if there was a power failure aboard the ship, you wouldn't crash down into the trees, but into a valley larger than Earth's Grand Canyon.

The wall screens also showed an outward view of the school. Two Hawks took off from the shuttle bay. Mason knew what was inside them: Rhadgast, as many as the school currently held, save two instructors who stayed behind to watch the students.

"I'm going up there," Mason said to no one in particular. Everyone looked at him. "I'm going up there, and I'm going to do whatever I can to help. If you want to come with me, meet outside my dorm—"

"What do you think you're doing?" a voice said behind him.

Mason turned around. It was Reckful, wearing a dark gray skintight suit Mason knew was meant for space. His robes were folded over one arm, and his Rhadgast helmet was held in the crook of one elbow. The faceplate was already throbbing with red light. Not purple, like when Mason had met him aboard the Will.

"I'm joining the fight. This is our one chance—you need *everyone*."

"You—" Reckful abruptly stopped. Sighed. Searched for words.

Mason held up his hands; Reckful's eyes immediately went to the gloves of Aramore. "Let me stop you right there— yes, it's dangerous. Yes, we may not make it. But with these gloves . . . I must have them for a reason. I can do something. Just get me up there." The gloves prodded him on, almost supplying him with the words. "Reckful, I think I can pierce their hull. I think I can destroy them."

He thought of how Broxnar had been able to shake off Mason's assault: *I have to let the gloves go deeper, that's all.*

Reckful scratched his chin and looked away, thinking. Torn.

Tom was furiously doing calculations on the Tremist equivalent to a dataslate. "The amount of energy required to move two planets is not something I can calculate. Their energy source is beyond what we can even register. Like they must have a controllable black hole in the center of their ship, an idea so absurd I'm embarrassed to say it out loud." His fingers continued to dance over the screen, and then his eyes widened. "Hold up. I made an error. They're not pulling the planets toward each other—they're holding Skars in place. Since Earth shares an orbit with Skars, it's going to eventually crash right into Skars on its own!"

Tom lowered the dataslate. "If we don't stop them, we lose this war right now. Billions will be dead by the end of today."

We don't need the planets to collide—once they get too close, the natural disasters on *both* planets will be enough to wipe us out! I'm talking earthquakes and tsunamis and continent-sized storms. And I don't want to say that's because the Tremist placed Earth too close to Skars, but, yeah, that's definitely why. If both planets weren't so close, we'd be having supper right now."

"Hey!" Risperdel said. "*Your* people built the planet gate in the first place!"

"To use on Nori-Blue, not a planet with billions of people!" Tom said.

"*Stop it,*" Merrin said, in a tone she must've learned as princess. It worked.

Mason looked at Reckful, daring to hope. He could see the gears turning behind Reckful's eyes and recognized when they stopped. Reckful struggled with the decision for a final moment. Then he said, "Does everyone know where the spacesuits are kept? The ones we wear under the robes?"

A few of the students nodded, looking like they were about to barf. Mason knew the feeling. *Bravery is nothing without fear. Bravery is nothing without fear.*

"Good," Reckful said. "If you want to come along, suit up and meet me in the shuttle bay."

➤ In the end, forty-five rhadjen volunteered to fight. Their bravery made Mason's heart swell and gave him strength. That lasted until they reached the shuttle bay antechamber and discovered that there were only six spacesuits left. The other suits had been taken by the instructors and visiting

Rhadgast that had been at the school. Those Rhadgast had been ordered to join the combined fleets of Tremist and ESC, to wait for a two-pronged assault.

Once again, the fleets were waiting to strike, and once again, Mason and his team were not content to wait. Especially when he knew the fleets would most likely fail, no matter how mighty they were.

Reckful handpicked his team: Mason, Tom, Merrin, Lore, Po, and Risperdel.

The room was filled with faces that were either disappointed or relieved, about an equal mix of both.

As the rhadjen suited up, Reckful pulled Mason aside. "What exactly do you think you can do with those gloves?" he asked. "I need to know before I take our best and brightest on a potential suicide mission."

Mason looked at his hands. *Give us a chance,* they seemed to say. Or did they actually say it? Maybe it didn't *seem* like they were talking at all. But no, that was impossible. If the gloves contained an artificial intelligence, surely that would be part of their legend.

"I think I can penetrate their ship," Mason said. "Were you at the battle above Nori-Blue?"

"Yes," Reckful replied. A troubled look crossed his face at the mention of it. "I was aboard a ship. It was over before I could be deployed."

"Then you know energy weapons aren't going to do anything, and this battle is going to be a massacre. We had to get close just to blow up their tractor beams with conventional weapons. They *won't* let us get close again—and last time, the tractor beams weren't twenty miles tall!" Mason could see the lingering doubt in Reckful's eyes. "Look, if you guys can provide me some cover, I'll use my gloves against the hull. If it works, we go inside the ship as a team and try to destroy it from within. If it fails, we all take off."

Reckful put his hands on Mason's shoulders, looked him in the eye. "I want to trust you, Mason Stark. I *am* trusting you. And frankly, I wouldn't do this if I didn't think it was absolutely necessary." He sighed. "I'm supposed to protect my students, not take them into battle."

Mason could only nod back: he felt pressure at the backs of his eyes. To gain someone's trust was a rare thing. Tom trusted him. Merrin trusted him. Who else? Mason would not let them down.

Mason changed into the Tremist spacesuit, which was dark gray and skintight, with veins of red stitched up and down the arms, across the torso, and spiraled down the legs. Like the stolen armor he'd worn aboard the Egypt, the suit shifted to fit him perfectly. Mason put his robes on over it. Soon he would see what it was like to use his Rhadgast belt in actual space, not a training room. He hoped the belt was as fast as the jetpacks he had used with Merrin and Tom during their assault on the planet gate.

The helmet came last. The curved faceplate was dark, but soon it would glow an opaque red. Mason had once feared the mask. Now it was his to wear.

"Mason!"

He looked up at the sound of his name and realized the room was almost empty. Merrin was waiting for him in the doorway. Mason looked down at the helmet one more time, and at the gloves that held the helmet. *Don't fail me.*

We won't, the gloves replied. There was definitely something alive in the gloves. But perhaps it was only the darker part of Mason's mind that answered.

Mason met Merrin at the door, and she put a hand on his wrist, stopping him. "We might not make it back this time."

Mason didn't know what to say. Merrin didn't seem to know either. So Mason just kissed her on the cheek and said, "We will." Merrin looked stunned, her mouth even making an O shape. Mason didn't linger: he took her hand and pulled her into the shuttle bay, where a Hawk was waiting for them, magnificent under the bright lights. The hull was covered in scales, the colors shifting between shades of rich purple and jade green.

"I wonder whose ship this is—it's beautiful," Mason thought aloud.

"Um, it's my dad's," Merrin replied.

Mason almost laughed at the idea of going to battle in the king's personal vessel, but the danger was too near. He'd be sure to return the craft in one piece. They walked up the ramp and through the corridors, which were only now beginning to gradually brighten. The ship was waking.

"We haven't had a chance to catch up that much," Mason said. "Have you been able to see your parents? I mean, your human ones." It was a standard tactic among soldiers to chat before a potentially deadly battle. Talking kept your mind off the dangers ahead, helped to calm the nerves.

"I've been busy with the coalition," Merrin said. "But yes, we've met twice. I was all ready to be mad and yell at them for lying to me for my entire childhood, but they were so happy to see me, and I realized that none of it mattered. They are still my parents." Merrin made a sound between a laugh and a sigh. "They're actually scheduled to visit the palace next month, to meet Father and my brother. I'm . . . hoping it goes well."

"It will," Mason replied. "He's different. You can see it in his eyes." Mason wondered if it had less to do with removing his armor than it did with getting his daughter back.

"I think you're right," Merrin replied.

The six of them gathered at the top of the ship, where a hatch would open to outer space. Reckful was in the cockpit down below. When he spoke, his voice sounded inside the rhadjen's heads, not through external speakers: "Everyone strap in. Put your helmets on and check the seal. We're going to do a short light-speed jump directly above the Fangborn ship. After that, Mason is going to do his thing. If he can make a hole in the Fangborn hull, we all go inside and try to stop them. If we can't, we go home, no exceptions. I'm going to cloak as soon as you're clear, but you'll be able to see me on your HUDs. Understood?"

Everyone replied, "Yes, sir!"

If we can't get inside, there won't be a home, Mason thought but didn't say. He slid the helmet over his head and felt it seal to the neck of his suit. He threw his hood up over his helmet, as the heads-up display snapped on. This time, he understood the flashing symbols. The suit monitored vitals of every kind, something Mason found extremely useless. With a thought, he cast them away until there was nothing to clutter his vision. The link the helmet made to his brain was a feeble thing compared to the gloves. All around him, faceplates lit up as they sealed. Tom's mask was bright red. Lore's, violet. As was Merrin's.

Mason strapped himself in as the ship took off. He felt heavier, then lighter, then normal, then heavier again as the ship rocketed up through the atmosphere.

Risperdel tried to put her hand over her mouth, but it bumped against her faceplate. "Oh, this isn't fun."

"Ever been in space before?" Merrin asked her.

"Hated it every time," Risperdel said. "Or at least, I hate being inside a ship. Guess that's not very Rhadgast of me."

Tom and Lore were sitting across from Mason. Lore nodded at him: "Stark."

"Yeah?"

"Whatever happens out there . . . you're all right."

"Isn't this lovely?" Po said to Mason's right. He was still messing with his straps. "We all make friends in time to be vaporized!"

Risperdel kicked Po across the aisle. "The power of positive thinking, Po. And next time, Lore, just say 'good luck.'"

"Be ready!" Reckful said to them. "When the ceiling opens, you need to move. Fast. Remember your training. You are no longer rhadjen, but Rhadgast." A chill went down Mason's spine: Reckful's words reminded him so much of Commander Lockwood's, when he'd ordered the cadets to retake the Egypt.

The sounds faded until there was nothing but the beating of Mason's heart and the slow and steady rasp of his breath. A warning on his HUD said they were now in a vacuum.

The Hawk was at light speed for no more than two seconds. Mason felt a building sensation throughout his entire

body, followed by a release that left him woozy, his eyes unfocused, and his toes tingling. He much preferred the cross gates used by the ESC, but faster-than-light travel had its advantages.

All the restraints unlocked and retracted automatically.

"Now!" Reckful said. The doors in the ceiling zipped apart, and Mason saw they were inverted above the Fangborn ship. As one, he and his team pushed off and entered space.

Chapter Thirty-five

The Fangborn ship was the world now, stretching out to infinity in all directions. Mason couldn't even tell where they were located on the ship, whether they were near the front or back. To the left and right, he saw the white light from the two tractor beams. They appeared like rising suns, one in the east, one in the west.

Mason looked over his shoulder, but the Hawk was already cloaked. Only a red outline painted on his HUD showed where the ship was. "I'm clear!" Reckful said. "Good luck!"

Through the com, Tom said, "Get it done, Mason."

Mason hit the Fangborn ship first, touching down with his hands, then swinging his feet flat against the hull. The ship wasn't moving, but he could feel how alive it was. He could feel whatever power was beneath his boots. His team spread out, covering all the angles, making sure no one was coming for them.

The gloves were eager now, sensing they'd soon be used. Mason put his palms to the surface of the Fangborn ship, which was smooth, a dark bronze streaked with black. He closed his eyes and poured energy through his palms and into the ship. The surface began to glow, spreading out in a circle. Lore backed away as the circle neared her feet. She used her belt to come off the surface as it passed under her.

After another moment, Mason took his hands away: there was no mark, nothing to say he'd done any damage. The circle of light under him faded to nothing. It was like the ship drank his energy and added to its own.

"Try again!" Merrin said. "If it doesn't work, we're outta here."

So Mason did. Drops of sweat hit his faceplate. His hands were burning up. And still there was no mark.

"I'm sorry . . ." Mason said. *Why isn't it working?*

"Reckful!" Po shouted. "We need an extraction."

"Oh, no," Tom said softly. Mason looked up. About one hundred meters away, Fangborn wearing massive spacesuits began crawling out of a hatch.

"Form up!" Po said. "Don't turn your back on them!"

"There's our entrance!" Lore said, pointing at the hatch. "If we can get around them."

But they never had the chance. The Fangborn were fast on land, but out here they didn't have to worry about things like gravity. Two of them launched off the ship, flying toward the team like missiles.

"SCATTER!" Mason screamed, as he leapt over a Fangborn that was barreling toward him, claws forward. The team split apart, flying in all directions, firing blasts of electricity when they could. Mason spun around in space as the Fangborn prepared to come at him again, but then he saw a sight that took his courage: small pod-shaped vessels were detaching from the hull of the Fangborn ship, rising up and zipping around, changing direction instantly with g-forces too incredible for the soft forms of human and Tremist to withstand. But for monsters like the Fangborn . . .

Mason watched as a pod zipped over to Tom, opened up at the bottom, and sucked him inside. Mason didn't think, he simply flew after the pod, preparing to unleash a blast that would hopefully disable it.

But then the pod began to glow. One second it was there, the next it was gone, a trail of blurry light left behind in the direction of Nori-Blue.

Chapter Thirty-six

Mason didn't cry out. He couldn't speak, couldn't move. People called his name so loudly his ears rang. Behind him, his teammates were scrambling into the Hawk. The pods were firing blobs of blue light at the king's ship, but so far it was absorbing them. His team had a chance to escape.

Positioned high enough above the ship, Mason could see over the edge many miles away. He could see Earth, shrouded in gauzy white light, its new orbit guiding it along a path to destruction. He imagined Earth and Skars finally meeting, crashing together and ending all life on both planets.

Thousands of miles away, his HUD highlighted where the fleets were gathering. The ships were tiny black specs against the small yellow sun of Skars. Far enough away to avoid the Fangborn's deadly weapons. They were afraid, Mason knew. With good reason. They were without hope, too. Also with good reason. Yet the fleets would still engage with the Fangborn ship, because there was nothing left to do.

And when the battle began, they would surely die.

Mason didn't have the strength to fight when Merrin bear-hugged him from behind and began to pull him back. He didn't have the strength to change until they reached the Hawk.

Mason caught the edge of the door with his fingertips and bobbed against their inertia. He shrugged free of Merrin and pushed her down into the compartment they'd come out of. The rest of his team was there. They were still yelling things, stuff like "*WE NEED TO GO! MASON COME ON! WHAT ARE YOU DOING?*"

Reckful screamed: "SHIELDS AT TEN PERCENT, WE HAVE TO MOVE!"

Mason knew what he had to do now. He'd always known, but he was afraid, and now Tom was gone because of that fear. Gone, but not forever. Mason would get him back, but first he had a ship to deal with.

Tom is already gone! His best friend was gone. More meaningless words.

Mason let the gloves take over. He opened the dark parts of his brain, every part of his mind, and closed his eyes as the gloves filled those parts, like water filling a cup. A voice said in his mind: *And now you will know the meaning of true power.*

His eyelids snapped open. Had Mason been able to see his eyes, he would've known they were now solid black.

Merrin was coming for him again, prepared to pull him down into the Hawk's compartment.

"Reckful," Mason said. Everyone went silent. "Close the doors." Mason pulled himself outside the ship . . .

. . . as the doors slammed shut. Voices filled his head, in his ears and in his helmet, but he muted them. Mason was a soldier, and he could do this. This was how he could live up to his legend—by actually being a legend.

Reckful was smart: the Hawk cloaked again, banking away and diving as it faded into the background stars. The pods were all around Mason, circling slowly like big cats. He called upon the shield again, forming a globe of pure electromagnetic energy around him. In the next moment, the globe expanded suddenly, then retracted. The pods were gone; all that remained were clouds of dust that sparkled in the sunlight. Mason flew high above the ship, miles high, then dived, circling down and around, moving impossibly fast, faster than the belt was capable of. But the gloves made the belt stronger, too.

The ship was enormous beyond comprehension, so Mason assumed any spot was as good as another. He was far enough away to see the entire thing at once. The fleets were moving in on Mason's left. The Fangborn ship was dispatching more pods, which were racing to meet the fleets head-on. The battle was seconds away from commencing.

"Mason!" It was Susan. She'd broken through on a priority channel, overriding his mute. "Mason what are you doing? Come back!"

Mason ignored her because he didn't know what to say. It was very possible his plan wouldn't work and he would still not be able to defeat the ship, even though he was letting the gloves go as deep as they wanted to. *It has to be enough,* he thought.

"Mason please come home. Please—"

Mason overrode the channel and silenced it. He was all alone in space now, his body veiled with energy as black as night.

The fleets were coming on strong, spreading apart, ready to cover the Fangborn ship from all angles. It was now or never. With a final breath, Mason shot forward.

He forged the lightning shield into a spear that enveloped his body, the shield somehow untethering him from space, taking away the strains on his soft tissues. It didn't feel like he was moving at all. But the readout on his HUD said he was traveling at just above twenty thousand miles per hour. The ship grew incredibly fast in his vision, until it became a solid wall of bronze. He blinked when he hit the Fangborn ship. When he opened his eyes, he was already out the other side. He spun around and saw the hole he'd created, easily a hundred yards across, venting atmosphere and debris. He saw the decks he'd cut through. But he didn't stop. He flew up and around, coming down from the top. He kept his eyes open this time, watching the decks melt away in front of him. Time seemed to slow. He saw glimpses of Fangborn scattering in the hallways, only to be sucked along by his passing. He burst through the bottom of the ship, creating another massive hole that was still tiny compared to the size of the ship. Just paper cuts, really.

But paper cuts large enough to hurt.

Sparrows and Foxes, the small fighter ships of the Tremist and ESC, zoomed through the holes like bees into a hive. A warning on the HUD said Mason was being targeted by some of the ESC ships—they weren't attacking him, but scanning. They had no idea what he was.

Mason didn't stop. He flew out and around and pierced the Fangborn ship again. He struck the room containing the power source this time: it was a room many miles high and wide (in truth, the borders were too far to see). The room was completely empty save for a small pulsing black orb in the center, contained within a globe of shimmery blue light. He only got a glimpse of the room, but once he broke through on the other side, it began to destabilize. The walls rent apart around him, but not from his passing, he thought. He felt gravitational forces on his body that didn't seem natural. The lightning shield protected him, but he was feeling the strain now. His limbs felt heavy, and his eyes throbbed with red pain.

Mason opened the top channel on his com: "ALL SHIPS BAIL OUT!" He was already outside the ship, many miles away. He spun around and saw the Fangborn ship in its entirety: it was a dying thing, venting gasses from dozens of holes, the small fighters zipping out of the exits as fast as they could. Suddenly a section of the ship snapped inward, as if an invisible fist twenty miles wide had punched it from the outside. Another segment concaved, sending more gases and great gouts of fire into space. Mason's com channel was alive with cheering from both sides. The fleets were hightailing it out of there.

Mason didn't have the strength to follow. So he had the best seat in the house when the Fangborn ship continued to crunch inward, getting smaller and smaller. Until it disappeared completely.

Chapter Thirty-seven

The white beams faded, and the planets returned to their normal appearances. If they were closer together, Mason couldn't tell.

A voice broke through the chatter: "Mason?" It was Susan again.

"Here," he said softly. He barely had the strength to speak. The gloves on his hands were throbbing with energy: they wanted more. Mason gathered his strength. *You've had enough*, he thought, and the gloves retreated, lessening the urge. Mason felt a small sense of relief at the fact that he was still in control. The gloves obeyed *him*, not the other way around.

But Mason didn't realize the gloves had been giving him strength all along. Once they retreated, Mason closed his eyes and slipped into a sleep as dark as the space around him.

Mason awoke on the Hawk. Through a window, he saw the space between Earth and Skars, still many millions of miles away from each other. The halfway point was alive with both fleets surrounding the Will and the Olympus, which had moved back to their positions. Even the shipyard building the new planet gate was back in place.

His friends were in the room. They were all smiling. A few video screens on the wall showed the celebrations taking place on both planets. One showed a replay of Mason coring the ship like an apple. He moved across the screen like a shooting star, entering the ship from one side and exiting in the next second, destruction trailing behind him. *So that's what it looked like.*

Po and Merrin were sitting on either side of his bed. "Nice job, buddy." Po said. "I knew you had it in you." His tone was casual, but he was staring at Mason with awe.

"*Did* you now?" Risperdel said. "I don't think any of us saw that coming."

"Tom," Mason said. His tongue felt fat and parched in his mouth, a slab of rock. "Water."

"Tom is . . ." Merrin started to say.

Mason knew where Tom was. *You don't leave a man behind.* That was something you learned on day one in the ESC.

Mason wasn't going to leave a man behind. And maybe he could find his father on Nori-Blue, if Erik Stark hadn't perished aboard the Fangborn ship. Mason couldn't tell what would be worse: to have inadvertently killed his father, or to come face-to-face with him on the planet where all of this began.

"Um, Mason, about your gloves," Po said. He was trying to give a reassuring smile, but Mason saw the concern in his eyes.

Mason looked at the gloves as Risperdel pressed a pouch of water into his hand. His robe was folded in a pile next to him. The material of the gloves had extended up past his elbows, over his shoulders, tendrils of it snaking out across his chest to connect with one another over his spacesuit. The gloves covered most of his torso now. He was terrified to see it—*this isn't right, this isn't what I wanted*—but the gloves felt . . . pleased. It was an odd feeling, one he didn't fully understand.

Everyone was staring.

Mason unfolded his robe and slid it over his head, hiding most of the gloves from sight. "No time to worry about that right now. I'm fine, I promise."

Merrin put her hand on his arm. "Mason . . ."

"Did anyone die?" Mason asked. He should've stopped his assault. Once the fighters were inside the ship, he should've left its final destruction to them. But he couldn't fight the urge for one final pass, and rupturing the core had immediately changed the objective from destroy to escape.

"A few of the fighters didn't make it out," Lore said, her voice somber. "A team of Rhadgast were fighting Fangborn on the way to the power room. They perished."

"Not his fault," Risperdel said. "They would've died anyway when they reached the core."

Mason felt feverish all of a sudden. "How—how many?"

"We don't know yet," Po said. He put his hand on Mason's shoulder. "It's over, Stark. Both our planets are saved. The newsfeeds are saying the orbits have stabilized."

Mason locked eyes with Merrin, who seemed to have already accepted what he was planning to do next. "It's not over, Po. Not until we get Tom back."

Mason stood up; a wave of nausea smacked him in the stomach. His vision blurred. He blinked it away, calling upon the gloves to steady him, a thing they were very willing to do. *When this is over, the gloves are coming off.* He waited to see if the gloves gave some kind of reaction, but they were quiet.

"They're not going to let you go," Po said. "Not with the gloves. They'd never risk letting the Fangborn get their claws on them. Reckful has been ordered to take us to the Will for a press conference."

"It sounds like we're all famous now," Risperdel said. "But yeah, they're not going to let you go to Nori-Blue, and they're certainly not going to authorize a mission."

"I'm not asking for authorization. Who can stop me?" Mason said.

Po didn't seem to have an answer for that.

But Mason wanted to be sure before he risked more lives. He reached down to his boot and removed the communicator Grand Admiral Shahbazian had given to him and Tom. Everyone gave him an odd look when he squeezed it in one hand, before he closed his eyes.

The incoming sensations of the room Mason was currently in—the dry smell of recycled air, the tiny vibrations through the soles of his feet—all of that faded away. He caught a glimpse of GAS's office, but Mason didn't want that just yet. He knew the answer he would get from GAS if he asked for help right now. Instead, he reached out across the galaxy for the other communicator. And he found it. It was inside Tom's boot, but it gave a picture of the room around it, painted in bluish hues and sharp white lines. The quality was much lower, since the device was not synced to Tom the way it was to Mason.

Tom was on his side, in a dirty cell carved from rock. The

door was a transparent force field. Outside, a Fangborn slinked by, dragging his claws along the force field, creating green sparks. Tom flinched away, shivering, then froze. He looked down at his boot, where the communicator was vibrating on a low frequency inside his heel. He pulled out the device and gripped it tightly in one hand. Two seconds later, Mason stood in the cell with Tom.

"Mason!" Tom said, but only in his mind.

"Are you okay? Are you hurt?"

"I'm okay—they roughed me up a little. But I'm fine. Did you win?"

"We won."

"Of course we did." Tom seemed to relax, which was odd to see considering he was currently inside an alien prison on an alien planet.

"I'm coming after you," Mason said.

"No! Are you crazy? They'll expect that. There are Fangborn *everywhere.* I'm in some kind of underground prison city."

"This isn't a discussion."

"You're right! It's a suicide mission. They—"

"What is it?"

"I don't think you should come, Mason."

"Why not?"

"Because . . . one of them told me . . . they said soon I would be like them. They're going to change me."

Mason's blood went cold. "I won't let that happen."

"There's nothing you can do about it! I'll be different. Even with the cure, you won't be able to get to me in here without getting eaten."

"*Tom.* If I was stuck in there, or Merrin was, what would you do?"

Tom didn't say anything for a long minute. Then he shrugged. "I'd come after you. But it's not worth it, Stark. If you can't think of yourself, think of your friends who might get hurt. Who *will* get hurt." A shadow fell across Tom. Mason looked to the right and saw two Fangborn outside Tom's cell.

The larger one spoke, the muscles in his throat undulating. **"It's time to evolve, little one."**

Chapter Thirty-eight

Tom looked at Mason, a mixture of resolve and fear on his face. "It's too late! Stay away, *please.*" He cut the feed.

Mason opened his eyes and dropped the communicator. He was shivering like Tom had been. He touched the pocket of his robe and felt the vials within. They had survived their trip through space. "He—he's on Nori-Blue. The Fangborn have him prisoner. They're going to turn him into a monster. . . ." Mason started for the door.

Lore blocked the way, her hands held loose at her sides. "Reckful won't take you to Nori-Blue. Are you prepared to fight him?"

Mason turned to face Po, Merrin, and Risperdel. "I have a plan, but I can't do it by myself."

The three shared a look.

Po shrugged. "If we don't go with you, they're just going to throw us in a cell and question us for days. Might as well."

Risperdel nodded solemnly.

The corner of Merrin's mouth twitched: the ghost of a smile. "Was there ever any doubt?"

. . .

➤ "We're going to need a little more help," Mason said to Merrin. They were docking at the Will. Mason felt a rush of air as the main door opened before the pressure could equalize.

"Luckily, I know a good crew," Merrin said.

Reporters both Tremist and human were waiting for them in the docking bay of the Will. They were crowded around the exit ramp with their cameras and their questions. Po was happy to take center stage, but once they saw Mason on the ramp they elbowed Po aside. Mason half considered using his shield to push them back.

What happened out there what did you see inside tell us about your gloves are you a Blood or a Stone?

Mason squinted against their lights and held up his hands. The words died away and the reporters seemed to hold their breath, waiting to see what Mason had to say next.

"I need a ship," Mason said. "Who wants to let me borrow theirs?"

No one spoke.

"You'll get an exclusive," Mason said.

➤ Five minutes later they were aboard a shuttle that belonged to the galaxy's number-one news network, MWNN. The Milky Way News Network had special clearance with the ESC (in exchange for a few positive puff pieces each year), which would make the next part of their mission easier.

"Better hurry," Merrin said. Through the window, they could see the Will's security forces moving toward them. They wore blue uniforms and carried handheld talons—the deadly energy weapons used by the Tremist—on their hips. Security must've been watching the news feed and realized Mason and his team had no intention of being part of a press conference.

Mason piloted the shuttle out of the bay, passing through the force field into space. Once clear of the Will, Mason dropped a cross gate. It expanded in front of them while their com logged over five hundred separate incoming frequencies. *I've got their attention.*

Only one of them made it through. "Where do you think you're going?" It was Grand Admiral Shahbazian. "I need you back here *now.* Nice work, by the way."

Mason decided to give GAS one chance. "Sir, I need a team of Reynolds to come with me to Nori-Blue. Cadet Tom Renner is currently a prisoner there. And I am going to get him back."

"Nori-*Blue*? Are you insane, Cadet? You clearly have some schooling left, son. We don't just execute missions on the fly. We require things like *intelligence* and *reconnaissance.* And *planning.* We currently have none of those things. Which means the answer is no. We can discuss a mission when you get back. But for now, you're a hero, son. Be a hero to these people."

Mason thought of the dead he was unable to save. Of the fighter pilots who perished because of his actions. His best friend captured because of Mason's arrogance. The people he had saved diminished the lives he had lost not at all.

"I'm no hero," Mason said, then he flew the shuttle through the gate.

. . .

➤ The shuttle appeared in high orbit above Mars. The computer flagged Academy I and II with little golden rings, highlighting them on the glass. Mason began his descent.

The com clicked: "Unidentified shuttle, this is ESC traffic control. State your business."

Po prodded his shoulder. "Say something!"

"This is Mason Stark," he said. "I'm here to pick up two cadets. Patch me through to Academy II."

Ten minutes later they were in the shuttle bay of Academy II. Having ESC ground under his feet again gave Mason a strange, tickly feeling in his chest. It was a good feeling. But so much had happened, he wondered if he could still be considered a cadet. Was he a cadet, or a rhadjen? Could he be both?

Mason was not surprised to see two Reynolds waiting for him in the shuttle bay. GAS wasn't going to give up that easily.

"Are you here to detain me?" Mason said to them. "Because that will go badly for all parties involved."

The Reynolds shared a look, but Mason couldn't see their expressions behind the blank masks. Their circular eye lenses brightened, flickering from pink to white.

"No, kid," the one on Mason's left said. "Well, yes. We are technically here to detain you." His voice came out raspy, modified by a computer.

"But we're not going to do that," the right one said. "Vice Admiral Bruce Renner was our commanding officer back in the day. We heard his son is in danger, and that you're not okay with that."

"Not okay at all," Mason said.

"So we're asking permission to come along."

Mason wondered if it was some kind of trick, a ploy designed to lower his guard so they could take him in peacefully. After the destruction of the Fangborn ship, who wouldn't be afraid of his power?

The left one removed his mask . . . and Mason discovered he was a she. A tumble of bright red hair fell around her shoulders. Her cheeks were dappled with freckles. She looked around Susan's age. "Kylie Sparks, at your service."

Mason shook her hand. The other one did not seem interested in removing his or her mask. "I need all the help I can get. Thank you. Find a spot on the shuttle."

Behind the Reynolds, the doors to the school hissed open. Mason peered over Kylie's shoulder and saw something that almost made him forget all the bad stuff that had happened. A real smile formed on his face. Because Jeremy and Stellan were here. The team was almost back together.

Chapter Thirty-nine

Jeremy and Stellan walked down the steps and sidled up next to the Reynolds. They were two of the bravest soldiers Mason had ever known, and two of Mason's closest friends. For this mission most of all, Mason appreciated how different they were. Stellan was purely logical and thought-driven. Jeremy was smart, too, but he liked to break stuff with his hands. They even looked completely opposite: Jeremy, dark hair and eyes, stocky and muscled; Stellan, willowy and tall, bone-thin, with hair so blond it was nearly white.

"Reporting for duty," Jeremy said with just a hint of sarcasm. "I hear the Fangborn decided to mess with one of our crew. The lore books will mark that down as a bad idea on their part."

Stellan, who was normally the first one to voice a doubt or make everyone take a second to think, was grim, his brow furrowed in anger. He would offer no objections. They were going to get Tom back, end of story.

Mason put his hands on their shoulders, pulling them

into a huddle. "I can't even begin to express how good it is to see you two."

Jeremy grinned. "They can't keep us apart forever." Something caught his attention behind Mason, and his eyes narrowed. "What's this?"

Mason turned: his new team was on the ramp of the shuttle, gloves glowing softly, rhadjen robes fluttering in the draft from the bay's climate control. The image struck him as so out of place—this was an ESC school, after all. Mason knew soon the time would come to choose between his old school and the new.

For now, his blood still belonged to the ESC.

"You brought Rhadgast *here*?" Jeremy said. He almost took a step back but seemed to catch himself. Jeremy never showed apprehension, even if he was feeling it.

"I must agree," Stellan said, "this is highly irregular."

"They're my teammates, same as you. I can vouch for them."

Jeremy's look softened, but only by half. "You've been gone a long time."

Maybe too long. How much time had passed? Not even a month.

"Look," Mason said. "They're cadets, they're soldiers. Just like us."

Jeremy raised an eyebrow. "Just like us?"

"Well, maybe not as disciplined as us. Or as disciplined as Stellan, I should say."

Stellan grinned. "I can be a rebel, too, you know."

"I know," Mason said. "Will you both keep an open mind?"

Jeremy nodded. "For you."

"I won't turn away help," Stellan said. "And I've been wanting to talk to a Tremist for a *very* long time."

Mason led them to the others. Po shook their hands eagerly and said, "More humans! I was hoping to meet more. I . . . that sounds strange, doesn't it." It only sounded strange because Po was now speaking English.

"Probably," Risperdel said, also in English. Their accents were slightly clipped and proper.

Lore didn't shake hands with anyone. Her mouth was a thin hard line. As the team acquainted themselves with Jeremy and Stellan, Mason walked over to her.

"What?" she said.

Mason didn't know where to begin. "You . . . it seemed like . . . you were, you know, not going to hate my guts forever."

"I don't hate you," she said, in a way that said she totally hated him.

Mason waited until she said more.

She sighed after a moment, and her shoulders relaxed. "My family has been Rhadgast going back past the days of the Divider. And I've lost uncles and aunts in our war with the humans, cousins, too. I know you saved us, but still more Rhadgast are dead." She shook her head.

"I never meant . . ." But the words felt hollow as he thought them. Meaningless.

"I *know* that. I know. And I know not everything is your responsibility, even if *you* don't. But it doesn't make it hurt less. You understand that, right? You did everything you could, and I honor you for that. Just give me more time. . . . I know we owe you our lives, Mason. I am grateful for that. And for you."

Mason drew breath to say something—he didn't know what—but Merrin appeared from around the corner. "Is everything okay?" She looked between Mason and Lore. Lore had her eyes on the floor, but then she lifted them to Merrin, and they were only slightly warmer than before.

"Everything's fine," Mason replied.

"Good. Because Tom is waiting for us." Mason felt a pang in his stomach—as if he had to be reminded? "Everyone is loaded up. Let's fly."

In the shuttle's passenger section, Mason faced his team. Kylie and the other Reynold were piloting them out of the Martian atmosphere. Jeremy and Stellan were mixed in with Po, Merrin, Risperdel, and Lore, a gesture Mason appreciated. They were all crammed in the seats, harnesses locked down tight.

Jeremy smiled at Risperdel. "Hi, what's your name? I'm Jeremy. Jeremy Cane. You may have heard of me. I was part of the team that assaulted the Fangborn ship above Nori-Blue. You know, when the Will and the Olympus were almost monster food? Yeah, that was me."

Risperdel was looking at Jeremy as if he were some kind of alien parasite trying to burrow into her skin.

Mason cleared his throat, and Jeremy faced forward, his smile fading into serious mode, with just the hint of a smirk left.

Mason didn't have some grand speech planned. He simply said, "Thank you for coming with me. Thank you for the honor of fighting at your side." Then he buckled himself in and tried to turn inward, to meditate, and to calm himself for what came next.

Merrin was sitting next to him. He placed his hand on hers, and she curled her fingers around his. He savored the feeling, tried to stamp it into his mind. Because the ride to Nori-Blue was short, and Mason didn't know how much time he would have left as a human.

Chapter Forty

Mason felt the strange static on his skin when they passed through the cross gate. He unbuckled his restraints and walked into the shuttle's cockpit. And there was Nori-Blue, massive and green, frosted with wispy clouds from pole to pole. In the southern hemisphere was the dark gray smudge of a storm.

"Where do you want us to put her down?" Kylie asked.

Mason popped his communicator into a slot on the console. All ESC coalition ships were required to have basic ESC functions, and this was one of them. A three-dimensional hologram appeared above the console: a photo-realistic picture of Nori-Blue, with a pulsing orange dot south of the equator.

"There," Mason said.

Kylie nodded, then fed power to the engines, bringing the shuttle in at a shallow angle for a smooth approach. The planet grew until all Mason could see was green.

The ship banked hard to the left, heading south. Mason was thrown sideways; he caught himself on the wall with both hands and barely avoided cracking his head open. Through the windshield was the storm Mason saw from orbit: a wall of charcoal clouds they were heading straight toward.

"You might want to buckle up, kid," Kylie said, her hands struggling with the twin control sticks.

"What's happening?" the other Reynold said. "I've lost control!"

Mason had an idea, but he dared not hope.

Allow me . . . a voice said in his head.

"Did you hear that?" Kylie said.

"Allow me?" the other Reynold said. "Allow who what?"

"Child!" Mason shouted. It was so good to hear the AI's voice once again.

You are off course. I'm afraid they moved Cadet Tom Renner and left his communicator behind in the cell. Luckily, I've been tracking them. I will fly you to that location now.

The other Reynold put a calming hand on Kylie's forearm. "Let him take over. I read the report—there's an ancient AI on the surface who helped the cadets gain the knowledge of the People. He's friendly, I swear." Mason still couldn't tell if the other Reynold was a man or a woman, as the mask modulated his or her voice into a grainy rasp.

Kylie took her hands off the controls, even though it was clearly the last thing she wanted to do. "Cool, I guess"

Very cool. And yes, please buckle up, Mason Stark.

Mason did what Child told him to do; it had worked out well so far. He went to the passenger section and sat back down next to Merrin.

"What was that all about?" she said. Child must've spoken only to Mason and the Reynolds.

He couldn't help but grin. "Our old pal Child is alive and well."

Merrin smiled, too. "I was hoping we'd see him again."

Kylie's voice broke on the com: "Get ready for a hot exit. This AI seems to think we aren't capable of walking."

Just trying to save time, Child replied.

Mason and the others readied themselves, lining up at the rear door. The shuttle was drifting down now on its landing thrusters, swaying gently from side to side, making the team bow their legs as if they were at sea. The rhadjen shifted from foot to foot, eager and a little nervous all at the same time. Stellan and Jeremy, however, were solid as rocks.

"Must be their first time storming an alien stronghold," Jeremy said.

"Hey, it's yours, too," Stellan replied. "*I,* however, have been here before."

"Yeah, yeah, we get it," Po said with a lazy smile. He was the only rhadjen who didn't seem nervous. "Earth Space Command is big and bad. Maybe when this is over, we can have us a little duel. What say you, human?"

Jeremy grinned wide inside the beard he was trying to grow again (it was still patchy and thin). "Name the time and place, I'll be there. You can even use those cute gloves of yours."

The well-intentioned ribbing stopped, because the shuttle door unlocked with a bang. Two seconds later, the ramp slammed down, and the smells of Nori-Blue rushed into the passenger bay. The team fast-marched down the ramp and into the storm. It was only windy at this point, but the air felt thick with rain ready to drop. Mason's robes tugged at him–what a poor garment to wear in a storm. He unbuttoned the front and shrugged out of it, letting the wind rip it skyward. Lightning flashed in the clouds, illuminating their target: a mountain, tall and wide and black. At the base of the mountain was an enormous arch and beyond that, darkness. The arch was as tall as a skyscraper, a quarter of the mountain itself.

"How was this hidden from our planet-wide scans?"

"I don't know," Kylie replied. "They *do* have a hundred-mile-long ship. I'd assume they have cloaking technology."

They did have a hundred-mile-long ship, Mason thought, *but not anymore.* Here on Nori-Blue, the surviving monsters would no doubt love to get ahold of the human responsible.

Stellan shouted "Your gloves!" when he saw how far Mason's had spread, how the tendrils crawled along his torso, gripping his chest and abdomen.

Mason shook his head: *Not now.* "Let's move!" he roared. "Stay close to me. We keep in formation no matter what happens! Once we find Tom, we're out of here! I'll try to repel them with my shield, but attack anything that gets too close."

They ran across the clearing. The trees around them swayed back and forth as if they were waving goodbye. Leaves filled the air, tiny razors zipping and tumbling sideways. Lore gasped as a line of blood appeared on her forehead. They were running for the arch at a full sprint now. This had to be the entrance to their city. Mason had no idea what he would find within, but he was ready to face it.

He was ready.

The team slowed as they approached the arch, but they did not stop. They entered the darkness willingly.

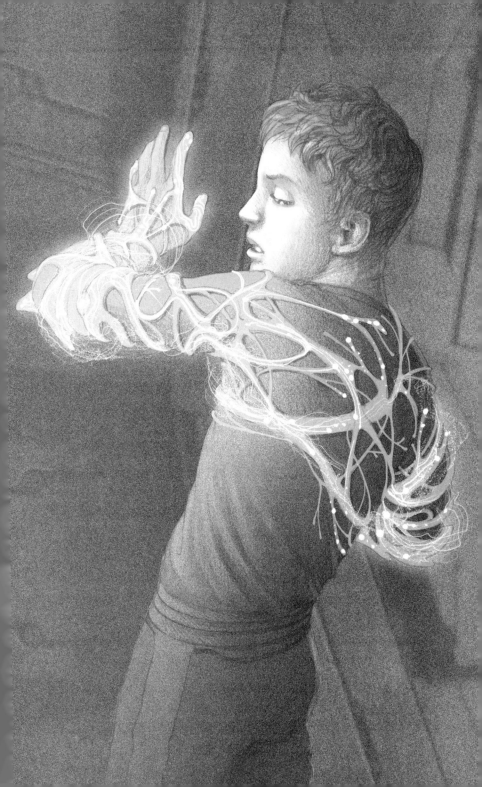

Chapter Forty-one

The sound of the storm became a howl behind them; the wind was cutting across the opening of the arch, like blowing over the mouth of a bottle. The darkness in front of them was absolute.

"Rhadjen!" Po shouted over the noise. "Light the way!"

The Tremist spread out and let their gloves come to life. Purple and red light filled the area around them, glowing brightly from their hands. They lit the way ahead, which was a tunnel too huge to be called a tunnel. It also revealed the enemy hidden in the gloom.

Fangborn were all around them.

The monsters were crouched low, ready to spring, their catlike eyes glowing yellow and green in the light, their fangs glistening with venom. A few of them leapt toward the group, but they never came close. Mason punched his fist toward the sky, releasing his will, and a column of crackling black light shot up and then curled down over the team, forming a dome out of electric bars. The Fangborn crashed into the dome and shrieked, falling to the ground in convulsions, some of them not moving at all. Mason kept walking forward, keeping his group under the shield.

The Fangborn retreated as his shield grew nearer, slowly at first, begrudgingly, then faster. The gloves were pleased Mason was using them again. He felt them pull tighter across his chest, felt the material branching down toward his legs. Soon he would be covered . . . if he allowed it.

At the end of the tunnel the darkness surrendered to light. The team kept moving, running now, the Fangborn hovering at the edges, not daring to approach Mason's shield. Some of the monsters sprinted away, probably to sound the alarm and get reinforcements. *My shield will hold*, Mason thought. Or hoped. *It has to, or we're all dead.*

Beyond the tunnel, the mountain was hollow. It seemed to stretch away to infinity in all directions, but if Mason squinted, he could just make out the walls, which angled upward to meet at several different peaks. Built into the walls of the mountain and all along the floor were hundreds of buildings carved from the rock. They clustered like needles, stabbing at the false sky above them. It reminded Mason of a cave floor, the buildings like stalagmites but carved into jagged shapes.

It was a city.

Mason could smell the Fangborn, but it was quiet, empty. Had they all been aboard the ship? Mason had a feeling this was only the surface, that the real city was below their feet, deep underground in caverns like the one the king's Hawk had fallen into.

Where do I go, Child? Mason thought.

You're on the right path, Child replied.

The team was on a primitive version of a street, no pavement, just flat stone that had been smoothed but not perfectly. They circumvented a jutting array of rocks and found that the road widened and continued for another hundred yards. Straight ahead stood an enormous building atop a hill, with many steps leading up to it.

"I have a bad feeling about this," Merrin said, and not for the first time since Mason had known her.

Mason didn't reply, not wanting to break the concentration on his shield. All it would take was a minor lapse for a Fangborn to slip through and eviscerate them. They kept walking toward the building, which resembled a palace more than anything. The stone it was carved from shone gold, with mighty pillars as wide as redwoods all across the front.

The gloves continued to shield them, and Mason slipped into a semiconscious state, putting one foot in front of the other. They climbed the steps as one and entered the palace as one.

They knew we were coming.

The room was vast, many stories tall, a hundred yards wide, but all it held was a throne. And Fangborn. The room was bisected by a rich crimson carpet leading to the other end, where more steps rose to an enormous throne carved out of rock. The throne was part of the floor, which was part of the mountain. Fangborn lined the perimeter, standing at attention, or at what resembled attention for a Fangborn. They were still hunched slightly, still ready to strike at any moment.

Atop the throne sat a Fangborn larger than the others. What else could he be besides a king?

The king spoke in a rumbling voice. **"Why are you here?"** It reminded Mason of distant thunder.

"I'm here to get my friend back!" Mason shouted over the crackling energy of his gloves. The Fangborn didn't seem as if they were about to attack, so he let the power fade from his gloves. The silence that followed was as big as the room.

Then: **"He doesn't want to go with you."**

Mason stepped closer. He felt Merrin's hand brush his arm, but he was moving too quickly. He wanted to see the king. At this distance, he was indistinguishable from any other Fangborn, save for a thick sash he wore across his chest. It was comprised of metal links wound together, like ancient chain mail.

"Yes, he does," Mason said. "Now tell me where he is."

"You destroyed our ship."

"So imagine what I can do to you."

The king began to laugh. He stood up slowly and stretched, then cracked his neck. He exhaled fiercely from his nostrils, creating twin plumes of steam.

The Fangborn began to close in from the perimeter walls, sauntering, one clawed foot after another.

"Uh, Mason?" Po said.

"Decision time!" Kylie said.

Mason lifted his fist, and the shield formed around them again. The king was still walking toward them. And he was still laughing. *What does he know that I don't?*

"There are many things your gloves can protect you against, but not everything. . . ."

From all directions, the Fangborn threw tiny rocks into the group. As they rolled by Mason's feet, he saw they were metal canisters. A few sparked off Mason's shield, but dozens of them made it through the electric bars and instantly began to spew a thick blue gas. It was chest height immediately, then above their heads a second later. Mason didn't even have time to hold his breath. The gas seemed alive. It flew up his nose, then down into his lungs, and he grew five hundred pounds heavier, then a thousand, and he fell asleep with the king's laughter ringing in his ears.

Chapter Forty-two

Wake up, Mason Stark. Please wake up? I need you to wake up, or you and your friends will be doomed, and I went to all that trouble helping you the first time around. Ah! Hello. Good morning.

Mason's eyes took a million years to open. He was on his back in a rock cell like the one he'd seen Tom in. The door was a force field. There was no sound but its gentle hum, no sight except for the rock wall on the other side of the force field.

You're not far from the king of the Fangborn, or the Usurper, as they call him. That's how the Fangborn rule—through strength. He is the strongest of them—Oh, but I digress. You must want out.

"Are they going to turn us into Fangborn?" Mason asked. His throat was raw from the gas, and it felt like an inch or so of liquid was sloshing around inside his lungs.

Haven't you been paying attention? No. Not if I have anything to do with it.

From the right, a small black orb drifted into view. It bobbed up and down, and a man appeared on the surface.

The skin of the globe was a video screen. The man waved. It was Child, an AI created millions of years ago to carry on the work of the People.

"It is beyond great to see you," Mason said. "How are the others?"

"They are alive, and human," Child replied. "Or Tremist, depending on what they were before you arrived."

"Can you get me out?" Mason said. His eyes scanned the corners of the force field for any weakness he could exploit, but he already knew there would be none.

"Well, yes . . ."

Mason sensed a *but* coming on.

"But in order to do so, I will have to deconstruct you on that side of the force field, then put you back together on this side. You will effectively not exist for a moment."

Mason's heart started to pound. He'd never even heard of that kind of technology. "Like, you mean on a molecular level?"

"Think smaller," Child replied.

Not like there was another choice. "Do it," Mason said.

"I must warn you, after this I will be at too low of a power level to assist you. In fact, I will cease to be operational. Forever. And also there is a fourteen percent chance you will be reconstructed incorrectly and die a horrible death."

Mason felt like he'd been slapped. He hadn't even spent an hour with Child in total, but Child was the reason Mason and his friends were still alive today. On the sphere was a skull and crossbones. The skull was laughing. Child had a grim sense of humor for an AI. Mason always wondered if he would have been friends with Elizabeth, the Egypt's AI, or just found her painfully dim-witted.

"Child . . . you know I can't let you do that. There's no way to open the door?"

"This may surprise you, but the amount of energy required to open the door is higher than it would take to deconstruct you. The Fangborn are working with powerful energies, and they aren't in the habit of letting their prey escape."

Mason looked at the rock wall around him. "Maybe I can blast my way out."

"Or heat the air so much your lungs are scorched from the inside out. Hmm . . . scanning . . . it would appear your gloves are trying to merge with your flesh. I would take them off immediately, or as soon as it is safe to."

"I can't," Mason said.

"You will have to try harder, then, before they are a part of you."

The Uniter was able to control them. So hopefully I can, too.

"Are you ready?" Child asked.

Mason didn't know what to say.

Child bobbed back and forth in a way that seemed happy. "Mason Stark, I have been alive, as you would call it, for a very long time. I have been alone for almost as long. I would like to see where machines go when they deactivate. I have fulfilled the purpose set for me by my creators. I am, in fact, content."

Mason felt pressure behind his eyes. He looked at the floor

and imagined what he would do next, and then he looked at the machine he owed his life to. "Thank you, Child."

Fourteen percent. There is a fourteen percent chance this ends right now. I will have to leave my friends behind in this place.

"You are most welcome. Stand by."

"Will it hu—" Mason stopped talking because the lights went out. The sensation throughout his body was brief and felt like fading into darkness. But then he saw light again. He stood on his two feet *outside* the cell. A wave of nausea ripped through his stomach, and he dropped to his knees, throwing up bloody mucus.

"Scanning . . . you are complete. Putting your blood back in all the right places was almost as difficult as reconstructing your brain. I am quite proud of myself." Child's voice was quieter. He was no longer bobbing, but rather stationary in midair. The surface of the sphere was flickering with static.

Mason tasted blood in his mouth. His left foot was cramped, and there was a ringing in his ears. He felt like he'd been in a spaceship crash. His heart was beating strangely in his chest—*bump, bump-bump-bump, bumpbump*—but after a moment it settled into a normal rhythm.

"Are you okay?" Mason said when he could stand tall again.

Child flashed a thumbs-up and drifted slowly to the ground, the static fading to black. "Be strong, Mason Stark. Your journey is just beginning." The sphere touched the floor and didn't move. It didn't seem to hold life as before; instead it now felt like an inert black ball. Mason kneeled next to it and picked it up with both hands. It was almost too heavy to lift.

Mason set Child on the ground. He didn't want to leave it there, but he had no choice. "I will be strong," he said, and then left the sphere behind.

Chapter Forty-three

Mason's had been the only occupied cell in the row—his team must have been held somewhere else. He found a tunnel that led to a set of crumbling rock stairs. The air stank of age and rock dust: the Fangborn probably weren't used to having prisoners. Mason climbed the steps and came across no monsters. The stairs led to a platform with no walls or doors, just a circular disk of polished metal. Mason stepped on it, and the disk pulsed with rings of red light on the surface. It began to rise, entering a vertical cylinder cut into the rock. A cylinder that led directly to the throne room, where the Fangborn king was sitting on his throne.

Mason was going to use his words first. That's what Stellan would have suggested, and Mason had learned to listen to him.

The Usurper noticed him, and stood up. **"Impossible . . ."**

"I did not come here to fight," Mason said. He made his voice strong. He was not going to throw away Child's gift.

The king moved toward him, slow and steady down the steps, one foot after another.

Oh well. It seemed like Mason was going to have to fight after all.

Mason remembered something Child had said to him long ago: *You are a Rhadgast. So clap your hands.*

Mason clapped his hands and held them together. A shaft of electricity sprouted from his closed fists. He pulled his hands apart and now held two blades, one in each hand. They crackled black and hot.

The Usurper laughed and kept walking down the stairs. He grabbed the links of metal around his chest and pulled hard. The chains split apart into two metal whips. The king whipped one sideways at Mason, who barely snapped his left blade down in time to parry. The chains sparked off his lightning sword but did not melt. And then another attack was coming, this one from the other chain high above his head. The chains were moving so fast they screamed through the air. Mason parried with both blades in the shape of an X, but the chain still curled around and slapped him on the back. Mason fell to one knee, his body on fire. But he did not unleash all of his power. He kept the gloves at bay. *Use your words.*

"Please," Mason said, rising to his feet. "I have destroyed your ship. I want this to end. Let us make peace. What can we do? Tell me what to do and I'll do it."

The Usurper let his chains rest on the floor at his sides, like coiled snakes. **"It is beyond your simple mind's understanding. We are trying to make you pure. We are trying to free you from your meaningless existence. You are not our enemy underneath that weak flesh and fragile bones."**

"That isn't your choice to make," Mason said.

"Nor was it ours. The universe is older than you know. We are not the darkest things in dark space, young one."

"But you tried to destroy our planets!"

"So that many would escape to space."

Mason understood. The planets would be destroyed, but there would be millions of survivors in space. Helpless, with nowhere to go.

The Usurper slapped the chains back onto his chest. "Your bravery pleases me, and your victory against us today was impressive. I will allow your friends to leave. But you must stay."

Mason fought the urge to tremble. The gloves loaned their strength; Mason could feel them infusing him with power.

"Why do you want me to stay?"

The Usurper hesitated, and Mason wondered if what he said next was going to be a lie. "We want your gloves. And they cannot be taken. They must be given willingly. In time, you will give them to us."

The same way Aramore's avatar gave them to me . . .

"And if I say no?" he said.

"You won't. We have taken precautions against your power. If you resist, you and your friends will surely die. The gas you inhaled is a poison. In less than one hour, it will feel as if your blood is boiling."

It seemed like Mason had to make a choice, but that was an illusion. There was no choice here.

"Is . . . my father . . . he was turned into a Fangborn many years ago. Is he here?"

"No, not here. But if you stay, I will bring you to him." The king grinned, showing his razor teeth. "He has been waiting for your return to this planet. Perhaps . . . we can make another deal. The gloves for your father."

He's alive! Mason thought. He could feel the cure vials inside his robes—the Fangborn hadn't found them. *Maybe I should use one on the king and see what happens.* But Mason didn't want to take the risk, not with the lives of his friends on the line.

"I'll stay, but you have to let Tom go, too. That's why we came here. Take it or leave it."

The Usurper was very still for a moment, and then he nodded at the two Fangborn standing guard by the door. The guards disappeared through the door, then came back a moment later with Tom bound at the wrists and ankles with heavy chains.

He was still human.

"Mason! What are you doing here?" Tom said.

"Rescuing you, of course."

Tom looked at the Usurper, then at Mason and back again. "What—how—why aren't you guys fighting?"

"We made a deal," Mason replied. A deal that made his stomach feel slippery, like it might drop through his other organs and sink down his leg. But it was a deal, and his friends would live to fight another day.

If I'm smart, I'll learn more about the Fangborn and find my dad, too. Susan would understand, and so would his mother. They both would have made the same call. Merrin would have, too. Merrin . . . they had just been reunited.

Mason faced the king again. "I want to take my friends to the shuttle myself."

The Usurper was breathing so deeply his muscular shoulders rose and fell with each breath.

"If you betray us, your shuttle will never leave the atmosphere."

It had crossed Mason's mind to try to get on the shuttle at the last minute, but the Fangborn hadn't lived for millions of years by letting their prey escape accidentally. There was something human about the Usurper's eyes, which were a piercing blue. It reminded Mason of the Egypt's engine—oh, how he missed that ship. What he wouldn't give to be back on it with his crew. *Both* crews, Tremist and human.

"Wait," Tom said, "what's going on? Tell me what the deal was. Mason! Tell me about the deal!" Tom shrugged the Fangborn's claws off his shoulders—no easy feat. He walked toward Mason as fast as he could with his ankles bound together. The Fangborn caught him after three steps. "Let go of me! Mason, what did you do? *TELL ME WHAT YOU DID!*"

Mason's face hurt from trying to stay placid. To see Tom this upset was harder than the actual staying-behind-on-an-alien-planet part. "Please, Tom," he said. "This is hard enough."

Tom fell silent, suddenly much paler.

More Fangborn came through the doors, each escorting one of Mason's friends, who were bound just like Tom was. They were all excited to see Mason at first, and then confused as to why he was standing next to the Fangborn leader.

Jeremy lifted his chained wrists. "What's the deal?" Stellan elbowed him in the side.

"Remember my words, boy," the Usurper said, handing

Mason a leathery pouch. **"Have them drink what's inside."**
He slinked away, bringing a group of the guards with him.

"What's happening?" Merrin said.

Mason gave Tom a sharp look when Merrin wasn't
watching—*Don't say a word.* Tom didn't. He seemed ready
to pass out, shell-shocked.

"No talking," Mason said. "I've cut a deal that will get us
out of here, but we're not allowed to talk." He didn't want to
keep lying to them.

They left the city with a group of twelve Fangborn following at a distance. Outside, the storm had grown angrier: the
shuttle was barely visible through the gray haze of rain that
flew in from all directions. It stung Mason's cheeks, and the
wind felt as if it were going to rip his hair out by the roots.

"I don't understand!" Merrin said. "It must be a trap—
they're not just going to let us go!"

"I said I made a deal!" Mason shouted back. "I'll tell you
on the shuttle!"

Mason jogged beside Po. "Do you trust me?"

Po looked at him through the rain. "Yes."

Mason ask Po for a favor, and Po agreed. The shuttle ramp
lowered at their approach. Mason looked over his shoulder at
their Fangborn escort: the creatures were huddled together,
crouched low in the grass, waiting. The lashing rain didn't
seem to faze them at all.

The team walked up the ramp, Mason being careful to let
them go first. For one brief second, Mason considered risk-
ing it all, just getting into the shuttle and hoping the Usurper
was only a good liar, that they really could escape and go
back to school together. Mason wanted to go back so badly

he was sick with it, almost feverish. *I want to go,* he thought.
I want to go.

But he decided to stay.

Back home he was a legend, but he hadn't earned it. Being a legend wasn't about valor. It wasn't about great deeds on the battlefield.

It was about sacrifice.

Mason could do that, for the ones he loved.

Merrin was suspicious; she was looking at Mason out of the corner of her eye, and her shoulders were tense. But she wasn't suspicious enough. As soon as she was inside, Mason hit the button to close the ramp, then dived off the side and rolled in the mud.

Jeremy almost made it off the ramp. Mason caught a glimpse of him running straight for him as the ramp angled upward and became less a floor and more a wall. It shut before he could jump through.

Po stood over Mason and extended a hand. "You're incredibly brave."

"Or stupid."

Po shook his head. "Brave. I'm honored to know you."

Despite everything that was about to happen, Mason felt a twinge of embarrassment. "The honor is mine," he said, pressing the leather pouch into Po's hand. "Have everyone drink what's inside here immediately. I want you guys to live long enough for a rescue."

Po nodded. "Consider it done. We'll be back before you know it."

Mason could hear pounding on the other side of the shuttle's door. It was probably Merrin. Then another set of fists was added—Jeremy, judging by how powerful they sounded. Mason was glad he couldn't see their faces. They would all forgive him one day.

Po pulled Mason into a rib-crushing hug. Then he left without another word, heading for a separate airlock on the other side of the ship.

Mason moved a safe distance from the shuttle, and soon the engines were warming up, their drone rising in pitch, battling with the crashing rain.

"What do you think you're doing?" a voice said behind him.

Mason spun around, almost slipping on the muddy grass. He blinked away rainwater and saw the other Reynold, not Kylie, standing ten feet away.

The Reynold ripped off her mask.

It was Susan.

This was too much—she was ruining everything. Mason had a plan, and he was sticking to that plan, and now she was here to mess it all up.

"What are you doing here?" Mason shouted. "Get back on the shuttle!"

"I'm not going anywhere without you, little brother. This is ridiculous. Open the ramp."

"What don't you understand? *I made a deal with the Fangborn.* If I go with you, we all die."

"I won't let that happen."

"It's not something you can control!" Mason knew how to convince her. "They poisoned us, Susan. We're poisoned. If you don't drink the cure that Po is carrying on the shuttle right now, you'll die. And then how will you rescue me?"

She stomped her foot in the mud. "Why do they just want *you*?"

Mason held up his hands. "They want these. They want the power. I crippled them today with *these*. Please, Susan, just let me do this one thing. Let me save us."

Susan stared at him for a very long time. The shuttle was at full power, hovering a foot above the clearing. Steam poured off the back, where the rain pounded the engines.

"I'm not a kid anymore. I am making this choice." But Mason saw they were too much alike. Susan would never leave him. Just like he would never leave her, not willingly. Susan saved him once before. She had stayed behind, and taken the risk. Now it was Mason's turn.

Mason raised his hands, palms out. "Get on the ship, Susan."

"You gonna zap me, little brother?" She took a step closer. "You're insane if you think that's going to make me leave."

Mason knew she was right. So he stepped forward, grabbed her wrist, and delivered a charge that locked up every muscle in her body. Susan stiffened, and Mason caught her before she could fall. He hauled her onto the shuttle and laid her down in the airlock Po had used. It was empty now. Susan was laughing, and then she was crying. "You little . . . I'm telling Mom." She tried to rise but was too weak. She lifted one hand, and it wavered, fingers reaching for him. "Don't . . ." she said.

"I love you," Mason said, and then he shut the door.

The shuttle didn't move for a long minute. Mason wondered what was happening inside. Were they arguing? Relieved? Screaming at each other? Scared? Probably a little bit of everything. Just when he thought the shuttle was going to land again, it took off, rising slowly at first, but then banking away from the mountain, angling toward the heavens.

The green light from the engines faded and was soon gone, but Mason didn't look away. He stood in the storm and let it thrash him, enjoying the sting on his face and the howl in his ears. His friends would come back for him, of that he had no doubt. But until then, Mason would be strong.

The boy worked in the mines day and night. With his gloves, he could melt the rock, shape it the way he wanted, or rather, the way he was instructed. The Fangborn were expanding under the surface of Nori-Blue. They were preparing. For what, the boy didn't know.

He woke each morning in his rock cell, his hands throbbing with the need to destroy. It scared him, but it was a problem for another day. The gloves had grown further, covering his entire body from neck to feet. Round his neck was a collar. If he turned against his captors, metal bolts would fire into his throat, killing him instantly. The boy had learned patience.

The Usurper had never brought Mason's father to him, but that was okay. Mason feared their reunion as much as he wanted it. Soon he would work up the courage, just like one day he would work up the courage to take off his armor.

Sixty-two days after he returned to Nori-Blue, the boy was melting out a new section of tunnel. The monsters lurked behind him in the shadows, always watching. He could feel their fear. But the boy had made a deal, and he would stick to it. He knew in his heart that there was more to come. And besides, using the gloves was a fine way to pass the time. Seeing the half-hidden fear in the eyes of the Fangborn around him was even finer.

As he smoothed the roof of the tunnel, he heard a rumble come from above. A deep sound in the stone. Was the tunnel destabilizing? No, Mason knew what he was doing. Pebbles fell around him, vaporizing when they touched the armor that had once been the gloves of Aramore the Uniter. The Fangborn scattered, taking separate vertical tunnels to the surface. The boy was alone for the first time in all those days.

The boy found a vertical tunnel and began to climb toward the surface. It was effortless. He'd grown stronger since coming here, making sure to keep up with his drills, to stay sharp. In the tunnel there was an alcove, one the boy had carved away himself. There he had hidden a cloth. Inside the cloth was a black sphere. The boy slung the heavy sphere onto his back and climbed one-handed, his fingers burning with the effort. It was a good burn. His heart was really pumping now.

At the top he shouldered away the flap of soil and grass, poking his head aboveground for the first time in sixty-two days. It was raining like before. The storm lashed at him, and his heart fell. The rumble had only been thunder.

But the rain woke him up. The sight of the alien clouds set his blood rocketing through his veins. And the breath of fresh air filled his lungs with fire.

He touched his collar. Sixty-two days. His friends hadn't come. This was his new life now. But the boy rejected that for the first time. It was his choice. He was not a boy; he was Mason Stark.

Mason pulled himself out of the hole. A great blast of lighting ripped the sky apart, turning everything around him blue-white. He heard a rumble again, a sound beneath the sharp bang of thunder. Was it really just the storm? He stood in the rain, enjoying it as he had sixty-two days ago.

Mason grabbed the collar around his neck and melted it off with a thought. He was a willing prisoner no more. Mason was going to die on Nori-Blue—he knew that now—but he wanted to die as himself. Not as this weapon he had become.

He began to stagger for the woods, the sphere that had once been Child heavy on his back, heading in the direction of the strange rumble. The trees swayed viciously in the wind. His armor sensed what he meant to do, and it contracted around him painfully. *No!* it screamed in his mind. *We belong to each other. You need me.*

I need nothing, Mason thought back. Nothing besides his crew.

He pulled at the armor over his neck and screamed. It felt like peeling off a layer of skin. He stumbled against a tree trunk, and the armor snapped back into place. "No!" he roared, fingers digging under the seam again. He kept running; he didn't know where or why. The woods were dark, water pouring down through the leaves. Tiny alien creatures the size of chipmunks ran from his passing.

Mason summoned his will and pulled again, and the gloves began to retract. The pain turned his vision red, and he splashed down into a puddle of warm water. But he didn't let up. The armor split apart into tendrils all at once, with a cracking sound that made Mason's ears ring. The ground around him was crawling with black lightning. He felt the material surging away from his skin, a slow liquid leaving fire in its wake. He squeezed his eyes shut. *I'M IN CONTROL!* he screamed in his mind, a supersonic thought with all of his will behind it. He was vaguely aware of a flaming tree next to him.

When he opened his eyes, the armor was gone. He was wearing black gloves and the skintight gray suit he wore in space. His skin was throbbing with heat and pain, as if he'd been dropped into the middle of a strong fever.

He could feel the gloves pleading with him. They didn't want to be removed. They would be good. They would obey. But Mason couldn't trust them. Slowly, gently, he pulled the gloves free and exposed his hands to the warm, humid air.

Mason heard the rumble again, a sound under the thunder. He looked down at the inert black sphere. The rain rolled off its surface, not a drop finding purchase. "I could really use your help, Child," Mason said, but the sphere was quiet. It always would be. Yet Mason would not leave his friend behind.

Mason moved toward the sound, feeling lighter but weaker. The urge to slide the gloves onto his hands again was strong—a moment was all he needed, just until the storm was over. Until he was safely away from the Fangborn. *Get a safe distance away, and then collect the rain,* he thought, his training kicking in. *Find a body of water. Make a shelter.*

The rumble grew louder, and Mason's heart began to pound with something he hadn't felt in a long time.

It was hope.

He began to move faster, feet quickstepping over the roots and mud pits. He shoved leaves aside, ignoring the ones that slapped his face. Soon he was running. There was a clearing ahead. He burst through.

Steaming in the rain was a Tremist Hawk. The ramp was down. People were gathered around it, assembling weapons, checking gear. Mason stood there and watched. Lightning flashed behind him, throwing his shadow across the clearing. The people noticed his shadow, and spun around, guns at the ready.

It was his crew. His entire crew. Tom, Merrin, Stellan, Jeremy, Po, Risperdel, Lore, and even Jiric.

Susan . . . and Mason's mother.

He was so filled with joy that he fell to his knees and began to cry. His friends had come back for him.

No one moved toward him; they were all frozen. But then Tom walked toward Mason slowly, almost like he was afraid to scare Mason away. He held up a hand to the crew, to make sure they stayed put.

The gloves were still in Mason's hand, and he still wanted to put them on, but the urge seemed silly now. So small compared to this.

Tom kneeled in front of Mason so that they faced each other. He was almost smiling, but not quite.

"Hey friend," Tom said. "Sorry we took so long."

Mason could only shake his head.

"A lot has happened. But we never stopped thinking about you. Not for one second."

Mason nodded. But he sensed there was more. "What is it?" His voice came out in a croak; he hadn't spoken in ages.

We need you, Stark. The treaty is over."

The words chilled Mason to his core. The treaty was over, all of his friends were here, human and Tremist.

"We'll brief you on the Hawk. You might need those gloves of yours still."

The thought of using the gloves once again made Mason pulse with anger and fear . . . even as the gloves seemed to pulse with pleasure and anticipation.

But he would do what he had to do.

Tom helped Mason to his feet. The crew was still staring at him. Mason could see his mother crying and Merrin holding Susan tight. Po was the only one openly grinning.

The rain had stopped now, but there was still thunder in the air. Tom slung an arm around Mason's shoulders, and together they walked toward the ship.